KILL...OR BE KILLED

Carr unsheathed the Gurkha throwing knife and hefted the carbine. Moving cautiously as the Kachins had taught him, he came within yards of the man. The Chinese, dressed in dirty, blue padded jacket and pants, was intent on whatever was ahead. A bolt-action rifle lay at his side...The man's head turned suddenly. His eyes met Carr's and he turned fully to reach for the rifle...

The Gurkha knife slashed through the air. It struck the faded blue fabric just above the chest, at the throat...The man fell and was still. Carr breathed again in a large gulp. He had not wanted a rifle shot to betray him.

THE
DRAGON
ROBE

CHARLES C. VANCE

AVON
PUBLISHERS OF BARD, CAMELOT, DISCUS AND FLARE BOOKS

THE DRAGON ROBE is an orginal publication of Avon Books. This work has never before appeared in book form. This work is a novel. Any similarity to actual persons or events is purely coincidental.

AVON BOOKS
A division of
The Hearst Corporation
1790 Broadway
New York, New York 10019

First Avon Printing, May 1985

AVON TRADEMARK REG. U.S. PAT. OFF. AND IN OTHER COUNTRIES, MARCA REGISTRADA, HECHO EN U.S.A.

Printed in the U.S.A.

WFH 10 9 8 7 6 5 4 3 2 1

To the courageous men who flew the Hump in the Forgotten War of the China-Burma-India Theater and to Mary Ellen, Penny, Kurt and Danielle.

Explanation

1. CBI — China-Burma-India theater of war.
2. Kuomintang (KMT) — Nationalist Party (China).
3. Kungch'antang — People's Liberation Party (China).
4. Myitkyina — Mitch-i-naw (in Burma).
5. Hump — Five-hundred-mile stretch of dense mountains and jungles between China and Burma.
6. Mao Tse-tung — Chairman, Chinese Communist Party. Pronounced *miaow* without the i.
7. Kempetai — Japanese secret intelligence organization.
8. Ding hao — "Very good!" Actually is *Ting hao*, with the *t* pronounced as a *d*.
9. Slopes — American slang for Chinese; also *slopeheads*.
10. Chinese P — Peking is pronounced Beking.
11. Cities — Names of Chinese cities on the map have in some cases changed since 1945. Despite this, their appearances are about the same. For the most part, roads on today's maps were nonexistent in 1945 in northwest China.

THE DRAGON ROBE

CHAPTER ONE

Northwest China
January 15, 1945

His eyes opened.

A black ball hurtled at him from space.

It smashed against his cheek without sensation. He tried to focus in the faint light. Another black ball.

He blinked in astonishment as his eyes converged on the dark shape above him. The ball came from a hand hanging inches over his face. His head jerked convulsively in dazed alarm. The ball splashed on his neck.

Where was he?

In the darkness into which he stared he made out the motionless body attached to the arm, a finger seeming to point in guilt at him. He tried to move, and pain burst from the recesses of his body. His head was on fire. His eyes moved without command.

Above, over his forehead, black trees shielded twinkling stars. At his right, as his eyes moved slowly, a body lay next to him.

Headless.

He heard the throaty whisper of a gathering wind. Another splash against his neck, and this time he felt its coldness. The sensation of life grew stronger. He struggled against a weird tiredness, a massive lethargy. Thoughts tumbled through his agonized mind.

His oxygen mask! Where was it? Why was it so quiet? Where was the roar of the engines?

"We've been hit!" He heard the sharp cry in his earphones, the intercom bursting into sound. "Pull up! Pull up! We're going down!"

His head moved, creaking loudly in his mind, sending tiny lightning flashes to his clearing brain. He stared through the thin mountain light at the overturned body pinned by metal two feet away from him, at the dark ugly wound where the head had been. There was a soft glint of the oak leaf on the shirt collar thrust out of the high-altitude flight suit. Body fluids, their downward journey ended, puddled around the neatly slashed alpaca flap of the flight jacket.

Major Holland.

He turned his head warily to squint upward, his eyes adjusting to the dim light. The dangling arm, unmoving, was graced by a bloody stainless steel identification bracelet hanging at the wrist. He'd seen it many times. Air Corps wings, officer grade, engraved name, rank, and serial number. Purchased in New York.

Captain Buchanan.

His body responded slowly. His hands in their heavy air-crew gloves pushed awkwardly at the debris covering him. He was wedged between cold metal, between his flight chair and his radio panel. He struggled free of his safety harness and rolled to a sitting position, brushing against the accusing hand. His headset was around his neck. He pulled it off stiffly.

How long had the captain been dripping on him? He ran a shaking finger along his leather helmet. Congealed blood. The cockpit was gone. He saw the dim shapes of trees moving in the wind. A space beyond, with stars. Night glow on the China mountains.

He was on his knees, over an abyss, breathing the cold, thin night air in long, uneven measures. He felt the lethargy leaving, pain pushing it aside. He remembered. The strange muffled sudden sound. Something striking the C-46. The frozen sight of Major Holland struggling with the controls. The terrible sensation of the downward plummeting. The intercom alive with startled voices. "Pull up! We're going down!"

The swift descent toward the dark mountaintops, the heavy roar of the two-thousand-horsepower Pratt and Whitney engines, the sickening screaming of metal as the plane struck the trees on its long glide downward.

Then the blackness.

He winced as he moved clumsily on hands and knees grated by the metal shards and shattered glass. He crawled an arm's length through the wreckage, over the smashed tree limbs and trunks that pierced the plane. He dropped several feet to the ground, steadying himself against the gaping maw of what had been the cockpit. He shuddered at the awesome sight.

The Combat Cargo C-46, huge and double-bellied, had cut a long narrow path through the trees lining the pinched mountain ridge. The wings, striking two stout trees on each side of the fuselage at the same incredible moment, were sheared off. They lay with their heavy engines to the left and right, far back, crumpled insanely against the mowed trees. The nose of the plane, sliced off by huge branches, was smashed backward up against the top of the plane.

He couldn't stop his shuddering. Something had carved off the major's head. The force of the crash landing had squashed the instrument panel and both pilots and their seats backward into the cockpit. The major and his left pilot's seat were disintegrated against the lower portion of the floor. The captain, wrapped in the remains of his copilot's right seat, was like a red-dampened rag doll, upside down, pinned hideously by the metal over the radio section. One arm was pulp. The other hung down, three fingers and thumb curled, the index finger pointing its guilt. Another small drop of blood fell from the finger.

He pushed himself away from the wreckage, unable to understand the enormity of its message. He shook uncontrollably, staring at the revolting sight of the upturned bodies meshed with the cockpit metal against which they had been impelled. He sighted along the fuselage, seventy-six feet long. The lower cargo deck under the main cabin floor had absorbed much of the tremendous force of the impact, its bulk completely flattened. The fuselage lay bent in its long fat middle at a twenty-degree angle. He smelled the high-octane gasoline, its vapors mingling with the hydraulic and deicer fluids.

He struggled to believe what had happened. The impact after the long downward glide of the C-46 had ripped the front portion of the cockpit upward, taking the two pilots into oblivion. His own seat, directly behind the copilot's, to the rear of Captain Buchanan, lay bent downward. An unexplained physical force had thrown his seat, in which he was strapped by his harness, to the floor of the cockpit. The floor itself was slashed off a foot in front of his radio operator's position.

Death had missed him by inches.

The major! He remembered him desperately pulling back on the controls, jabbing his feet at the rudders, jabbing back the throttles, feathering the propellers and extending full flaps, trying to slow the rapid descent. And the captain, shouting into the intercom, helping the major, watching the narrow mountain ridge rising to meet them. The suddenness of the disaster left them with no time to scramble into their parachutes and bail out.

Staring at the frightful cavity of the nose, he tried to think of the time. It couldn't have been more than a minute. Why hadn't they exploded on impact? The wings, striking the trees on either side of the plummeting fuselage before being ripped off, had borne the first brunt of the crash. The wingless fuselage had slid in a bumpy, jarring path a half block long before more trees slammed into it, ripping the cockpit upward and capping most of it on top of the fuselage.

He couldn't believe they hadn't been incinerated in the plane. The others! His mind functioned with pitiful slowness. Hands out to steady himself, he made his way on limp legs back up into the maw, looking for Nick Engels. Shoots of pain jabbed through his body.

The crew chief lay next to his twisted floor-bolted seat. A long strip of blood-red aluminum alloy stuck crudely out of his chest. His oxygen mask was ripped off. His face, head propped up on a curled metal sheet, made him look as if he were soberly examining the strange spear that pierced his short, muscular body.

He leaned against what was left of the door that connected the pilot's cabin with the main cargo compartment, looking with blinking eyes at what remained of his friend. He knew he should be crying and wondered why he was not.

The main cabin, with its sharp V shape, lay beyond in a terrible darkness. He tried to force himself to think. The VIP? Where was the VIP passenger? He gulped the night air, trying to clear his head and appease his shuddering body. Somewhere in that awful darkness was a very important officer.

He groped dazedly for Nick's right leg. The crew chief usually carried a flashlight in the flight-suit pocket below the knee. It was there. He fumbled with it, trying to find the switch. The light startled him. He turned it into the main cargo compartment. The officer, strapped in at the navigator's table in the front section near the cabin door, sat in the gloom, head bent oddly. It lay almost on his shoulder.

"I'm Master Sergeant Carr," he said. "Sir. Are you all right?" His voice was a metallic echo. No answer. He shook the man's shoulder and the head rolled loosely. Carr straightened in quick nausea. It was the first broken neck he'd seen. The thought galvanized him. The major's head! Where was it?

He started to search, playing the light around the wreckage within the cabin. He stopped abruptly, dimly aware that he was on the edge of insanity.

Insanity with death all around him.

He forced himself back out into the open, switching off the light. The wind moaned in the trees overhead. He sought the familiar North Star and the Dippers. The cold air whipped against his face. The moving tree limbs above him made an eerie sound; portents of an approaching storm brewing in the Mongolia reaches to the north, ready to spring.

They're dead and I'm alive.

He unzipped his heavy flight jacket and felt inside for the shoulder holster. He pulled out the .45 automatic. I'm a survivor, for the third time. For the third time. His mind repeated the words in torment.

We were on fire over the Hump, in the night, both engines hellishly aflame. We all got out. The C-46 exploded seconds later. The pilots died in trees, their bodies ripped as their parachutes swung them mercilessly into the deadly branches. The crew chief came down into a lake, unaware that it was there, and drowned. I came down in a clear area. I walked out. One hundred miles. With the help of the Kachins. That was the second time. Four months ago.

When was the first time? Yes, in Texas. Eighteen months ago. On my final checkout in an advanced trainer, with an instructor in the front seat. A tire blew as I brought it down onto the runway. We ground-looped and caught fire. They got me out. Not the instructor.

I saw his charred body.

Why did they all die and not me?

He pushed back the ejector of the .45.

I've survived three times. I've had more than a thousand hours over the Hump. I've flown dozens of different aircraft. I've served as an enlisted ferry pilot on assignment. I've flown C-46's while the pilot or copilot napped. I came to Burma and China with thirty others. Over a year ago. Half of them are dead. I'm twenty-four years old, and this is the end of me.

I'm alone on a China mountaintop.

He raised the .45 and put its muzzle to his temple.

U.S. Air Corps
Combat Cargo Headquarters
Myitkyina, Burma

Colonel Max Ribbands pointed a finger at the map hanging on the Quonset hut wall.

"Here," he said, "this is the last position Carr sent. We've radioed Yenan and Chengtu. They lost them at the same time Carr slammed out his Mayday." He looked with disgust at the dark brown elevation area where his finger lay. "A twelve-hundred-mile flight. Extra fuel tanks in the cabin. Ground speed averaged one hundred and sixty miles an hour. They were five and three-quarter hours into the flight. That's about nine hundred and thirty miles. They only had two hundred and seventy miles to go. An hour and three-quarters and they'd have made it!"

He slapped the map sharply. "What the hell went wrong! Best crew we had. Holland, Buchanan, Engels, Carr!" He turned to Major Henry Foxx. "And Moffett! Christ, the Dixie Mission has enough trouble without this!"

Major Foxx moved closer to study the map. "That's just at the edge of Shensi province. Damned big mountains up there. I doubt if the Japs had night fighters that far north. We sent them on a straight line from here to Yenan, give or take some in-flight adjustments." He shook his head. "The Chiang Kai-shek boys might have been on to the mission. Still, that's a funny area for them to have their fighters out at night."

"Son of a bitch!" the colonel said over a cigar slammed into his mouth. "Top secret! OSS wanted their man Moffett sneaked in at the dead of night. Dark arrival. We play their game and look what it got us. A damned fine C-46 down and a damned fine crew with it!"

The major scratched his neck and glanced at the wall clock. "It went down at 0109. It's almost 0200. Radio says there's been no radio traffic up there, except the Mayday. If it was shot down, damn it, somebody did it without flipping on a radio."

Alongside the clock was a tear-off calendar. January 15, 1945. The 4th Combat Cargo Group had been in Myitkyina, Burma, only a short time. Before that, it had flown from other bases, carrying war equipment over the Hump into China to supply the Nationalist government, the Kuomintang, headed by Generalissimo Chiang Kai-shek and headquartered in Chungking, China. With the Burma–Ledo Road closed by the Japanese armies, Chiang was dependent on the unarmed cargo aircraft. The American bases in China, where fighters and bombers flew to fight and harass the Japanese armies in China, depended on the cargo planes.

The major kept his eyes on the clock. Another hour and three-quarters and the big C-46, the largest cargo plane in service, would have made it into Yenan. Yenan. He wondered what the place looked like. He had heard about it, often. The base of the Chinese Communist Party and the Chinese Red Army. Chiang, with his Nationalist armies, was locked in a terrible conflict with the Communist Red armies. It was, he reflected, a strange situation. Japan's armies held all of China's coastal areas. Chiang and his Nationalist armies were basically in central China. The Red Armies were behind a massive blockade manned by hundreds of thousands of Nationalist troops that held them in the mountainous northwest area of China. A blockade that had been in effect for years. On which Chiang had expended great amounts of his U.S.-supplied war materials, instead of using those materials against the Japanese invaders. It was Chinese fighting against Chinese over who would control a land of 450,000,000 people, an ancient land that stretched 2,700 miles east and west and 2,600 miles north and south.

The colonel walked around the headquarters Quonset in irritation, glowering at the dusty floor, at the backs of the officers on night duty working at their tables, working on papers, pretending not to be listening. ''We've got to get a rescue team up there from Chengtu. We'll have to do a drop. If the Japs or the Kuomintang slopes get to them first, we'll have a hell of a time!'' He lighted the cigar. ''Goddamned super-secret flights!'' He turned to the major. ''Okay, get busy on it. If Chengtu can do a chute drop, how do they get them out? Find out if we have any native agents in that area. OSS might have some, those crazy bastards. Get me the last reports on the Jap and Kuomintang concentrations. Find out what our intelligence has got. We've got to get those men out of there if any of them are alive!''

The major reached for the telephone.

''If any of them are alive,'' the colonel repeated bitterly.

''Remember the Mongolia storm?'' the major said, hand on the phone. ''We sent them in just ahead of it.''

''Christ!'' the colonel snapped, remembering. ''Check weather. Maybe there's still time to get a rescue team in there.'' He peered at the map. ''A storm coming and they're in that god-awful miserable shitty spot. Even the Chinks stay out of it!' He bit heavily on the cigar.

The major picked up the phone.

Carr's finger touched the trigger.

For a long moment he held the .45 to his temple, then he lowered his arm. He shook his head in dismay, standing at the edge of memory, remembering the Illinois cornfields, deep green in the prairie sunshine. He thought of his father in his American Legion uniform and the World War I medals. He heard his mother's voice calling over the sound of the tractor he was repairing.

He ejected the cartridge, picked it up, took out the clip, and replaced the cartridge in the clip. He clicked the automatic on empty, slammed the clip back in, and holstered the weapon. He no longer shook. The coldness of the mountain night nipped at his lungs, face, and hands. The harsh sounds of the irritable wind in the trees, the snapping of branches together, brought him back to the center of his emotional control. The memories of home! He was in command again, risen from the dead, coming out of the long darkness of near derangement. His functioning mind forced him to decisions. He would walk out, as he'd done before. This time he would have air charts and equipment, none of which he'd had when they'd exploded over the Hump.

He'd found inner resources then, he would find them again. He thought of the Kachins who had passed him along from area to area, guiding him out of more than a hundred miles of mountains and jungle to the safety of the air base at Myitkyina.

He remained motionless, thinking of the death he'd seen in Burma and China. The sight of Jap fighters attacking a convoy of unarmed Combat Cargo C-46's in the unusual early-morning sun over the Hump. The plummeting aircraft with black smoke billowing from their wings. The race to get into a distant cloud cover to escape the Zeros, bullet holes appearing in the fuselage.

He thought of his year in the China-Burma-India theater of war, scenes flipping through his mind like an old newsreel. A neglected, forgotten theater of war. Largely unreported by U.S. news media. Where men disappeared into vast reaches of jungles and mountains. Where men were housed in tents in the midst of unbelievably bad conditions. India, with its teeming millions in countless small villages across a parched, barren land. Burma with its tortuous rivers and deadly jungles. China with its sprawling land mass filled with nearly half a billion people starving, fighting pestilence and disease, uprooted by a macabre war.

The long hours in C-47's and later the larger C-46's over the dangerous, unpredictable Hump, the thickly clustered range of Himalaya Mountains between Burma and China, a terrible reaching trap that ensnared the cargo craft carrying vital supplies from India and Burma into China, from shabby, makeshift bases on one side to even worse ones on the other. The frantic pace of flight after flight, a few hours of sleep, a hurried meal, and more flights. The sounds of the intercom in his ears, the constant vibration of the overloaded planes, the messages sent and received from his radio operator's desk behind the copilot, the taste of the oxygen flowing into his mask at the altitudes above ten thousand feet. He'd been a sergeant, a three-striper, with the Troop Carrier Command, a staff sergeant and another stripe with the Army Transport Command, bypassing tech sergeant and being promoted to master sergeant and six stripes with Combat Cargo the month before arriving at Myitkyina. Six stripes because of his ferry pilot work and his volunteer teaching of the loran, long-range navigation, to newly arrived replacements.

He thought of the meager hospital at Myitkyina where he had recovered from his walkout. Where men lay near death from snake bites, dysentery, malaria, hyena attacks, and gunshot wounds. The British, American, Indian, Chinese, and Kachin jungle fighters whose bodies were ripped by mortar fire shrapnel, trip-wire explosives, machine gun bullets, knives, and swords.

He studied the sky. His death on this China mountain would be futile. He was a survivor. For the third time. He had to do something to get down from that high level. First, the VIP, the man responsible for the mission. He must be carrying something that would give the reason for the high-altitude flight in an unarmed transport of the 4th Combat Cargo group out of Myitkyina under the cover of night.

His distress signal would have been monitored by U.S. planes and installations, perhaps by the Nationalists, the Communists, and even the Japanese. Who would reach the wreckage first? A rescue team from the American air base at Chengtu an hour's flight away? A team from the Communists to the north? A patrol of the Kuomintang Nationalists from the east?

Or would the approaching storm from the north keep them all away? The realization that daylight was only a few hours away, and the storm not much farther, stirred him into movement. He pulled the flashlight from his pocket and went back into the stricken fuselage. He moved past the bodies, unable to look at them again. He laid the light on the contorted navigator's table and searched the VIP.

Under the winter woolen-issue shirt of the officer, after the bulky alpaca-lined altitude flight jacket had been removed, he found a packet of documents sealed in plastic. He opened it with fingers turned red by the cold. He held the papers near the light. Lieutenant Colonel Ambrose Moffett, Office of Strategic Services, Washington, D.C. An official identity sheet. An agenda sheet. Papers in Chinese.

The identity paper said Moffett spoke Chinese. The agenda said Moffett was to meet with Chairman Mao Tse-tung, Ambassador Chou En-lai, and General Chu Teh. Carr drew a deep breath as he unfolded a sheet marked "top secret." He sat down on the gritty cabin floor, holding the light to see better. Moffett's mission was outlined. A highly secret meeting under top security to inform the Dixie Mission and the leaders of the Chinese Red Army of an intelligence breakthrough made possible by sensitive spying at the Kuomintang headquarters at Chungking.

Blinking rapidly, Carr read: "The Nationalist high command has approved a proposal by General Tai Li to capture Mao Tse-tung, Chou En-lai, and General Chu, bring them out of Shensi province, and deliver them to Chiang Kai-shek in Chungking. If they are taken alive, on arrival in Chungking they will be given their choice of public execution or of ordering their armies placed under the control of Generalissimo Chiang Kai-shek immediately."

Carr read on. "Our intelligence unit in Chungking has not determined the method devised for the capture. It was learned, however, that it will be done in such a way as to make it appear that the American Military Observer Mission (Dixie Mission) in Yenan was responsible for turning over the Communist leaders to the Nationalists."

Carr's breath was belly deep. It was desperation at its worst. The Nationalists, called Kuomintang, had been fighting the insurgents, the Chinese Communist Party with its Red Army, for many years. The Kuomintang had suffered innumerable defeats at the hands of the Japanese invaders. It had nearly 800,000 men blockading 600,000 Communist soldiers in northwest China. It needed these men to fight the Japanese. If the Communist leaders could be kidnapped, if their capture could disintegrate the Red armies, more Kuomintang forces could be thrown against the Japanese.

He breathed deeply again. The war against the Japanese had been going poorly; untrained and stupidly led Chinese soldiers were often no match for the superbly trained and well-equipped invaders. The Red Army, fighting a guerrilla war in the north and northeast, had scored victories against the Japanese. They had evaded the Kuomintang, and when they had fought, in three great campaigns, they had beaten the Kuomintang on the battlefield.

Now, more desperation. A senseless attempt to bring the Chinese Communist leaders out of their lair, to humiliate them, to execute them. He thought of the tons of war supplies Combat Cargo

had carried over the Hump, flying high over the Burma–Ledo Road
closed by the wily Japanese; aviation gasoline, oil, ammunition,
jeeps, disassembled bulldozers, medical supplies, food, artillery,
machine guns, aircraft engines, truck engines. Everything. Even
Kotex to be used as oil strainers for the engines of the 14th Air
Force fighters in China. And Kuomintang troops to fight in Burma
against the Japanese there. And VIPs.

He reread the English documents. He'd heard scuttlebutt about
the Red Chinese, that Mao and the others were loosely guarded in
Yenan. Under a surprise move, the plot could be carried out. The
results would be a great clash between the Red Army and the Nationalists, which maintained a blockade of the Communists somewhat to the south of Yenan.

He stuffed the papers back into the plastic folder and placed that
inside his own wool shirt, in the back under his shoulders. He
rezippered his flight jacket. American intelligence officers in
Chungking, the headquarters of Chiang Kai-shek's military and
political forces, had uncovered the kidnap plot. It was not information they would trust to a radio message to Yenan. It might be intercepted and decoded by Tai Li's men.

Carr was puzzled. The "top secret" paper mentioned no date for
the kidnapping, nor the date when the information was first
learned. The intelligence coup must have been recent, he thought.
Thus the quick dispatch of Moffett from Myitkyina. Now he knew
why Moffett had left from Myitkyina in Burma rather than from
Chungking, where the China-Burma-India headquarters of the
United States were maintained by military and diplomatic officers.
The U.S. command did not want the generalissimo to learn they
had uncovered the plot.

Carr knew the generalissimo would enjoy having the three Communist prisoners brought to him. In 1936, Chiang himself had been
taken prisoner at Sian, and blamed Chou En-lai for playing a role
in that escapade. Alerted by gunfire, he had run from a building
and severely hurt his back falling into a pit, where he had been captured by the soldiers of the "Young Marshal," Chang Hsueh-
liang, commander of the Shensi-Kansu-Ninghsia Border Area, the
blockade line against the Chinese Red Army. Carr had heard the
story from a war correspondent during a Hump flight. Chiang, in
Sian to inspect his troops manning the border that hemmed in the

Red Army in the north of China, gained his freedom after his capture by the Young Marshal. He agreed with the Communists—an agreement in which Chou En-lai reportedly played a role—to a united front under which the Nationalists and the Communists would fight their common enemy, the Japanese.

The Young Marshal, after releasing Chiang, had flown with him to Nanking, the generalissimo's headquarters at that time, and had in turn been placed under arrest. The governor of Shensi province, Yan Hu-ch'eng, who had acted with the Young Marshal, had been murdered in a prison camp years afterward.

Carr placed the light on the navigator's table and went through Moffett's clothing carefully. Nothing. There was no reason to search Major Holland, Captain Buchanan, or Nick Engels. They would carry nothing in connection with OSS intelligence. He recalled Moffett coming on board, carrying only a parachute, the one next to his lifeless body. He pulled the parachute free of the debris and opened the seat pack. Among the survival items were a .38 pistol with a strange sealed packet taped to it. He undid the packet. A silencer tumbled into his cold hand.

He stood on rubbery legs, wondering what the OSS man had intended to do with the weapon. He slid the units into a pocket and looked at his navigator's hack watch. The luminous dials told him it was twelve past two in the morning. How long had he been unconscious? He calculated it was fifteen to twenty minutes. It would be light in three hours. With the light there might be a search patrol. If the storm did not come before that.

He went outside and walked along the crumpled, heavily dented fuselage, playing the flashlight on it. What had caused the crash? Had they been hit by a night fighter equipped with a cannon or a rocket? At the tail unit he saw the hole. The outward ripped metal around the gap, almost large enough for him to crawl through, indicated there had been an explosion in the section just ahead of the tail fin and elevators.

He stood on a shorn tree stump to look in the hole. The light played on the remains of an explosive cylinder placed where it would destroy the hydraulic controls of the tail unit. He smelled the ugly odor of the explosive. He moved the light around, looking at the twisted metal and torn hydraulic systems.

It had taken a little more than five hours for the time bomb to go off. It had been set by a chemical delay fuse. He'd seen them at Chungking when he'd helped unload supplies. A box, falling from a truck, had broken open and Nick Engels, an inveterate prier and pack rat, had snitched one for study. He'd explained it to Carr.

The fuse, no larger than a pencil, held a wire made taut by a spring. An acid vial, of various strengths, could be broken to allow the acid to dissolve the wire until it broke. The small spring snapped shut, activating the fuse, which exploded a small container of Composition C.

The thickness of the fuse wire and the strength of the acid would allow the detonation in a matter of days, hours, or minutes. Carr, swallowing hard, moved away from the jagged hole and leaned against the heavily crumpled fuselage. Someone had set the explosive but misjudged the timing. If it had gone off while they were over the northern range of the Hump, there would have been no survivors. Here, on the smaller mountains of north China, there had been a remote possibility, one that produced a single survivor.

The blast was meant to sever the hydraulic controls that operated the huge tail-fin rudder and elevators. The controls, he'd seen, had not gone completely, nor had the hydraulic fluid burst into flames. Torn impacted metal had jammed the rudder into an exact rest place, so that the plane could move neither to the right or left but had to continue straight on. The elevators had been frozen into a slight glide setting, putting the plane into a long sweep down toward the mountain ridge instead of into a nose-over plunge toward earth.

The pinched ridge, strangely, had acted almost as a runway for the C-46. It lay directly along the downward path of the plane. Looking at the scene in the night glow, Carr shook his head in disbelief. Major Holland, fighting that long glide, had been able to keep the nose up long enough by using wing flaps, cutting power completely, skimming the trees, switching off electricity, until the craft lost the last of its lift and slammed into the cushioning trees.

Carr fought his sick feeling. Someone at Myitkyina had placed the small explosive cylinder in the tail section where it would not be found in a preflight inspection. Someone who had access to the

guarded plane. The tail section could be entered, under that cir-
cumstance, by someone going through the small door in the rear
bulkhead within the cabin itself.

Sabotage!

Carr felt a rising anger. So much for security! He remembered
the Chinese laborers who had swept out the plane and cleaned the
toilet container. There had been Nationalist agents in the cleanup
crew, he was certain of that.

He carried the thought with him as he explored the wreckage beyond the fuselage, playing the light on the unbelievable wrecks of
the wings. The massive four-bladed propellers of the engines were
bent into grotesque shapes. Metal ripped from the bottom of the
craft and the wings littered the crash path, mixed insanely with
shredded trees.

He walked on ground sodden with high-octane aviation fuel, hydraulic and deicer fluids, stepping on metal shards and pieces of
trees. He saw that the slope of the ridge, going down, not up, had
helped the plane avoid a direct head-on impact into the ground. A
turn of luck that had left one man alive.

He walked back, stepping around the larger pieces of debris,
feeling a furious anger at the men who had sabotaged the C-46.
They were agents of General Tai Li, Chiang Kai-shek's intelligence chief, a man called the Chinese Himmler, the man who now
plotted to kidnap the Communist leaders from Yenan and blame it
on the American Dixie Mission.

At the devastated cockpit area he steadied himself. He had a
great deal of work to do before daybreak and the storm. His dislike of the Nationalist Chinese, corrupt and inefficient, had
hardened into hatred. He went into the main cargo cabin to
gather the things he would need to make it off the mountain. He
would not put out ground markers for the search-and-rescue
team from Chengtu. He would not stay to greet them or whoever made it to the wreck. He had Moffett's packet. With the
storm coming, could the brass in Myitkyina send another plane?
He doubted it. The responsibility of getting the packet to Yenan
was now his.

He felt a terrible resolve as he worked in the light of the issue
flashlight. He would find a way to repay General Tai Li for his
treachery.

Japanese Intelligence Center
Northern Szechwan Province

Lieutenant Renya Oshima took the paper from the radio man and traced lines on the map spread on the field table under the kerosene lantern.

"Ah," he said softly, "here are the coordinates. The plane is down here. We will move as soon as it is light." Sergeant Masumi Mutagachi shifted his sturdy bulk under his despised Chinese clothes. He regarded his superior, seeing the somewhat frail body, the smooth, darkened skin of the face, the delicate hands, the thick black hair cut Chinese-style, and the irrational look that often appeared in the officer's eyes.

"The storm?" he said, affecting his obedient posture. "And is it wise to leave here? Our mission is to stay covert, to recruit more fifth columnists who advise us of the Communists to the north and the Kuomintang in this area."

The lieutenant was displeased. "Damn the storm! That plane can only be American. I will radio headquarters for permission to investigate it. The storm will give us good cover." Mutagachi bowed and left the tiny brick and thatched-roof building that housed the secret task force of the Imperial Japanese Army assigned to penetrate into China's vast reaches and organize spies and informers. The wind whipped his clothes about him in snapping sounds. He stared through the night gloom at the distant mountains looming over the intervening land. The stars were brilliant, but he worried about the approaching storm.

He knew the mountains were sparsely inhabited, but they held nomads and tribesmen who hated Japanese. There was perfidy everywhere, and he shuddered with a sense of dread as he studied the black land mass to the north. Up there, somewhere, was an American aircraft. Down here, an unpredictable officer.

He grimaced as he made his way to another building where his men were sleeping. Having been aroused by the lieutenant, he knew he could not return to sleep. He would organize the patrol as ordered. Still, his mind was on the vast possibilities of discovery once they left the comparative safety of the small village from which they operated, disguised as Chinese.

He plodded over the uneven ground, bending against the wind, feeling a deep sense of dismay. The lieutenant was overly ambitious. Lately the man had been acting queerly, as if a small Chinese demon had slipped inside him. Mutagachi coughed as dust rolls struck him. The lieutenant and his ambition, driven by the unseen demon, would get them all killed in this miserable part of China!

Under the lantern light, Lieutenant Oshima wrote his request to General Sato Ishimura for permission to take a small patrol of his intelligence force and investigate the downed American craft. It would provide valuable information. What was the plane doing in that area so late at night? Where was it going? What was aboard it? He studied the night's radio reports. The fixes on the position of the Mayday signal came from his radio operation and from another clandestine unit eighty kilometers to the northeast. There had been no other radio traffic in that area at that hour. Now the Americans were sending coded signals, obviously in connection with the crash.

The puzzle intrigued him. He straightened, thinking of the possibilities. He could take a patrol deep into enemy territory! An escape from the detestable recruitment of Chinese to betray their warlord masters, their landowners, their political leaders.

He entered the small adjoining room and handed the message to the sleepy radio operator. Watching the man send the dispatch, he felt a surge of elation. The general would see the advantage of his breaking cover for so important an objective. He knew that General Ishimura, aging rapidly, suffering poor health, needed something to make him look better in the eyes of the general staff in Tokyo.

Ishimura's fortunes, related as they were to those of Lieutenant General Masaki Honda, commander of Japanese forces in Burma, where things were not going well, were faring poorly. Taken from a combat role and placed in intelligence because of his ability to speak Chinese, Ishimura felt the samurai's fierce longing for combat.

The last time Oshima had conferred with the general at the

Kempetai base at Lini in Shantung province, he had heard all this from the disgruntled, balding, overly fat Ishimura. The American plane, if it held intelligence material about the Chinese Red Army or about the Nationalist army under Chiang Kai-shek, would be a priceless card to play to win better assignments for them both.

Oshima was sitting cross-legged by the tiny fireplace, warming himself from the winter cold, watching the flames and drinking the last of his tea, when the young radio man entered, bowed, and handed him the reply from the general. He read it and smiled. "You are permitted," the message said, "but no more than four days. Remain in radio contact."

The tea never tasted sweeter.

It was snow.

The first dry flakes fell, stinging his reddened cheeks, as Carr crawled down from the plane carrying the decrepit barracks bag. The bag was heavy, but he had no choice but to take all the survival items he could. A light canvas sheet left over from a free-fall drop to a Gurkha battalion in Burma; the drogue chute from his own parachute; long lengths of nylon shroud lines from the chute. These would make a tent.

From the parachute seats he had all the first-aid supplies, toilet paper, a hand compass, and packaged food which went with the C and K rations that he and Nick always carried on board. From Nick Engels's crew-chief compartment he had a full water container, a mess kit, extra flashlight batteries, three cans of Sterno, and a metal holder.

Miraculously, the items had not been damaged. Nor was the carbine with its seven extra clips. It had taken all of Nick's persuasive tactics to get the weapons officer at Myitkyina to allow them to have it instead of the standard .45-caliber burp gun, an automatic weapon that could spray but seldom hit anything with accuracy. Most C-46's carried one.

His search with the aid of the flashlight had turned up his two jungle knives, now strapped to his legs near the ankles, air charts, the code book and ship's log, his Air Corps binoculars, a hatchet, a half-dozen clips of .45 cartridges, and three hand grenades that

Nick had unaccountably hidden in his tool kit. There was a lensatic compass to help plot his position in the China mountains, and sealed packets of matches. And three small packets of salt that Carr always carried with him.

In the bag were the personal effects of the dead men. He hadn't wanted to leave them behind for looters. He swung the bag onto his back, held there by nylon cord as a backpack. He hefted the carbine. He glanced at the place where he had buried the dead men's weapons. They would have added too much weight to an already heavy load.

But he had packed Moffett's pistol and silencer, unwilling to bury the unusual weapon. He stood before the cockpit area, looking up at the sky. It seemed to be lightening, ever so little. From his study of the air charts in the cabin, he knew he was at least two hundred miles northwest of the American air base at Chengtu, from which B-29's flew to bomb Japan. He was about the same distance from Sian to the northeast. Yenan, his destination, lay to the north and west of Sian about 250 to 270 miles. He would need the food and survival gear to get him there.

If bandits, nomads, deserters, animals, or the storm did not get him, he could make it.

He had done all he could. The bodies lay together in the wrecked cabin. He had pried them from their blood-splattered metal tombs and dragged them into the cabin. He had made certain their dog tags were visible. He had placed metal pieces over the door and the smashed windows of the cabin to keep out any prowling animals.

There was nothing usable left in the wreck. The radio transmitter and receiver and the crystal panel tuners were smashed beyond repair. The natives would find the plane and hack it apart, carrying off the aluminum to be used for shelters.

The snow was heavier. He swept up handfuls of it to remove the dried blood from his face and his leather flight helmet. Then he set off. He looked back once, peering through the snow, wondering if he had forgotten anything. He turned back to the trail along the ridge, feeling an incredible loneliness.

In two hours, trudging through the thickening snow, he felt it was safe to make camp. The fierce hate that filled him as he moved served to override his pain. His savage thoughts concentrated on General Tai Li, whom he had once glimpsed in a long black limousine at the Chungking air base. They concentrated on the inept security at Myitkyina that had allowed Chinese agents to learn of the flight and sabotage it.

He found a space sheltered by thick trees. He tied a drogue line between two of the trees, slung the nylon chute and canvas sheet over it, used the hatchet to slash stakes from tree limbs and hammer them into the harsh ground to peg the nylon and canvas down tight. He had a shelter. He crawled inside with the barracks bag, carbine next to him, and made a meal, heating the opened tin of K ration over the Sterno on its holder.

The storm hit with full fury, so brutal that it removed all visibility when he opened the entry flap to peer outside. He cleaned the tin, punched several holes in the bottom with a knife, inserted one of the four small candles he'd found in Nick Engels's tool kit, and lighted it. It would keep him warm within his wind-whipped tent. In the candlelight, he looked again at the air charts to prepare his troubled mind again for the time when he would break camp and move on. He was comfortable in his winter-issue woolen uniform, covered by the thick flight suit with its alpaca lining. His air-crew gloves had a thin silk lining covered by a thick woolen insert inside a leather covering. He strapped his leather flight helmet under his chin. With the candle heat and his clothes, food, and water, he would survive the night.

He felt the wind beat against the simple tent. The howling outside comforted him, despite the raging soreness in his body. He was far enough away from the wreck to avoid capture at that site. The storm would continue throughout the day, making it difficult, if not impossible, for searchers to scale the high ridge. Or for animals to be on the prowl. He lay back and curled himself around the heat of the flickering candle, the carbine near his hand next to the .45 automatic pistol.

He closed his eyes and was asleep instantly.

Major Foxx, groggy from a sleepless night spent between the headquarters Quonset hut and the radio shack, looked up to see Colonel Ribbands coming through the screen door.

At that moment, the Myitkyina air-raid siren burst into life. Jarred into quick motion, he followed the abruptly turning colonel out of the door, one step ahead of the other officers of the 4th Combat Cargo group who'd worked with the major through the night. They ran through the thick, warm morning fog and leaped into a deep trench, panting heavily.

"Son of a bitch!" Ribbands yelled, shaking a fist at the sound of the Japanese Betty overhead. "Why can't our guys get that bastard!" He ducked as the antiaircraft battery opened fire. No one in the trench had a steel helmet, and they protected their heads with their arms. A stick of bombs exploded several hundred yards away, shaking the ground. Loose dirt tumbled into the trench.

"Well," Foxx said, "he's on time, anyway. It's all the Japs can do to let us know they're still around. We've been here a couple of weeks and 'Pissing Sam' has only missed one day." The roar of the bomber faded. The hit-and-run attack was over. The siren trailed off and the men returned to the Quonset hut, shaking dirt from their tropic uniforms. The early-morning fog from the Irrawaddy River forced them to use the high radio antennas, which they could see, as guide marks.

Inside, Ribbands said, "I talked to the C.O. He's pissed off at me. He thinks it was equipment failure. Intelligence told him there were no Japs or Chinks up there last night."

"It could be." Foxx wasn't certain.

"How'd you make out with Yenan and Chengtu?"

"The storm is a number oner, Colonel," Foxx said. "Snow, the kind that drifts. It's cold up there. The overcast is up to fifteen angels, and some of the peaks in that area are at twelve and fifteen. It's going to clear later." He sniffed. "The Reds can't get anyone organized on that side of the blockade right away. It will have to be the search-and-rescue guys from Chengtu."

Ribbands pulled up a chair and sat down. "The OSS came to see me. Got me out of the sack. They don't think it was equipment failure or pilot error. I told them to go see the C.O." He glanced quickly around at the other men, all busy at their desks. "They think something must have happened here. They don't want Chungking to know about it. We're under wraps."

"What do they think happened?"

"They think someone got on board. Perhaps a delayed explosive."

Foxx was startled. "The coolies? The sweepers?

"They got the M.P.'s and Gurkhas and rounded them up. Two of them are missing."

"Oh, shit!"

"They're out in the jungle chasing those two slopes." Ribbands moved his bulk. He wore a clean khaki uniform, shirt opened at the neck. He brushed a hand through his salt-and-pepper hair. His light blue eyes looked at the fly-specked ceiling. "It's fun and games like this that are killing me. We just moved into this damned place. Jap bomber in the morning. Jap snipers in the hills. Now, on top of all we've got to do to get cargo over the Hump to Chiang Kai-shek, we've got this cloak-and-dagger mess." He stood up abruptly. "I'm going to see the Old Man. Keep on top of the storm where the plane went down. Let me know as soon as Chengtu gets a team in there. We've got to find out what happened."

He slammed the screen door behind him.

Carr set off along the ridge, his heavy paratrooper's boots tramping down the dry snow.

He and Nick Engels had long since quit wearing the native-made jungle boots on flights. They'd traded cases of beer for the boots in Kunming. Looking at the low overcast, he knew the inevitable search-and-rescue team would have difficulty finding the wreck. He thought of the base camp at Myitkyina. They would be in a flap, trying to find out why the plane went down. He thought of the tented city alongside the Irrawaddy River, the rope-laced bunks, foul-tasting water, malarial mosquitoes, snakes, water buffalo, Gurkha guards, Sikhs, Punjabi, Hindus, Muslims, betel-nut-red-teethed Kachin hill men, Tokyo Rose and her broadcasts, the BBC news, the Armed Forces station in Calcutta.

His eyes moved warily as he plodded through the deep, dry snow, every movement painful. He thought of the combat lessons he'd had from the Gurkhas, playful and boyish, who taught him how to throw their curved knife, how to use their battle stick. And the little brown Kachins, the wily jungle fighters who taught him on his walkout how to tend to leeches, snake bites, insect bites, stomach distress, and how to use their razor-sharp sword, the *dah*.

And the British advisers who roamed around the base; they had taught him the Japanese jujitsu and their own hand-to-hand combat techniques. He and the other American airmen, who knew little or nothing of such things before they arrived in Burma; returned the favors by showing the natives and the British something about American baseball and football.

He'd fought with himself about leaving the wreck. The first rule was to stay. But he couldn't stand to be near the four bodies. He'd committed himself. Yenan it was. He knew, dimly, that his survivor syndrome was at work.

Leaving the ridge, he came across animal tracks. It was difficult going down, but he had chosen the best spot he'd seen. It was almost midday, dark under the overcast, when he saw the pugmarks of a tiger, larger than his gloved hand placed over one of them. Other tracks appeared to be those of wild dogs and smaller animals.

He made his way down the small mountain, slipping often in the mud where the thinner snow had already melted. Near the bottom, he chose a course that ran to the northeast. In minutes, some instinct made him stop and move into the protection of a rock outcrop. He was close to the valley floor. He used the binoculars and saw a winding dirt road below, puddled by melted snow and sheltered by small trees and bushes. There was no sound ahead of him, but he caught a movement. Through the binoculars he saw the Chinese man, a dark form against the rocks, kneeling, peering over a large boulder, watching something in front of him, unaware of Carr behind him.

To stay where he was meant losing valuable time. If he moved, the Chinese might see him and raise an alarm. Carr let the backpack down easily and placed the binoculars on top of it. He unsheathed the Gurkha throwing knife and hefted the carbine. Moving cautiously, as the Kachins had taught him, he came within yards of the man. The Chinese, dressed in dirty blue padded jacket and pants, was intent on whatever was ahead. A bolt-action rifle lay at his side. Ahead, Carr made out what appeared to be a small cave dug into the slope, partially screened by mountain shubbery.

The man's head turned suddenly. It was encased in a fur headpiece of strange appearance to Carr. His eyes met Carr's, and he turned fully to reach for the rifle. He stood, trying to throw the bolt. The Gurkha knife slashed through the air. It struck the faded blue fabric above the chest, at the throat.

Carr saw the intense shock in the man's dark eyes. One hand still held the rifle. Carr lunged, swinging the carbine. It thudded against the fur headpiece. The man fell and was still. Carr breathed again in a large gulp. He had not wanted a rifle shot to betray him. He looked with a mixture of uneasiness and triumph at the form at his feet. The man's long hair glistened greasily. His face was scarred from smallpox and what appeared to be an old knife wound across one cheek. Carr knelt by the man, feeling for a pulse; there was none. He pulled the knife free, wiped it on the soiled jacket, and sheathed it. He moved carefully to the boulder to look over it.

He counted four men, creeping in what appeared to be an assault line. They signaled silently to each other. Their objective was the cave. They moved crablike, concentrating on their quarry. They wore uniforms of the Nationalist army and carried bolt-action rifles. The sight of the uniforms destroyed his notion that he would be able to make his way quietly out of the area. The man he had killed, he believed, had been a scout for the four soldiers. They were part of the Tai Li group, and that meant they had something to do with the sabotage.

Carr moved over the boulder to follow the men, putting the carbine in its firing position. As they rose to run forward he did the same. There was no shooting. Loud voices rose in triumph. The men had their prize, an old man and a young girl. They dragged the pair from the cave and danced around their captives, who looked at them with stoic expressions. Chinese civilians!

One of the men ran into the cave. He emerged, throwing straw mats, blankets, and small baskets into the wet bedrock clearing. He laughed gleefully in a high-pitched tone. Another soldier struck the old man with a rifle butt, yelling at him, taunting. The old man went down, a splash of blood tinting his long white hair and his wispy white beard.

The men turned their attention to the girl, roughly stripping her quilted pants and jacket from her, throwing her on a mat, talking to each other excitedly about her nakedness. The fat one, who acted as their leader, thrust his hand into his trousers and pulled out his hardened penis. He waved it back and forth, grinning with great expectation, and fell upon the girl.

Carr stood, firing first at the man who still held a rifle. He saw him jolt and fall. The others, in shock, moved to pick up their rifles. He shot them both, firing twice into each. The leader rolled from the girl toward his weapon. Carr fired again. The fat soldier's face shattered. Carr went to one knee, swinging the carbine in a wide arc, looking warily for others. He heard no shots or the sound of running feet.

He walked past the dead men. The nude girl, astonished, lay still, head off the ground, staring at him. He motioned to her clothes, and she quickly put them on. He marveled at the smoothness of her light tan skin, almost ivorylike, the suppleness of her slender body, her long black hair, and the dark, almond-shaped eyes in an exquisite oval face. Her lips were red, full, and beautifully shaped. He couldn't guess how old she was.

He went to the old man and motioned her to help him. He kept his eyes moving around the area, his finger on the trigger. She knelt by the old man, helping him to sit up. He moaned. She talked to him in high-pitched staccato Chinese. She patted his face and his eyes opened. His arms moved awkwardly, and she tried to straighten out his legs. She helped him to his feet, and Carr steadied him with his free hand.

The girl turned to Carr. She said something in Chinese. He shook his head. He pointed to the sky and made the sound of an airplane.

"Are you an American?" she said.

Carr was stunned. He almost dropped the carbine. "American? Yes! My God, I can't believe it!"

"How did you get here?" she asked. The old man's eyes blinked, and he held a thin, age-spotted hand to his head.

Carr pointed south with the carbine. "Our plane crashed during the night on that ridge up there. I'm the only survivor." He swallowed hard, looking at her magnificent eyes. "Thank God you speak English! I was wondering what I was going to do with you. Who are those soldiers? Why were they after you?"

"They're Nationalist deserters. We've been hiding from them and others like them for days. Someone from our village must have informed on us. It is our ancestral village."

"Is it near here?"

She indicated a distant place. "Over there, about ten li."

He remembered. "That's about three miles." His eyes swept around again. He had just killed four of Chiang Kai-shek's men. No, he had killed five. "There was another one, up there." He indicated the boulder.

"Then he was the one who brought them here. What did he look like?" Carr described the man's pocked and scarred face. "Yes, that would be Ku the Miserable. He sold us out."

Carr looked at the bodies. He felt no remorse, especially in light of the gang rape they had been about to indulge in. "We've got to get out of here. Can he walk?" She spoke to the old man in Chinese, and he nodded, his eyes showing obvious pain. "Wait here," Carr said. He raced back to get the barracks bag and binoculars.

"There's a truck down below," she said when he returned. "I saw them come in it. But we did not know where else to go. There are other groups looking for us. My grandfather is too old to run. We hid, hoping they would not find us in the cave, but Ku the Miserable must have told them exactly where we were."

Carr took the old man's arm, not surprised at its frailty. Together he and the girl helped the old man down the rest of the treacherous slope, wet and slippery, along a narrow overgrown footpath. The old man grunted often in pain, the gash in his head still bleeding.

There was no sentry. The truck was in a grove of ugly-looking trees. It was smallish, an old Ford, with a dented cab

and an uncovered, rotten wood-stake bed. Its tires were worn
and it had been poorly maintained. Rust covered it in patches.

The air was warmer at the lower level, despite the heavy overcast. Carr removed the heavy flight suit and threw it in the back.
He fished out a leather A2 jacket, old and worn, given to him by a
pilot returning after many Hump hours to the States. He threw the
backpack onto the back of the truck, noting the wooden case fastened at the end near the cab. No time to look into it. He helped the
old man and the girl into the cab and ran around to the driver's side.
He turned the ignition switch. The engine coughed and rattled into
life.

"I'm going to Yenan," he said, feeling a great elation. "Can I
drop you somewhere along the way?"

CHAPTER TWO

Lieutenant Renya Oshima, arms folded in disgust, stared at the small van that concealed his radio equipment. It was mired in the mud of a deeply rutted road. He watched his five men, all he could spare, dressed in their Chinese clothes, massed to push it from the deep hole in which its front wheels were almost hidden.

He heard Sergeant Mutagachi shouting harsh, guttural orders in Japanese and was grateful there was no one around in the desolate area to hear that Japanese voice deep within enemy territory.

Smallish but muscular, he appeared to be Chinese, a genetic effect given to him by a grandfather who had served in a diplomatic post in Peking and brought home a Chinese bride. He affected the Chinese haircut and mannerisms. He spoke the Chinese national tongue, learned at the Kempetai training camp near Tokyo. He was proud to be a member of the Kempetai, the secret intelligence organization.

He studied the map again, aware that a map and the actual terrain often did not match. He looked at the coordinates marking where the Mayday signal of the American plane had been fixed. He glanced at the ugly low purplish overcast and then at the white cover of the peaks ahead. It would be difficult to climb to the top. If he were successful the effort would be well rewarded. He thought of General Sato Ishimura and the last conference he'd had with him at the Kempetai center in Shantung province, dining on rice and fish, with excellent tea and several cups of hot sake. "Your mission in northwest China is one of high value to us," the general said. "We have done well in organizing fifth columnists. There are always Chinese who wish to betray their masters. Infil-

39

trate as far west and north as you can. Find those who would join us.''

There was that despotic crooked smile that revealed rotting teeth in the old man's puffy, heavy-lidded face. Dental care in the field was rare, and the general had not been home in a long time. Nor was his dysentery completely cured. He suffered frequent internal disturbances. He sat, short, stumpy legs crossed, eyes bloodshot, holding the tiny cup of sake. His rumpled tunic was open at the throat over a bulging belly. A white ceremonial band was wrapped around his glistening bald head. An air of evil drifted from him, keeping Oshima on the alert. In the Japanese way, he belched heavily in appreciation of the meal.

''We face great difficulties in Burma,'' the general said. ''The American Stilwell has been recalled, and Wedemeyer operates as the commanding general of the American forces in the China theater. General Honda, my beloved relative, has had too many defeats. We lost Myitkyina last August, and now the enemy threatens to open the Burma Road.'' A huge sigh from the overflowing belly. ''We must know more about the American B-29 base at Chengtu.'' A bomblike fart. ''Your mission is to find out all you can about the Americans. You will need all of the Chinese spies and informers you can recruit. You will have enough Chinese yuan and opium to help you. You will have excellent radio equipment. Your men speak Chinese, as you do. You must not fail us.''

The lieutenant came out of his reverie to find the sergeant bowing. The radio van was loose and moving again. They were ready. The lieutenant got in the small, dirt-covered sedan and eyed the mountains ahead, waiting for the sergeant to get behind the wheel. The car dipped as the heavy Mutagachi did so. The snow tops of the mountains penetrated the gloomy cloud layer. The car, followed by the van, both bearing the Chinese markings of a Szechwan rice-buying combine, bumped and jerked on the unfriendly dirt-and-mud road.

The long meeting was nearly over.

Colonel Ribbands sat looking at the C.O. of the Myitkyina base. ''Oh, shit!'' he said. ''Why didn't you tell me?''

The C.O. shrugged. ''The OSS would have my ass, Max, if they knew I'd let you in on it. They couldn't send it in code to Captain

Beard in Yenan. It might be intercepted and broken by Tai Li's men. Or by the Kempetai. They wanted one of their own, Moffett, to take it in and face-to-face it with Mao, Chou, and General Chu.''

"It cost us a good ship and our best crew," Ribbands said testily.

"OSS has no doubt that Tai Li's agents here picked it up. They heard someone who was loose-mouthed.''

"Why don't our people in Chungking tell Chiang the deal's been uncovered?''

"Max, it would blow a very sensitive operation OSS has inside Tai Li's group there. If Chance Beard can catch them in the act in Yenan, it gives a Mao a club to hit Chiang with.''

Ribbands shifted uncomfortably. "What happens now?''

"We send another crew and another OSS guy.''

Max almost spat. "You know what the weather's like up there? We're sweating in heat here and they're freezing their balls off in northern China. Yenan and the whole area are socked in. We can't send another C-46 with cabin fuel tanks in there now. Not until the weather clears." An idea struck him. "Why don't you get the Dixie Mission pulled out of Yenan? Move them to another place up there. If Tai Li's goons are successful and no Americans are around, they can't blame the snatch on us.''

The C.O. shook his head. "I've been through that with OSS and our own intelligence men. The Dixie Mission has been there since late last July. They are to find ways we can justify dumping Chiang and putting the U.S. behind the Commies. Hell, Max, the Commies are fighting the Japs, and Chiang's only concerned with fighting the Commies. With those conditions, look how lousy the war against the Japs has been going in China.''

"I see it," Ribbands said. "Since they jerked Stilwell home— that was last October—we've got to keep those guys in Yenan. It's got to pay off for us." He coughed. "I still don't understand why they can't radio the kidnap plot to Beard. Our codes have been holding up.''

"Max, look at it this way. The Gurkhas caught the two coolies who were on the cleanup crew. Obviously they were agents. They put up a fight in the jungle and were killed. The cabin fuel tanks and loose talk must have tipped them off. They had nothing on their bodies. Our radio sweep logs show there was no radio done around here on a clandestine basis before or after Holland and Buchanan took off. That means the agents did not have time to radio Tai Li's relay men about the fact Moffett was being sent to Yenan.''

Ribbands thought it over. ''That means Tai Li doesn't know we know about the plot.''

''He didn't learn about it by radio. If those agents sent a courier overland it would take days or weeks to get to another of their radio links.''

Ribbands relaxed. ''All right, so it's static for a little while. If you want to get another ship up there to tell the Red slopes to keep their heads down, I'll have one ready for you.''

The C.O. spread both hands. ''It's tricky. OSS tells me Moffett was carrying a packet with everything spelled out. I've contacted Chengtu. They've got to get a team in there and get that packet before someone else finds it. I'll keep leaning on them. You get a ship ready. OSS will have someone with another packet.''

Ribbands stood and moved toward the door. ''Max,'' the C.O. said, ''what you heard stays here.''

Ribbands grimaced. ''Sure.'' He left the C.O.'s quarters in the little brick and stone house, one of the few still standing at the Burma air base.

Radio Operations Hut
U.S. Air Force
Chengtu, Szechwan Province

''Red Dog, this is Fox Able.''

''Red Dog, Fox Able. Read you five on five.''

''Fox Able, say your position.''

''Red Dog, Fox Able at code six six point three niner niner up and oner eight point three seven down. Do you read?''

''Roger. How is the weather?''

''Thick soup. Cleared on ridge but ridge has a thick white top. No sighting. Elevation five zero oner oner. Over.''

Static

"Fox Able, Fox Able, Roger on weather."

Static

"Fox Able, Fox Able, respond to Red Dog."

"Sorry, Red Dog. We think we've found it! Hold the line. We're going down for a better look."

Static

"Ah, Red Dog, Fox Able here. We've got it in sight. Two hundred feet over ridge. Long gash on cheek. Read me?"

"Roger."

"Bird in nest, bird in nest!" Static. "Affirmative on fixes, affirmative!"

"I read you, Fox Able. Any sight of the shepherd and his flock?"

"Negative, Red Dog. Colorado quilt. Negative on patches."

"Roger. Give me a five-second button-down for double fix."

Clear tone. "Ah, Roger, Fox Able, we have you. You are cleared for return. IFF four, IFF four. Do you read?"

"Roger, Red Dog, affirmative IFF four. Over."

"Thank you, Fox Able. Well-done."

"Roger and out."

The radio operations lieutenant finished his rapid writing in the log book and stood up. "That goddamned soup up there! That B-25 has been gridding that area for two hours in a stinking overcast you can cut with a knife." He looked at the radio men around him. "They found the C-46 but no one's moving around. No ground panels laid out. Snow has covered the wreck."

He waved the log book. "Now we know exactly where it is. I'll take this over to command. They'll get a search-and-rescue team in there."

"What about the storm?" one of the men said.

"Screw the storm!" the lieutenant said. He left on a run to the jeep standing outside the hut.

They came to a fork in the rutted, muddy dirt road, and Carr downshifted the ancient truck.

It had been a strange, silent dash along a twisting, hilly route. They'd seen a few peasants trudging along the way. They had looked up, startled, to see the speeding truck and moved quickly to one side. They appeared tired and emaciated. Their clothes reflected their poverty. Some carried reed baskets, others long sticks to ward off wild dogs. Others carried bundles slung from shoulder yokes. Old people walked with the aid of sticks. There were a few children among them. They plodded stoically on their way.

"Any idea where we are?" Carr shouted over the noise of the engine. They were several hours away from the cave site and the five dead men. "This piece of junk is heating up. We need water for the radiator. I want to see how much gas we've got. And we haven't eaten."

The girl, holding her grandfather's bloodied head on her shoulder, said, "The one to the right cuts back to Hanzhong. The other goes to Baoji." He drove the truck into a grove of misshapen trees.

"We're far enough away. Let's take stock." He killed the engine. "How's your grandfather?"

"He does not feel well."

Carr got down, carrying the carbine. The hill area was an uninhabited, lonely-looking place, covered with heavy clouds and a fine chilly mist. The tire tracks in the mud road bothered him. An easy trail to follow. He removed the old barracks bag, one he had always carried on flights, from the truck bed. He opened it and pulled out the water bottle, a blanket, and the first-aid supplies. He helped the girl down and then the old man. He carried him to a clear, dry, rocky place under the trees and laid him down on the blanket. He washed the clotted wound carefully, dabbing disinfectant on it, and taped a bandage over it.

"Both of you," he said, "drink some water. I'll heat up some food." He busied himself with the Sterno can and holder, opening three cans of K ration, watching the surrounding area with caution, never letting the carbine out of reach. He opened his leather jacket so he could reach the holstered .45. He restrapped the knives to his legs near the ankles. He watched the girl as she helped the old man drink from the water and struggle with the unusual taste of the heated K ration. He laid out the air chart.

"Hanzhong and Baoji. Baoji is on the road that goes near Yenan, right? Is it a big place?"

"Fairly large."

"Can we get around it?"

"There are trails, yes."

He studied her. "We've got a problem. I'm sure this heap will get as far as Yenan. We still have about two hundred miles to go—that is, I have." She seemed so small and vulnerable in her cotton padded clothes and the cap she had pulled over her hair. "The problem is what do I do with you and your grandfather? Where do you want to go? Where will you be safe?" He paused. "And why were those deserters after you?" He jabbed the mess-kit knife into his tin and began to eat.

Her dark eyes reflected her worry. "What is your name?"

"Douglas Carr." He found himself mesmerized by her eyes, jet-black, and the incredibly smooth ivory complexion of her face. He thought of her sensuous body under the shapeless blue padded pants and jacket. "I'm a master sergeant in the United States Air Corps. Do you know Myitkyina?"

She nodded. "Burma. On the Irrawaddy River."

"We're based there. We left late yesterday on a mission to Yenan. We have an American military observer mission there."

"What happened?" She folded her arms, and he noticed how small and finely tapered her hands were. Patrician. Smooth, creamy, with well-cared-for, long fingernails. "Why did you crash?"

"Chinese Nationalist spies at the base. Put an explosive device in our tail section." He felt himself trembling. The can in his hand shook. "It locked the rudder and elevators into position. We came down on a glide. Not nose over." He struggled with the thought. "The pilot and copilot were killed. My buddy, Nick Engels, our crew chief, had a long piece of metal through him." He swallowed. He couldn't talk about the major's severed head. "I don't know why I wasn't killed." He looked at her, seeking understanding. "It's the third time I've survived. I can't believe we didn't burn. I know the pilot used the cabin tanks. He alternated them with the wing tanks. They must have been empty."

She reached out and put a hand on his trembling arm. "But why would the Nationalists place an explosive device on your airplane?" She plainly was confused. "They are your allies! You supply them with so much military equipment!"

Her light touch brought him out of his disturbance, and he felt a sense of guilt. "We were taking a very important officer to Yenan. They didn't want us to get there."

She removed her hand, stood, and backed off a step, as if she were guilty of a transgression. "That is all you had on the airplane—an officer? Not war equipment for the Red Army?"

"He was an influential person. He's dead. Broken neck. He carried an important message to the political and army leaders in Yenan."

She studied him for a moment. "In the truck, you did not talk. You were busy driving, to help us escape. My grandfather and I talked."

"You spoke in Chinese."

"We speak Kuo-yu, our national language. He does not speak English. We wondered why you, an American, wanted to go to Yenan. It is so far away."

"I have to deliver the message." Carr felt foolish standing with the food tin and mess knife in his hands. "I don't know if the message has any value now. They may have radioed it, or sent another plane. But the idea keeps me going. It's something I can hold onto until I get out of the mountains."

"Why didn't you stay with your plane? Wouldn't your people have come for you?"

"I couldn't. Not with them dead." He stared at her. "I was so low, right after the crash, seeing them. I almost put a bullet into my head."

She blinked, unable to understand his emotions.

"Your eyes bother me," he said. "Are you afraid of me?" She had seen him kill four men. Knew he had killed another. He stood, knives strapped on his legs, carbine at his feet, the .45 showing plainly. He thought of the terror on her face as the fat soldier had mounted her.

"No, I do not fear you." Her voice was barely audible. "I fear for our safety, for yours. But we are grateful. Please understand. If you had not shot those deserters we would be dead."

"Why were they after you?"

She sighed and glanced uneasily around the gloomy area. A thin breeze blew a wisp of her hair across her forehead. "It is a long story. Let's sit by him and I'll tell you." The old man, finished with the tin of unfamiliar food, had wrapped himself in the blanket and was lying asleep. Carr and the girl sat Chinese-style, on their haunches, and finished their tins as she talked.

"My grandfather is Ho Ling-chi. He is a member of the Central Committee of the Chinese Communist Party. Have you heard of him?" Carr wondered again about the strong British accent that flavored her light, rising voice. He shook his head. "My father was Ho Li-san. He is dead. We came to bury him at our ancestral village. It was difficult for us to come to that place with so many Kuomintang troops and deserters looking for us."

"But why?"

"Chiang Kai-shek would very much like to see us dead or in jail." She paused, looking forlornly at the landscape. "My grandfather, at the turn of the century, established an export business in Kunming. He shipped lumber to foreign nations. When my father came of age he took over the business. He was very successful. That was before the Japanese invaded us in 1938 and captured Peking, Shanghai, Nanking, and Tientsin. We had a house on the lake at Kunming. When the Nationalists were driven back by the Japanese and made Chungking their headquarters, we were forced to flee."

"When was that?"

"In 1938. I was fourteen. My father sent me to Calcutta, where I was raised by a cousin who is an officer of a British shipping company. I attended school run by the British. Now I have been a student at the Calcutta University. I attend the All India Institute of Hygiene."

Carr grinned. "You have no idea how it strikes an American to hear a Chinese girl speaking with a British accent. That makes you twenty years old. I thought you were much younger."

She was embarrassed and turned her head briefly. "My father wanted me to be safe. He worried about the Japanese and knew that someday they would move from our coastal cities, which they started to occupy as early as 1937, into Thailand and Burma. He felt that Calcutta, under the British, would be safer for me."

"How did he die?" Carr instantly regretted saying it.

She closed her eyes. "My brother." Her voice broke. "My brother Ch'en, in 1938, when we fled, went with my father to Shensi province to join my grandfather. My grandfather had visited Russia after their revolution. He became impressed with Leninism, with Karl Marx. My father and brother had always been sympathetic to the People's Liberation Army. You Americans call it the

Red Army. After my father's business was taken over by the Kuomintang, they wanted to be with Chairman Mao in Yenan. They were accepted.''

"Is your brother still there? You mean, what you're saying is that you and your grandfather want to go to Yenan with me?"

Her eyes glistened. "In my country, the son is all important. Only the son can inherit. Daughters are nothing compared to the son. Ch'en was very brave. I loved him very much. He volunteered to return to Kunming last October. He was to pretend to be a coolie at the air force base. He was to join another Red Army volunteer and use a radio and a courier to keep the Red Army advised of the movements of Nationalist and American airplanes.''

"Your brother was a spy in Kunming?"

"He was in the Red Army and it was his duty." Her voice was defiant and her eyes half-lidded.

"What happened to him?"

"There is a general, Tai Li, who is in charge of Chiang Kaishek's secret police." Carr stiffened at the sound of the name. "He has always hated my family. He had a special group of men whose duty it was to watch for my grandfather and father, for my brother and me. Great rewards were offered. Ch'en, my grandfather told me, did very well until he was betrayed by a former schoolmate who saw and recognized him. He was captured, tortured, and put to death.''

Carr didn't know what to say.

"My father, knowing only at that time that Ch'en was a prisoner, made a terrible mistake. He thought he had friends at Kunming, that through them he could go there and buy my brother's freedom." She paused to swallow hard. "He contacted his friends through the underground. They said they would help. My grandfather tried to dissuade him from going, but he was stubborn. He wanted to bring Ch'en back."

"He was captured?"

"No, when he got to Kunming the friends did help, but by then my brother was dead. We don't know what the KMT did with his body. My father stayed all of last month, trying to find out where Ch'en's body was. His friends feared for their own lives and warned him to leave. In despair he did. He had to be disguised as a villager because for so many years he had been a prominent businessman there. He bribed a corrupt postal official to take him to Chengtu, where he met two undercover soldiers of the Red Army who were to take him back to Yenan. They had to pretend they were simple village people. They left Chengtu in a cart drawn by two mules, planning to get through the blockade which the Kuomintang has along the Wei River. There are paths around Baoji and places across the river where the Red Army people go through at night.''

''Why didn't they make it?''

''North of Chengtu, near Hanzhong, a patrol of the Kuomintang fired at them. For no reason at all. Just shot at them, laughing, and went on their way. Father was hit in the upper right leg. The soldiers from Yenan did what they could for him, but they had no extensive medical supplies. Father bled too much. There was no hope of getting him through the blockade in that condition. He asked them to take him to our ancestral village. It is near Baishuijiang. They took him there. It required three days over the hills and the mountain range. The wound became infected. He died from loss of blood and fever the day they reached the village.''

Carr knew what she was feeling. He sought words to comfort her. ''You said you were at the village to bury Ho Li-san. If you were in Calcutta and your grandfather in Yenan, you both had a long way to go.''

''It was arranged through the post and our friends at Calcutta. The British concealed me on an RAF plane on a flight to Chengtu. I was put in a large wooden box before they unloaded. That night, the British let me out and took me to an American building. They talked to the men there. They made a deal for the Americans to take me the next morning to Hanzhong. It involved a case of Scotch whiskey.''

Carr half-stood as he saw a movement beyond the girl. It was swirling mists in the distance. He sat down, feeling foolish. She darted a glance behind her at his sudden movement. Carr pulled the carbine closer to him.

''That's where you were to meet your grandfather?''

''The Red Army has many friends in Hanzhong. My grandfather was accompanied by four soldiers dressed as villagers. They brought us to our village and left us there for the burial ceremonies. They returned to Hanzhong and were to come and get us a week ago. I don't know what happened to them. This is the road they were to come on.''

"This Ku the Miserable. He's the one who informed on you? Why did he do it?"

"The Kuomintang secret police are everywhere. The soldiers, even the many groups of deserters who are nothing but bandits, know they can get money and favorable treatment from General Tai Li's men if they inform on anyone who is against the Kuomintang."

"Ku was a Chinese Judas."

"I have heard of your Bible. In school, they told some of its stories. Judas was the one who informed on your Jesus."

Carr reached for the carbine and stood. "Look," he said, "if we're lucky, we'll be together awhile. What's your name?"

"I am Lui-ch'ao. My Indian friends called me Loo. It was easier for them."

"May I call you Loo? It's easier for me, too. Your Chinese is tough on my ears. It is Mandarin you speak?"

She stood next to him, and he was aware again of how attractive she was. '' 'Mandarin' is a foreign term to us. We spoke Kuo-yu, our national tongue. What you refer to is Kuan Hua, and that is widely used because it is an old civil service language."

He glanced at the silent form of the old man. "I'm glad you're not afraid of me. I know what you've been through. I feel like I don't have any insides. I'm just a shell. I can't get over the crash."

She looked up into his face. "You are a warrior. You carry so many weapons and you are nervous. I see a great anger within you."

"Damn right I'm angry! My plane was sabotaged! My friends died! My own people had lousy security, I ache all over, and I feel a hatred I can't control!" He stopped, ashamed of his gush of words.

"We have been here too long," she said. "Do you not fear what I do?" She pointed to the south, along their back trail. "That other soldiers might come?"

He hefted the carbine. "It never left my mind. Let's get your grandfather back into the truck. Wake him up and I'll check the gas supply."

"To get past Baoji and to the area at the blockade where we must cross the river to get to the road to Yenan, we must go ahead. There is a pass which will take us across this mountain range. When we get across, we will be just south of Baoji.'' She turned to go to her grandfather.

He packed the barracks bag again and swung it on the back of the truck. He got and examined the long wooden box bolted to the floor behind the cab. The rotted flooring and box were rutted and scarred with use. He lifted the lid. Three large cans of gasoline and a large jar of oil made him give out a whoop. There was a long length of inch-thick rope, oily and dirty; a Japanese light machine gun and stand, feeder rolls of cartridges, a rusty shovel, and a wooden box filled with ten Chinese hand grenades. Four thick straw mats were piled together.

He yelled from the truck as Loo guided her grandfather toward it. ''Things are looking up! Plenty of gas! A machine gun! All we need is some water for the radiator and we've got the show on the road!''

Jumping down, he saw again the telltale tire marks in the muddy road. He helped them in and ran around to leap into the cab, place the carbine at his knee, and start the engine. He snapped his fingers, then climbed up on top of the cab to scan the road behind him with the binoculars. The higher level gave him a clear view of the long hilly incline. He jumped back behind the wheel and shifted rapidly, pressing hard on the accelerator.

''You've got a well-tuned sense, Loo,'' he shouted over the chugging engine. ''Someone's right behind us. I could see a military truck.'' He steered the bouncing vehicle along the road. ''I'm damned if I'm going to let those filthy bastards get us!''

The fading roar of the B-25 told him he was near his prize.

Lieutenant Oshima knew from listening to the plane, hidden by overcast, that it had been gridding the crash site. The sound of the twin-engine B-25 was all too familiar to him. Another plane would come soon to drop parachuters on the ridge. He would not have much time. He placed a guard at the van and car, concealed with branches hacked from trees close to the base of the ridge. He hurried the sergeant and the three other men up the difficult slope, made precarious by the melting snow and the lack of trails. Drenched in sweat, feeling the biting cold, breathing hard in the nearly mile-high altitude, he reached the ridge before the others. He unholstered his Mauser, a cherished captured weapon. He stared at the wreck.

"Wait!" he ordered the others when they joined him, panting from the long climb. He walked through the snow, still dry and hard at the top of the ridge, marveling at the damage. The cockpit gaped in hideous fashion. He stepped up onto its shattered ledge, studying the large pieces of snow-covered aluminum strung across the entranceway into the main cabin. He sought evidences of booby traps and found none.

He undid the wiring and pulled the metal fragments away, jarring the snow loose. Cautiously, pistol ready, he entered the dark tomb. There was barely enough light from the shattered windows in the fuselage to see the four bodies laid side by side on the cluttered floor.

"Sergeant!" he shouted, and the perspiring soldier pounded on heavy feet to his side. The sergeant carried a Nambo machine pistol, small enough to be hidden under his padded Chinese jacket. "Your torch!" The sergeant fumbled for it. Its light played on the bodies. They stared at the headless corpse and the dark brown stains on the flight suits.

"Get the others in here and search with care," the lieutenant said. "The Americans will send a team in soon. They will come by parachute, because there is no place for them to land." He had seen too many dead men to be moved by the four Americans at his feet. His mind worked on the discovery that one American or more had lived. Someone had placed the bodies together. Mauser at ready, he jumped down from the wreck and walked around it. He stopped at the hole well past the V-shaped fuselage, near the huge curved tail fin and the elevators. He pushed himself up on the shattered tree stump and peered inside the hole with the sergeant's torch, seeing the devastating damage inside.

He got down, confused. Had the plane been hit by a large aircraft shell? A small rocket? Or had it been sabotaged? The outward bent surface of the plane indicated the latter. He walked through the snow, leaving small neat footprints, to where the misshapen wings and giant engine nacelles lay. Snow covered them, but it was evident what had happened. He made a careful

note of the number painted on the tail fin in his personal daily
log book, then retreated.

At the cockpit area he learned the men had found nothing.
There was no military or political intelligence on the bodies or
in the plane. Everything had been removed. The sergeant was
clearly frightened. "Nothing!" he said. "How could this be?"

The lieutenant spat out his disgust. "Fool! These planes carry a
crew of four. There are four bodies. There are no war supplies.
Where are the papers? They must have had maps and a log book. It
is required of them!" The shaking sergeant could only glance
wildly around the desolate site.

The lieutenant pushed the man to one side roughly and went into
the plane. After a half-hour search he knew the sergeant was right.
Among the debris there were only unimportant items: pieces of
canvas tarp, ropes, empty food tins and cartons. The IFF set, fastened to the rear bulkhead of the long cabin, had exploded on impact, as it was set to do. The Identification of Friend or Foe device
was useless to him.

He unfastened the warped panel at the rear bulkhead and
played the torch over the control area of the elevators and fin.
He saw where the explosive device had detonated. He left the
plane in great irritation. The snow made it impossible to find
tracks. In the dust of the cabin floor he had seen only one large
set of footprints, marred by those of his own men. He con-
cluded that one man had lived through the crash. One man who
had laid out the bodies, had strung metal from the wreckage
across the entrance and windows. Why? The open parachute
seats were mute evidence that the man had removed the supplies, had taken all that was useful. The radio and flight equipment were totally destroyed. He had made this journey into
enemy territory to find a wrecked American plane without any
intelligence information on it! The thought brought acid surging into his stomach.

"Sergeant!" he shouted. "Get the men! We leave!"

The wide-eyed sergeant, still shaking, came over to him.
"Should we patrol? It is an empty airplane with four dead men.
Where are the others? Perhaps they are hiding and we can find
them."

The lieutenant almost slapped the fat, shivering idiot. He had never seen the man so disturbed. "We are out of time," he said, glancing at his watch. "Get the men on the move, now!" He followed them down the same path they had made getting to the ridge, slipping and sliding, swearing to himself as he formulated his radio report to the general. It would not be a report well received, he knew, and the acid in his stomach surged again. From afar he heard the drone of an airplane, the familiar sound of a C-47. By the time the plane was overhead and circling down through the thick overcast, he and his men were in their vehicles and moving away. "Drive north," he ordered the sergeant, who was struggling with the wheel. He glowered at the startled face turned toward him. "North, I said!"

He had no choice. The man who had walked away from that wreck was one whom the gods favored. A man who was capable, intelligent, who exited alive from a mangled aircraft on a remote China mountain ridge. A man who had taken a prize away from Renya Oshima. A man on foot, carrying the intelligence coup he needed to keep face with the general. A man who could not have gone far, who was headed north with only a few hours of lead time. There was only one place the American plane could have been heading.

Yenan.

The man was trying to get to Yenan. There had to be a strong reason why a lone American, on foot in a terrible wilderness, would attempt to do that instead of heading to the safety of Chengtu or waiting for rescue from the crash site. He carried something of importance to the Chinese Red Army. It was not weapons. It was papers, papers of interest to the Kempetai. The report would have to wait.

He shouted to the sergeant to drive faster in the gloom. The American would have left the ridge, gone down to the uninhabited valley, where he could be more easily seen. There was no alternative. He had to capture the American and find the papers he was carrying. The weather was worsening. It was midafternoon, but it was getting darker. Was another storm forming over the ugly mountains? Was his luck changing for the worse?

"Can you drive?" Carr yelled over the laboring engine.

Loo shook her head.

He glanced over his shoulder through the glassless rear window of the cab. The pursuing truck clearly was gaining on them, and he cursed the old vehicle. Ahead were more curves. It was darkening rapidly, with the deep gray overcast seeming to settle down for a rest on the earth.

"Decision time," he said to himself. "Do we run or do I make a fight?" The last word appealed to him. He stopped the truck around a bend, leaving the engine idling in neutral. He grabbed the machine gun and fitted the tripod stand to it. He loaded it with a string of cartridges and hefted it along with the carbine. With three hand grenades bulging in his pockets, he ran back to the lip of the bend. He grunted, lugging the weapons to the highest place of concealment he could find, behind a fallen tree.

He had barely enough time to set up the machine gun before the truck was in view. He saw two soldiers in the cab, four more standing with rifles in the open bed. The truck was virtually a replica of the one in which Loo and her grandfather waited for him. He pulled the pin of one of the grenades and lobbed the grenade down onto the road in front of the racing truck. The blast reassured him. The truck skidded to a halt in the mud and swung sideways. The left front wheel was blown off. He knelt and fired the machine gun, thankful that it worked. He raked the vehicle, back and forth, seeing bullet holes appear amid puffs of dirt flying from the truck.

Two of the soldiers leaped from the truck bed. He found them with deadly aim in the open. The man next to the driver, who was slumped over the wheel, opened the door and raised a rifle. A bullet zipped into the log in front of Carr. Carr aimed the machine gun directly at the man. He was thrust back against the truck and slipped slowly to the ground.

Carr pulled the pin of the second grenade. He stood, throwing it carefully into the truck bed. By the time the explosion came he had gathered the machine gun, carbine, and himself and was running back toward his own truck. Loo's face was white. The grandfather's eyes were wide and startled. "What happened?" she said. She and the old man stood close together at the cab's side, watching his running approach. He laid the machine gun in the back and herded them into the cab, breathing in large gulps. He drove away rapidly, spinning the nearly treadless tires in the thin mud of the road.

When his breath was near normal he released his tight grip on the wheel and looked at them. A small red dot was in the center of the old man's bandage. Loo sat with her arms around him, holding him from the jarring of the road. "More Nationalist soldiers," he said, finding it difficult to talk. Despite the chill of the late January afternoon, sweat ran down his body. "I figured they were buddies of the bastards who found you."

"We heard the explosions and gunfire!" Loo's voice was shaky. "What did you do?"

"I ambushed the sons of bitches!" he said. "They would have caught up with us. Four of them are dead. I don't know about the other two. I doubt they made it." He flicked on the headlights to see the road better in the sudden darkness. "Look, we've got to find a place to hide tonight. Does your grandfather know anything about this country?"

He listened as they talked in Kuo-yu. She turned to him. "There are some small villages ahead. The first one is dead."

"What?"

"It has been ruined by fighting over many years. It has a bad name. It was never rebuilt. The people of this district stay away from it because it has evil spirits."

"How far is it?"

"At least ten miles. About thirty lis, he said."

"Ask him if he thinks we'd be safe there tonight."

She spoke softly, and the answers were even more indistinct to Carr. She had to lean her head against the old man's to hear his tired voice over the clattering of the truck. "It is off the road, a quarter of your mile. We can stay there if we do not offend the spirits. He says we are travelers. We are different from those who live in this district."

"Ask him if he knows whether troops or guerrillas or bandits are in the area around the village, the dead one."

Again the slight whispers. "He says one never knows. We must stand sentry during the night, because that's when evil men and evil spirits come." Following the old man's directions, they found the remains of the ancient village. Carr turned the truck from the road and drove down a narrow path overgrown with weeds and wild vegetation. He stopped the truck. In the headlights he studied the ruined buildings. He saw no footprints in the mud, no movements except branches weaving in the breeze. He took the carbine and flashlight and prowled around the place, noting the desolation and disuse of the village. It had eleven wrecked bamboo and wood huts and the remains of a large building that must have served as a community center.

He went back to the truck. "There's one over there with most of the roof on it. The walls are standing." He moved the truck to the side of the building, cut the lights and engine, and helped them down. He set up a makeshift camp inside as Loo held the flashlight. The straw mats were beds. The drogue chute and canvas tarp became their covers.

He carried in all of the weapons, unpacked the rest of the barracks bag, and lighted the Sterno on its holder. He opened three cans of C ration, which Loo heated. He helped the old man onto a mat and bent to examine the wound after he peeled the bandage away. He ran his hands over the body. "Good God! This poor guy is nothing but skin and bones! Hasn't he been eating? Has he been sick?"

She looked over her shoulder at him as she squatted near the heater. "We were almost out of food when the deserters came. I was ready to go back to our village and seek food and water and find out what happened to our friends who were coming to get us."

Carr sat back. "Well, his head is scabbing. I don't feel any broken bones. I'll wash the wound and put some more sulfa on it." He busied himself with the first-aid supplies and taped a fresh bandage over the wound. The old man's eyes never left his. Carr thought he saw a flicker of approval in them. He helped the old man into the flight suit. "It's too big for him," he said, "but it will keep him warm tonight." He looked at Loo, who handed him and her grandfather a tin and mess-kit utensils to eat with. "How does your grandfather feel about Americans?"

"He doesn't like them."

"Does he trust me?"

"No. You worry him. You carry those weapons. He has seen you kill men. He knows what you did back there." She glanced quickly at him in embarrassment. "He feels you are a warrior who likes to kill."

Carr felt weariness and frustration. "Hey, look! I'm a flier. Honest, I can fly anything with wings. I've had some training in combat. All of us had it. Back at Myitkyina the Kachins and Gurkhas taught me some things." He gripped the hot tin. "Fliers aren't killers. Not in the sense he's thinking of. Those soldiers would have killed us. Do you understand that?"

"I understand, but it is difficult for him. He has seen so much killing. The Japanese. The Kuomintang. He has lost his son and grandson. He mourns for them. He finds himself in the hands of a tall, blond American wearing knives and shooting guns." She tossed her head. "No, he does not like Americans."

Carr ate for a while. Then he said, "I can understand why he worries about me. I never shot anyone in my life before today. First I'm scared to death, and afterward I feel a thrill. It's all new to me. I don't understand it." He looked at the old man eating with a spoon. "But Americans have been friendly to the Chinese for a long time. We've had missionaries over here." He sought other points. "We're helping you fight the Japanese."

Her eyes gleamed in the light from the Sterno. "You Americans! You help the generalissimo!"

"What's wrong with that?" He knew he was being defensive.

"We hate the Kuomintang and Chiang Kai-shek. You support a corrupt regime that has killed many thousands of our people!"

"Well, who the hell are those guys in the Nationalist army?"

She glared at him. "Have you seen those soldiers? Do you know who they are? They are farm people, taken from their homes at rifle point and tied together. They are put in a jail to keep them from running away. They are forced to fight. If they don't, they are shot."

"Come on! I've flown a lot of them. They didn't look like prisoners to me." He was arguing without knowing the reason.

"You do not understand. Chiang does not use all of your equipment to fight the Japanese. He uses much of it to fight the Red

Army. He wants to kill every Communist. He has already killed vast numbers of us!''

Carr leaned against a flimsy wall for support. Her outburst worried him. ''Look, I know all about the war between Chiang and Chairman Mao. I know your people don't trust the guys in Chungking. That's why we have the Dixie Mission in Yenan. The mission is trying to find ways America can help the Red Army. That's why I want to get to Yenan.'' His resolve returned. ''By now, our search-and-rescue team has found the wreck. I don't know what's going on between Myitkyina and Yenan. All I know is that I'm alive, I've got a packet, and I want to get to Yenan.''

''You would have been wiser to go to Chengtu. Your people are there.''

''So are the Nationalists. Who would have found me first, them or my people? I couldn't take that chance.''

''You could have waited for your rescue team. Your message must be important. Is it so important you could not wait for rescue?''

''Hell, I don't know if it is or not. We were sabotaged. That makes me think it's important. Besides, I just couldn't stay there.''

She finished her tin of food. He forced himself to eat his. They cleaned the utensils and drank from the water bottle, the silence deep between them. He broke it, glancing at his watch. ''It's nearly eight. I'll take the first sentry. Two hours. Can you handle an automatic?''

''Show me how.'' He took the .45 from the shoulder holster and explained how it worked. She practiced it with dry fire. He slapped a clip into it and moved a cartridge into the chamber. ''This is the safety. Push it off and pull the trigger. It will kick up, so hold it with both hands.'' He watched her as she lay on her mat and pulled the nylon chute and tarp over her. He went out into the cold night air with the carbine. He waited outside the windowless, doorless building until his eyes adjusted to the inky blackness. The cloud cover was low.

He moved around the village, thinking of the evil spirits the Chinese feared. One had gotten into Loo. He was convinced she didn't like him. He walked the perimeter, noting that the only path through the thick undergrowth was the one they had taken in. In the dimness, he saw a few animal tracks. Others looked like bird marks. In the daylight, he knew, their tire marks could lead other evil spirits to them. They would have to be up and moving long before that.

He filled the gas tank and reloaded the machine gun. He found an old clay basin filled with rainwater. He smelled it. He used an empty gas tin to fill the radiator with the water. Satisfied, aching with every movement, he squatted with his back to a large tree a short distance in front of the decayed building in which Loo and her grandfather slept. If anyone came in during the night, they would use the path.

For the rest of the two hours he reviewed the incredible turn of events in his life. He thought of Nick Engels. Major James Holland. Captain Rollo Buchanan. Lieutenant Colonel Ambrose Moffett. The disastrous plunge to the mile-high mountain ridge. The sight of Ku the Miserable turning to see him. His bullets hitting the four men at the cave. The excitement of the ambush of the others in the pursuing truck.

"It isn't happening," he said softly. "How can this be happening?" He thought of Loo's naked body, the strange sound of her English and Chinese words. The look in the old man's eyes. The cold kept him shivering in his leather A2 jacket. Loo was beautiful. He had never met anyone like her in his life. It seemed he had known her forever. He fantasied making love to her, and his head jerked up as he nearly went to sleep. He gripped the carbine for comfort, feeling that Loo's dislike of him made any meaningful relationship impossible.

When his time was up, he went back into the doorless building, eyes heavily lidded, shoots of pain throughout his body.

The faint glint of the .45 automatic told him she was pointing it directly at him.

He handed her his watch. "Good girl!" he whispered. *"Ding hao!"*

He collapsed on his mat, laughing without sound, the carbine cradled in his arms.

She rose, hearing his heavy breathing. He'd said, *"Ding hao!"*—"Very good!" She smiled faintly and went outside to her sentry duty. She'd slept fitfully. She realized that in her waking moments she had been thinking of the strange, heavily weaponed American flier. What was there about this big man that attracted her? She looked around the dead village area, eyes already adjusted to the darkness. But she couldn't keep from thinking of the American.

He would never find her as attractive as she found him.

CHAPTER THREE

OSS Detachment 101
Field Headquarters
Myitkyina, Burma

Captain Joe Karras studied the red sweep hand of the wall clock as he waited for the team of three cryptographers to decipher the last of the messages from China.

Its dusty face told him it was 0432 hours. A long night. He flexed his narrow shoulders as the last of the sheets were handed to him. "Good work, fellas," he said in his mild New Jersey accent. "Get your tired butts out of here and have your minds go completely blank." He smiled thinly. "Like mine is normally." He watched them leave and pulled his rickety chair closer to the table with the overhead green-shaded light.

Karras, who always appeared to be working as a trial lawyer in a Trenton courtroom, had been among the first to be accepted in the Office of Strategic Services when it was formed in June, 1942, under the Joint Chiefs of Staff. He brushed back his sparse brown hair, trying to ease the worry he felt about the reorganization of the OSS that was currently under way, sending shock waves through its agents. His long narrow face, decorated with a small mustache and a scattering of thin pockmarks, reflected the exhaustion he felt.

He pulled a tin of Chinese tobacco to him, bought on his last trip to the CBI headquarters in Chungking, stuffed his favorite pipe, and studied the codes-deciphers as he lighted the pungent stuff. He picked up a pencil stub and began writing the condensed summary report for Colonel Chick Gregory, head of Detachment 101, grimacing heavily as he thought of the order barring OSS from operating in north China and Manchuria. He wrote:

"At 0105 hours, January 15, radio/radar operator M/Sgt. Douglas Carr, in C-46 8429, sent a distress signal that the aircraft was going down. He screwed down the key for fixes. The Mayday was picked up by both airborne and ground directional radios. The crash site was fixed approximately north of the village of Baishuijiang in the vicinity of where Kansu, Szechwan, and Shensi provinces have borders.

"This is mountainous country, not heavily populated. The search-and-rescue team from Chengtu, after a recon by their B-25, parachuted onto the long narrow ridge where the wreck was located. Elevation about 5,000 feet. The storm had left a thick cover of snow. Lt. Clyde Rellis, under our instructions and covert as a medical corpsman, went in with them. His objective was to retrieve the Moffett packet.

"The team found Lt. Col. Moffett laid out in the severely damaged main cargo compartment alongside S/Sgt. Engels, Capt. Buchanan, and Maj. Holland. Lt. Col. Moffett had a broken neck. The major's head was severed in the crash. It was found in the crushed metal of the cockpit, the front part of which was torn off. S/Sgt. Engels's chest had been pierced by a length of aluminum shard, and this had been removed and placed to one side. Capt. Buchanan was crushed to death.

"M/Sgt. Carr was not present. The team searched the wreck thoroughly. They found no weapons, food, water, or ammunition. No personal effects. No papers. The log, air charts, and the packet were missing, the latter known only to Agent Rellis. Some Chinese had been there prior to the team's arrival. There were small footprints in the dirt in the compartment and around the wreckage, made by Chinese shoes, not Jap. The trail of these men, apparently six in number, came from a road bordering the ridge. A discarded cover of tree branches was located where two vehicles had parked alongside the road while the Chinese scaled the ridge to where the C-46 was located. The cover was obviously to shield the vehicles from aerial recognition.

"The C-46 was sabotaged by a very small amount of Composition C with an acid-spring fuse to the detonator, located in the tail section. The explosion locked metal into elevators, causing a slight downglide position. The tail fin was frozen into a straight-on position. The aircraft came down in a direct line with the ridge, which sloped away from its path.

"The positions of the wing flaps, engine power controls, and the electric power controls indicated the pilots were able to slow the plane to a point where it smashed in atop a long row of scattered trees. The wings came off first. The fuselage slid another hundred yards, striking more trees, which ripped the cockpit off and up over the fuselage, which itself was bent in a fairly sharp V shape. M/Sgt. Carr's radio operator's seat was bent down to the deck, apparently shielding Carr. Both pilots were thrown up and back by the impact. The cabin fuel tanks, installed for the flight, which was past the range of the C-46 wing tanks, had been drained. Maj. Holland obviously had alternated the cabin tanks with the wing tanks, leaving the latter empty. That is why the fuselage did not burn.

"It is Agent Rellis's view that Carr survived, perhaps with some injury, but capable of collecting the Moffett packet, air charts, log, and survival items. The parachute seats were opened and all items removed. The personal effects of the deceased, except dog tags, were removed. The tags were laid out carefully. There was no message left by M/Sgt. Carr, possibly because he did not know who would find the wreck first. All radio equipment, including the IFF, was destroyed, including the Mae West distress unit.

"M/Sgt. Carr had not placed out ground markers. Where is he? Why did he leave the plane? Did he leave because of the Chinese? Agent Rellis found indications that Carr had made an effort to seal the cabin by wiring pieces of shard aluminum over the cabin door and smashed windows, possibly in the thought of keeping out wild animals. These had been removed by the Chinese.

"The questions that remain are: Where is M/Sgt. Carr heading? Who were the Chinese? Were they secret police? Bandits who had vehicles? Why did Carr leave? The fact that he took the survival items, including the carbine, which he had permission to carry on board and which was not found, indicated he had a long journey in mind. This could be to Chengtu, but the scouting parties on ground have not located him in that direction. Villagers nearby, interrogated by the backup ground team sent out to bring in the parachuters and bodies, said they heard gunfire further down the ridge, to the north, about midday. A search of that area, below the snow line and almost at the valley floor, produced the bodies of five Chinese. Four were soldiers of the Nationalist army, and the fifth was an armed civilian. The villager had been knifed in the throat. The soldiers were killed by carbine caliber bullets.

"A truck, which the villagers said the soldiers had driven into the area the night before, was missing. Other villagers to the north reported that a truck similar to it was seen on the road that goes north and east from the ridge, and on the east side of the ridge.

"The backup team, at the site where the five bodies were found, said there was a cave there that had been occupied by at least two persons. Those persons were not in evidence, but campsite articles were strewn about—straw mats, baskets, a small amount of food, some pieces of clothing. Tracks in the mud showed that a large man wearing paratrooper boots and two Chinese left the area and went down the final phase of the slope to where a truck had been parked. The truck was gone and its tracks were overrun by a second truck, possibly the one the villagers had reported seeing loaded with Nationalist soldiers. The villagers believe these men to be simple deserters, roaming as bandits. They had been seen in that area a number of times and in that truck. They had committed crimes such as rape, theft, and assault.

"The two teams returned to Chengtu with the bodies. As soon as the weather lifts (there is low overcast over the entire area) an effort will be made by spotter aircraft to follow the path or paths of the two trucks and locate them."

Karras stopped to knock the dead ashes from the pipe and refill it. He glanced at the form that held the military record of M/Sgt. Douglas Carr, piecing the man together from the information on the sheet. He wrote:

"Attached is the record of M/Sgt. Carr. A review of it indicates he is a very resourceful individual. He is a native of Bloomington, Illinois. Graduated 5/42 from U. of I. with a major in agricultural engineering and a minor in radio communications. He had a private pilot's license and a ham radio operator's license while in school.

"He entered cadets in 6/42. Took advanced training at Randolph Field, Texas. He was charged with landing too hard on his final graduation check. The plane blew a tire, ground-looped, and the instructor was burned to death. Carr was pulled out alive, burned slightly."

Karras paused, considering his choice of words. He gripped the pencil. "As the decodes became available to me, it was apparent that M/Sgt. Carr was alive and had the Moffett packet. I made telephone inquiries at Chabua and Myitkyina. I found a Lt. Will Jackson who had been in the same graduating class at Randolph with M/Sgt. Carr. He said the major who headed the inquiry was a brother of the instructor who died in the crash. After the inquiry, M/Sgt. Carr was sent immediately to the radio school at Sioux Falls, S.D., where his previous radio training enabled him to finish in several months. He was sent to Bergstrom Field, Texas, where he received radar training, was assigned to Troop Carrier, then assigned to Army Transport Command in India. From there, transfer to 4th Combat Cargo Group, 16th Squadron. He has more than 1100 combat hours over the Hump. A DFC and Air Medal with cluster.

"Last September, a C-46 he was in caught fire in the left engine while they were over the Hump carrying a cargo of jeeps and ammunition to Kunming. Search-and-rescue, after a long period, found the pilots hanging in trees. Ants had eaten their flesh. They died from broken bones that had torn through the skin and from loss of blood. The crew chief came down in a lake. Natives pulled him out when he bloated and came to the surface.

"Carr, the report states, went out second. He came down in a cleared area. He gained the help of the Nagas, who turned him over to the Kachins, who guided him out 115 miles through jungle and mountains to this base. The report said at that time that M/Sgt. Carr carries small packets of salt with him on all flights. It was this salt trade-off and his ability to survive that enabled him to walk out. He lost thirty-one pounds, had leeches sucking him dry. His atabrine held off malaria until he was in the Myitkyina hospital. He was back flying in three weeks."

Karras flipped the sheet over to read Carr's description again. Six-one, blond, blue eyes, twenty-one years old, muscular, adaptive, back to 171 pounds. He sat slumped, looking through a bluish cloud of smoke, thinking about Carr, wondering where he was headed in the north China mountains. Carr had the Moffett packet and was on his way to Yenan.

He finished the report and stood, feeling slightly ill from lack of sleep and food and the headiness of the Chinese tobacco. He would deliver the report to the colonel and ask permission to have Clyde Rellis and some handpicked men comb the area from the crash site northward toward Yenan. How could Carr get through the blockade the Kuomintang had fashioned against the Red Army? How could the idiot expect to make it 270 miles to Yenan through some of the wildest country in China?

Carr had to be found and the packet retrieved. The hell with the stinking weather up there. He fished out the last meteorologist's report. Another winter storm was forming on the heels of the first. The hell with it. He took the report and on legs that refused to work properly left the OSS quarters.

Lieutenant Oshima groaned in his sleep, and Sergeant Mutagachi peered at him anxiously in the darkness.

He stood near the small mud-smeared car where the lieutenant lay curled on the rear seat, wrapped in a blanket. He shivered in the cotton-padded Chinese clothing, wondering if it was time to wake the officer. He squinted around, seeing nothing in the stillness of the predawn hour. He heard the stamping of the other sentry trying to warm his feet. The other men were asleep in the van, huddled close together against the night's damp coldness. It was day two of their patrol.

The sergeant, unable to control his nervousness, relieved himself again, listening to the sound of his own water. He cursed silently the decision of the lieutenant to attempt to capture the American. He cursed the miserable China mountain area in which he found himself. He was hungry, and his fat, short frame punished him with its insistent demand for food.

He jumped, gripping his Nambo machine pistol in alarm, as the lieutenant moved and sat up. The officer opened the car door and blinked, trying to clear his tortured mind. He stepped out, holding the blanket around his shoulders.

"Wake the men," the lieutenant ordered in a low, raspy voice. "See that they are fed. As soon as it is light we will move out." He coughed. "Two on sentry at all times!"

The sergeant, grateful the long night was almost over, padded heavily toward the van.

* * *

Carr bent over the old man, listening to the faint breathing.

He went to the open door, stretching, and saw Loo standing against a tree, the .45 automatic in her hand. She pointed with it. There was a strand of white smoke at the end of the path, faint against the lightening sky.

He checked the carbine and motioned to her to stay where she was. He scouted the perimeter of the village. He saw nothing in the drying mud except his own tracks. He joined her. "There wasn't anyone there last night," he whispered.

The level of her voice matched his. "They came after we changed the last time. I heard a few sounds."

"Why didn't you wake me?"

She looked down the path. "I waited to see if they would come this way."

"Don't take chances like that again!" he snapped. "Get in with your grandfather. Wake him and give him water. Tend to his needs." He went to the barracks bag and got two clips for the carbine.

"What are you going to do?" she said nervously when he emerged from the old building.

"We can't get the truck out of here except by the path. We can't waste time. I'll go take a look. Pack everything in the truck and wait for me." Her eyes told him to be careful. Staying close to the trees and tangled bush lining the path, he moved silently to the thick foliage at the juncture of the road.

He smelled the smoke, heard the Chinese voices. A horse whinnied softly. Crouching, he inched his way closer, peering through a low bush. There were five of them, sitting around a fire. One of them stirred a pot with a smooth stick. Rifles were strapped to their backs. They wore Chinese clothes. With one difference. Their headbands were those of hill bandits.

Carr counted six horses, tethered on a small grassy area. He squinted to see beyond the horses. Four women, their hands bound behind them, squatted together, tied in a group by a rope. Carr studied the dirt road. The drying tire tracks, smoothed by the night's mists, were not so readily noticeable. He saw no tire tracks to the north of the juncture. There were only hoof and sandal prints from that direction. The bandits had come during the night, along the road, herding their captives, and had stopped for their morning meal. If they had noticed the tire marks, the marks had meant nothing to them.

He was at the edge of the clearing, on one knee, behind the shrub, peering at the men across the road, when a sound made him whirl, startled. A fat man shuffled out of the bushes, carrying a small load of dried firewood. They faced each other ten paces apart.

Equally shocked, the fat bandit opened his mouth to shout. Carr swung the carbine, leaping forward. It crashed against the man's shoulder, knocking him down. The firewood scattered in the thick grass. Carr pounced on the man, pressing the carbine against his throat. A soft gurgle, a thrashing of the body. Carr leaned back and smashed the butt of the carbine into the man's head. He heard the skull crack. Then he jumped up and leaped through the bush, flipping the carbine onto fire.

The five men, hearing the sounds, rose, alarmed, moving to get their rifles from their backs. Carr raised the carbine and fired at them carefully, seeing them jerk back with the impact of the lead. Puffs of dirt came from their soiled clothes at the holes. He fired again at two men, wounded and knocked backward, who were struggling to get up. He aimed at their headbands, turning them into sudden crimson.

He heard the carbine sounds echo in the surrounding hills. The horses reared and crashed into each other. Their boulder-tied leather tethers held. The women lay in a heap, their eyes frightened. Carr shoved in a fresh clip and looked around quickly, expecting others to come running. He remained, half crouched, weapon ready, totally alert. Were other bandits nearby? The pot, knocked over, had put out the cooking fire. A thin plume of smoke rose from the embers.

He whirled at the sound of the truck coming down the path. Loo drove with one hand, holding her grandfather with the other. She braked to a stop near him. He sighed, tension draining from him. He looked up at her through the dirty windshield. "I thought you couldn't drive!" he shouted over the noise of the engine.

"I watched you," she said. She put the gear in neutral, patted her grandfather, leaped down, and looked with awe at what she saw. She walked over to the women, Carr trailing behind her, nervously scanning the morning mists, finger still on the trigger of the carbine. She spoke to the women, and they answered in a long stream of words. Carr cut them loose. They were all talking at the same time, gathering around Loo, gesturing to the north. She said something, and they began stripping the clothes from the dead bandits, gathering their rifles and food sacks, untying the horses, moving quickly while keeping up their singsong chattering.

"What was that all about?" he said, aware suddenly of the shaking of his hands.

"They were taken captive two days ago in a raid on their village. They were abused many times by these men. They're from the north. They were going to be sold. Their men were killed. Their homes were burned by these bandits."

He looked at the naked, blood-streaked dead bodies. "Where were they taking these women?"

"There are land groups south of here," she said. "They buy men and women to work the land. These probably would have ended up in a brothel for the Kuomintang deserters. They are all fairly young." She got into the truck. "I put everything in the back. Let's get out of here."

He swung up behind the wheel and shifted gears, carbine across his lap. "What now? How do we get to Yenan?" He glanced at the old man, who almost seemed to be smiling. "What's with him?" He listened as they spoke to each other.

"He heard me tell the women to take the horses and weapons and go back to their village." Loo bent past her grandfather to look at Carr. "He admires the way you dealt with the bandits, the way a merciless warrior treats his enemies." Her voice became softer. "You are shaking. You do not look well."

"I'm okay."

"No, you're not. Are you ill?"

He gripped the wheel tightly as he drove, foot heavy on the gas pedal. "Maybe I am. We crash. I'm the survivor. I lose a fine buddy and three officers. In two days I've killed eleven men!" He tried to control his shaking. "I can't believe what I've gotten into! It's a damned nightmare!"

They rode in silence for a long time. His stomach settled down. He felt stability coming back. The terrible road took

them over a succession of hills and around steep bends, upward
toward the mountain range to his right, the one they had to get
over. To call it a road was a compliment. He thought of the
truck he had ambushed. It had come swiftly after them. That
meant there was some kind of control in the deserter unit. He
wasn't certain the men he'd killed in the truck had been regulars
or deserters. Whichever, someone was trying to capture them.
Other soldiers might be after them, having found the ambushed
truck, knowing he was responsible. If they had any radio communications they could set up a roadblock along the way and
ambush *him.*

With the haze lifting slightly, he could see better, but the thick
blanket of gray cloud was still low to the ground. Was another
storm coming? They had seen no one although Carr thought he'd
spotted peasants hiding behind the tree stumps and rock outcrops
along the way. Everything that grew in the desolate area seemed
stunted and unhealthy. He saw paths from the road leading to villages, whose rude thatched roofs he could see in the distance. A
few stray dogs, looking wild and hungry. Only a few low-flying
birds daring the winter's cold.

Loo spoke to her grandfather. "We are worried that more
soldiers will attempt to trap us," she said to Carr. "There is a
main pass far up there." She pointed. "But it could be dangerous for us to go there. He knows of a small pass, used by the hill
people. He will show us where we must turn from this road to
reach it."

They drove for another hour, fording small mountain
streams, chugging up steep hills, hitting rocks in the road.
Going around another sharp bend, Carr braked suddenly.
"Good God! Look at that!" The charred remains of what had
been a small car lay smashed against a blackened tree. Its windows and body were riddled with countless bullet holes. Carr
put the gear in neutral and slid to the ground, carbine ready. He
walked warily to the car. He stared with nausea at the four cre-
mated bodies inside. He turned as Loo joined him. There were
no movements in the mist-shrouded hill area. He looked back at
her. Something about her alarmed him. "Get back," he said.
The forms appeared unidentifiable. They sprawled in their
torched positions within the ugly black interior.

Loo straightened, unable to take her eyes from the disaster. "They were the ones coming to take us to Hanzhong and from there to Yenan!" Her voice was barely audible.

Carr walked around, studying the ground. He saw the ambush site, littered with cartridge casings. He picked up one of them and saw its Chinese markings. "Loo," he said, "they set up here, behind these bushes. When your friends came around the bend they opened fire. Your friends never had a chance. Their car hit that tree. Whoever did it splashed gasoline inside the car and torched it after they took the weapons from it." He bent to examine the trampled grassy area. "They had a radio. Hand-crank job on a stand. Used automatic weapons. Sandal tracks all over. They had a truck. See those empty gas tins over there? The tracks show they drove it north, where your friends came from."

He felt a presence near him and turned. Ho Ling-chi, trembling, stood looking at the torched wreck, an unreadable expression on his face. Loo spoke to her grandfather in soft singsong Chinese. The old man walked to the car, peering intently at the corpses. He uttered whispery moans. "He is mourning his comrades," she said. "Even as they are, he recognizes them. I knew this was their car."

"Get him back in the truck," Carr ordered. "Now! The bastards that did this have a radio. They're probably waiting for us up north. We've got to get off this road. They might have another group coming behind us to catch us in a pincers." He ran back to the truck and grabbed the air charts. "Get him in and help me with this map!" He breathed quickly in near dread. Loo helped the old man up and came to him, leaning over the map spread on the hood. "Here," Carr said. "This is where we are. Now where the hell is that damned little pass you said was around here?"

She pointed to the map. "From what Grandfather said, it is here. This narrow place." Behind the wheel, following her directions, he turned east onto one of the narrow footpaths that joined the road, but not before he had craned his neck and looked out the rear cab window and seen the top of a truck far to the south, coming down a steep incline.

"They're behind us again," he shouted. "They're trying to trap us between them and the ambushers up ahead on that road!" Sweat ran down his face. The truck bounced sharply along the narrow footpath, smashing against cloistering trees and bushes. He drove as fast as he could. Branches smacked against the dirt-streaked windshield. The old man grunted from time to time as the truck bounced mightily over rocks in the path and skidded around sudden turnings. Over the roar of the engines he shouted, "Are there villages along here?"

She motioned "no" with her hands, then grabbed her grandfather in time to keep him from pitching forward to hit the dashboard when the truck lurched over a deep hole in the path.

"Where we turned off was rocky. My guess is they won't know we've left that road. They'll go on up and meet the other sons of bitches. Then they'll know for sure we're on this route. How many other paths lead to the pass?"

"One other. From the north."

"Ask him how far it is to the pass. It looked like ten or twelve miles on the map." Loo spoke to her grandfather and translated for Carr.

"He knows this country. He used this pass several times when he was young. There is an old wood bridge on this path, by now very old and not too strong. For people on foot. When we get there, we must leave the truck and go on foot."

Carr thought of the impossiblity of getting a frail old man and a tiny Chinese girl over the pass on foot. And when they were over the high ground, how would they travel on to Yenan? He glanced backward again, seeing only the weaving trees closing the footpath behind them, hearing the whacking of new tree branches against the battered truck and the noise of its protesting engine. "We need another ambush of our own," he shouted. "Ask him about that."

He heard more quick Chinese. "At the bridge," she said. "The best place is at the bridge."

He wiped sweat from his eyes. They hadn't eaten or taken water. They'd left six bodies behind them. He swallowed hard, cursing the incredible nightmare he was in.

Lieutenant Oshima stood by the radio van, reading the transcript the operator had just finished.

He turned to Sergeant Mutagachi. "He's picked up some strange Chinese transmissions. Apparently they are trying to set a trap for someone."

"Someone on foot? The one we seek?"

The lieutenant, messages in hand, looked at the coordinates he'd marked on the map placed on top of the car. "Very strange. The distances are too far for the man we seek on foot. They seem to be after someone in a moving vehicle traveling north on the other side of this range." He looked at the map markings. "Who could they be after that would make them transmit in voice, back and forth, like children?"

"The Chinese are stupid," the sergeant said. "They fight like children and run like cowards."

"They were transmitting from these two points a while ago," the lieutenant said. "Now they transmit only from this point here." His finger marked a point south of where Carr had found Loo and her grandfather. "So they have a headquarters in this south area and patrols with radios up here to the north." He looked at the high peaks ahead, then turned his attention back to the map. "From their last signal, they seem to be chasing their quarry along a path leading to this small pass." He marked it with a pencil.

To the sergeant he said, "We'll move up to that pass on our side. I am curious about their quarry. If that person comes through the pass I want to be there to greet him. It may be the American. Put the men on full alert and let's move out quickly. The American is crafty. He may somehow have gotten a vehicle." He strode on his thin bowed legs to the decrepit car. He heard the van start up behind it. He got in as the puffing sergeant slid behind the wheel.

He settled back as they moved out, feeling pleased and with a growing sense of impending victory building within him.

U.S. Military Observer Group
Dixie Mission
Yenan, Shensi Province

Captain Chance Beard was working in his headquarters room, dug deep into the loess cliffs of Yenan, when he heard the footsteps coming through the tunnel that led to the outside.

"Friend or foe?" he said. He sat back on the bench and rubbed his thick-haired head, which sat atop a very stout frame larded with small rolls of fat. Lieutenant Fraser Dillon, the signals officer for the Dixie Mission, came through the tunnel. "Cryptos for you, Chance," he said. He looked around the familiar room hewed deep into the hillside. The walls were lined with finely hewn stone. Beard sat at a rough wooden table, perched on a sturdy wooden bench. Tallow candles sputtered on the tabletop. There was an enameled washbasin in one corner. Beard's clean but rumpled woolen-issue jacket was draped over the kang, a wide solid board lined with felt and placed over two cement ends.

Beard reached for the paper and his code book. "Sit, Dilly. I'll see what this is all about. Who's outside?"

"Just *pa lus* moving around. No guards. Place is quiet."

Beard concentrated on using the OSS decode system. When he was finished he looked at the signals officer. "Background?"

"Our own receiver. The Reds alerted us it was coming twenty-six minutes ago. I copied it myself."

"The Reds will have copied it, too. Tai Li's men here in the Ministry of Communications in the Postal and Telegraph Administration of the Kuomintang will have copied it."

"Standard practices."

Beard lifted his decipher sheet. "Ever hear of an Ambrose Moffett?"

Dillon shook his head.

Beard rubbed his stubby nose. "This is hotter'n a long rifle at a Kentucky turkey shoot," he said. "Ever since Major General Patrick J. Hurley came up here our mission has been ground up like a ham loaf. We came here last July to do weather reportin', to try to get more on the Jap order of battle, get some intelligence on targets and bomb damage, and see if there was some way the good ol' U.S. could help the Commies, right?"

Dillon pulled up the other small bench and sat down. "Right."

"Hurley upsets the applecart. The Commies control nearly ninety million Chinese. They're blockaded up here by eight hundred thousand Kuomintang troops. General Stilwell wanted to work with them. Roosevelt dumped him and brought in General Wedemeyer as chief of the American forces in China and chief of staff to Chiang Kai-shek." Dillon waited. Tall, slight, redheaded, and freckled-faced, the Texan was used to long speeches by

Chance Beard of OSS and by Colonel Dean McHugh, head of the Dixie Mission. Both men were a lot alike.

Beard went on, a thoughtful expression on his face. "Hurley comes in as a special emissary from Roosevelt in November, two months ago. The Commies agree to a five-point proposal where they'd throw in with the Kuomintang to defeat the Japs. They'd get recognition from the coalition government and foreign supplies would be distributed equally. Okay? A good break for the ol' U.S.A. Chiang turns it down, the bastard! We propose bringin' in OSS teams to train the Commie guerrillas for demolition and diversionary tactics. We suggest the possibility that we give the people's militia one hundred thousand pistols. What happened?" His words were laced with roughness.

"Both ideas went down the drain."

"Right! So now we've got both Hurley and Wedemeyer throwin' rocks at each other and the Commies thinkin' we're a bunch of idiots. Hurley is tryin' to blame us for the mess. Mao Tse-tung and Chou En-lai tell us they'd like to go to Washington for a secret meetin' with Roosevelt." Beard's dark eyes glowed in the candlelight. "What a deal that would have been! Hurley sticks a knife into it. Where does that leave us?"

"With shit on our face." Dillon's words were definite.

"Now comes the stinger." Beard held up his decipher sheet. "This is top-secret, Dilly. One-oh-one finds out about a Tai Li plot to kidnap Mao, Chou, and General Chu Teh!"

Dillon was surprised. "Oh, Christ! They'd never get away with it here!"

"Well, how's that for broken rocks? This Ambrose Moffett, I remember him vaguely from a meetin' I was at in New Delhi, he's comin' in to fill us in and to face-to-face it with our hosts. It's that sensitive. The C-46 he's in goes down about an hour and a half out of here. One guy makes it out, a master sergeant named Douglas Carr. He's got the packet Moffett was bringin'."

"Chance, is this the first you've heard of it?" Dillon leaned forward. "I mean, what the hell are they doing? Where was the C-46 coming from?"

"Myitkyina. Can you believe it? They fitted it with cabin tanks. Sent it in ahead of the storm that hit south of us. Wanted to stay away from Chungking or Chengtu and Tai Li's guys."

"This Carr. He the crew chief or radio?"

"Radio."

Dillon rose to look at the maps pinned on the wall, held in by nails driven into the mortar between the hewn rocks. "I don't believe it, Chance. If the C-46 went down, say two-fifty, two-seventy miles from here, he'd be in some really bad mountain country. That storm swept through there. He'll never make it out. How the hell's he going to get through the blockade?"

Beard rose and looked at the map alongside Dillon. "What's even crazier, one-oh-one says he's hooked up with two Chinese."

They were silent, until Dillon turned away from the map. "What do they want you to do? What about Colonel McHugh?"

"I'll go route him out now. He's over at the General Chu's headquarters. They want us to sit on this until they get back to us. They're tryin' to find this Carr. He's out there in no-man's-land runnin' around with a packet that could get us in a lot of trouble if it falls into the wrong hands!"

"Anything I can do?"

"Stay with your radio operations, Dilly. This thing's hot, and God knows what they're cookin' up at Myitkyina." They went down the tunnel, Beard slipping into his uniform jacket and carrying his greatcoat and cap. "McHugh will bust a gut when he hears this!"

They saw the bridge as the path widened and straightened out. Carr drove up to within a few feet of it and killed the engine. He felt immensely tired.

In the late afternoon, a thick mist rolled over the saddle of the pass, chilling them and turning the area into a darkish gray caldron. The narrow old bridge was the single link between the two sides of the pass. He went to the edge of the bridge, staring down into the murky gorge below, realizing it was many hundreds of feet deep. The planked bridge sagged alarmingly. It looked weakened with age. It was suspended from each side by a network of four-inch-thick woven ropes fastened to rusty steel pillars sunk into deep holes bored into the bedrock.

He tested it gingerly, forced to use the flashlight in the misty gloom. The heavy cloud layer still held the sun at bay. He saw where recent repairs had been made, with new thick planking and reinforcement rope here and there and stout steel wire added at a number of spots. He wondered if it would hold the truck. Carbine in hand, he went to Loo. She had the Sterno can working. The old man, his thin white chin whiskers blowing in the rising breeze, sat on a fold of parachute cloth, sipping water from the mess-kit cup. He looked at ease, despite the bandage on his head, his expression noncommittal.

Carr unloaded the truck, carrying everything across the bridge in ten trips. "I've measured it," he said to Loo, who squatted at the Sterno. He knelt next to her, taking a steaming tin of food. "I've got a crazy idea. We need the truck on the other side. If I can lighten it, it may go across."

She looked at him intensely. "The truck is too heavy. It will crash through."

"I said the idea is crazy. If we're across and it goes down, it will take the bridge with it. That'll keep the bastards from following us."

She brushed back her long gleaming black hair, a totally feminine movement. Her old cotton cap lay on the ground near her. He could smell her dried perspiration, and the closeness of her bothered him. He wondered what he could do to make her like him. It seemed a lost cause.

"We must go on foot," she said. "Your idea is insane. How can we drive the truck over? It is too wide for the bridge. We will go down with it."

He ate his K ration, drank from the water jug, and handed it to her. "Your grandfather's eaten, had water. I'll take him over to the other side. You bring this stuff. I'll show you how I think we can do it." He picked up the old man, pleased that in his tired condition he could do even that. Matching his steps with the swaying bridge, slowly and with growing confidence, he made it. He placed the old man on the ground in a small clearing well past the bridge. Loo joined them, carrying the cooking items and water jug.

"Here's how we'll do it. No telling how close those guys are. It's getting dark. They may burrow in for the night and come at us in the morning. We can't take that chance. I'll strip off the stake sides and hack the bed down to the width of the truck. It will just fit."

"If it breaks through, we will lose you." There was no emotion in her voice.

"I'm not going to be in it." He explained his plan, and she helped. They ran long lengths of the drogue-chute shroud lines to the truck, parked with its front wheels on the first plank of the bridge. With the hand ax, Carr hacked at the rotten wood of the bed. The dry wood splintered easily. In an hour he had the bed trimmed to the sides of the cab. One nylon line ran through the right window, tied to the bottom of the steering wheel. A second line ran into the left window, tied to the top of the wheel. A third line ran under the open hood to the accelerator control.

He started the engine, put it in drive, and the truck moved slightly, then stopped, idling. He got out, crossed the bridge, and took two of the lines. "Remember," he said, "if it goes to your right, pull your line gently and keep taking the line in as the truck comes toward us. Easy does it. If the truck goes to the left, I'll pull my line. I can rev it up with this other line."

She was nervous, moving about in her padded clothes, the cap back on her head, her hair tucked under it. "Have you ever done anything like this before?"

"Did something like it with a tractor back home. Damned thing got stuck in the mud, and we didn't want to be in it if it turned over on a slope. Rigged it up with ropes like this and got it out." He grunted. "Didn't have a damned bridge, though." He tested the accelerator line. The idling engine picked up. "Here we go!" He pulled the line gently. The truck moved.

"Your line!" he said grimly as the truck veered to the right. She pulled and the truck straightened out. He slacked his line to allow the movement. The truck moved to his side, and he pulled the line as she loosened hers. They quickly worked out the sensitive controls, pulling the lines as they did. Slowly, the truck made it almost to the center, then one wheel bit deep between two of the planks. The entire bridge swayed heavily.

"Off!" he said, and they lessened the pull on the lines. "Wait until that miserable son of a bitch stops swaying." He stared critically at the moving bridge and was surprised when its swaying stopped suddenly under the weight of the truck. "Once more," he said quietly. He pulled the accelerator line. The engine sounded loud in the grayish gloom and the cold mountain air. Carr won-

dered how far the sound was carrying. Would their pursuers hear it
back along the two paths that led to the bridge and the pass?

His accelerator line was taut, and the truck lurched forward from
the plank gap. Loo tugged quickly when the wheels turned right,
then Carr tugged as they turned left. Between them they steered the
rumbling truck forward until it reached the hard-packed ground. Its
rear wheels were still on the last of the planks. "Hold it!" Carr
said. "If I don't get in the cab the damned thing will take off." He
motioned to the steep drop-off behind them. The path went down-
hill rapidly from the bridge, curving down the quickly sloping,
rocky mountainside.

He threw the lines to one side. "Stand over there with your
grandfather. It's the only way I know to get the truck off the
bridge."

Cautiously he entered the cab, keeping the door open. He
pressed his boot gingerly on the accelerator, and his heart raced as
the truck backed up a foot. Then it moved forward and was off the
bridge. He slumped over the wheel, foot jammed against the brake
pedal. She came to the open door, looking up at him in the dim
light. "I don't believe it," she said.

He found the strength to shift and move the truck carefully down
the narrow winding path to a fairly level place. He turned off the
engine and got out, shaking violently. She followed him and found
him leaning against the cab. This time there was concern in her
voice. "Are you ill?"

"Just scared," he said through chattering teeth.

A sharp gust of wind suddenly whipped their clothes, and they
looked up at the quickly waving trees overhead. "The weather will
get worse," she said. "What do we do now?"

Carr fought his trembling. "We can't go down this slope in the
dark. They can't get across the bridge with their truck. When it
gets light they'll come across on foot. I'll set up my ambush." He
tried to smile. "It had better work."

She pointed to her grandfather, who was squatting between large
rocks to avoid the gusty wind that blew dust up in swirling clouds.
"He isn't worried. I'm not worried. It will work."

He looked back at the bridge, feeling strength returning.
"You're damned right it will work!"

CHAPTER FOUR

The storm had missed them, but it brought quick, inky blackness to their mountain.

With the sound of the wind came the chugging of a laboring engine on the other side of the pass. Carr had scouted, flat on the ground, seeing the wavering headlights approach, seeing the riflemen hop down from the truck and investigate the old bridge. He knew from their movements that they would bivouac where they were. They would not send a patrol over in the night. It was too dangerous.

He had crawled away, then stood and gone back to the truck. They had slept that night on straw mats on the back of the truck, wrapped in nylon cloth and the canvas tarp. Loo and Carr shared sentry duty again, two hours on and off. Long before the first hint of light of their second day together, Carr fashioned his defense. He had a choice of trying to snake the old truck down the precipitous trail in the dark, which he didn't fancy, or making it hard, if not impossible, for the soldiers to follow them when it became lighter.

With the roll of thin wire he fixed hand grenades to two trees on each side of the path. He linked them with a trip wire staked an inch above the loose dirt on the hard rock path. He sprinkled dirt on the trip wire to camouflage it. Further down the path he jammed two grenades in the side of the slope and ran a pull wire to the truck. He hoped the blast would send rocks across the path, barring the way of the soldiers. He set up the machine gun on top of a rocky bulge, high enough up from the path to give him a clear view when the soldiers came across the bridge. He worked in the darkness, feeling his way, thankful for good night vision. He loaded the carbine clips and made certain the .45 was fully loaded.

He went back to the truck. "Loo, get in the truck with your grandfather. It'll lighten up soon. When they come across the bridge to this side I'll have them in my sights. I'll fire short bursts at them to send them back. That will give us some time. I'll leave the machine gun. We'll go down as fast as we can. If the map is right, we should break out in four or five miles at the main road."

She nodded her understanding. Carr crawled up to his perch at the machine gun. He regretted not being able to take it with him, but he had no way of knowing how many of the men could get past his trap. He scanned the upper reaches with the binoculars. He picked up the first movement. Three, then four men, rifles at the ready, came across the bridge, the end of which he could just see. They were dressed in Chinese army uniforms. Nationalists! In all, twelve men were in a knot on the east side of the pass, looking down the steep slope of the mountainside in the growing light.

Someone gave an order. They began to move along the sides of the path. He pressed the trigger of the machine gun, allowing for distance and windage. He saw bullets smash into the lead group. Three men fell. The others ducked back toward the bridge. He fired again in shorts bursts. Two more of the shocked men fell. Something came flying through the air at him. He hugged the rock in desperation. Grenade! The blast jarred the area in front of his shielded position. He emptied the machine gun, spraying the end of the bridge. Shaken, he slid down, grabbing the carbine, and ran down the path. He pulled the wire he had laid in the road. The two grenades exploded, sending a shower of rocks into the air. He heard the rumble of a landslide.

He leaped behing the wheel, slamming the door and releasing the brake. The strange-looking vehicle moved quickly, and he steered it around the bends of the downward path, heavily tree-lined, snaking along a course between the rocky outgrowths of the mountainside. They were more than a mile away when a booming sound followed them. He looked at Loo and her grandfather, a grin on his face. "Trip wire worked!"

The truck careened down the steep slope. They were nearly at the bottom when Carr caught sight of the main road. He braked to a stop, bringing the binoculars to his eyes.

"What is it?" Loo asked anxiously.

He pressed his foot harder against the brake pedal and steadied his hands. The binoculars swept the road below. "Four vehicles down there. Two trucks, a van, and a car. Listen!" There was a cacophony of noise from below.

"She breathed sharply. "Oh, no!"

"Nationalist soldiers," he said, "shooting at Chinese civilians!"

It was a battle.

Lieutenant Oshima knelt behind a boulder, directing the fire of his men. He saw the Kuomintang soldiers running through the tall grass, firing at him, popping from rock mound to rock mound. The soldiers had hailed them, motioning for them to stop. Chancing it, the lieutenant decided to keep on going. The two KMT trucks, each bearing three men, circled around and followed them, swinging from the road into the grass to go around and head them off. They began firing from the backs of the trucks, and the lieutenant, knowing now the impossibility of escape, gave orders to return the fire. He had hoped that fire from civilians would stop the patrol. It hadn't.

"Get the knee mortar going!" he shouted. He fired his Mauser, knowing the distance was too great for any damage to the soldiers. The noise on the grassy plains was deafening. His four men and the sergeant had taken a position to his right. There was a great amount of shouting on both sides. His men worked their automatic weapons. The mortar was set up, and it appeared to drive the enemy back. He was beginning to feel more reassured about his pinned-down car and van when he heard the unmistakable sound of an incoming mortar shell.

"Offspring of prostitutes!" he shouted, throwing himself flat against the ground, gritty soil slamming into his face. He heard Sergeant Mutagachi shouting orders, and his own mortar began whuffing shells back. He counted the fire, knowing that his ammunition reserves were dwindling rapidly. He crawled toward the sergeant. "Space them out!" He raised himself to a half-kneeling position to see better. There still were six soldiers moving around. A bullet sang past his head and zinged into a large boulder behind him. He flopped down and reloaded the Mauser. He knew they were in for a long day. He hoped the Chinese ran out of ammunition and mortar shells before his men did. He looked around quickly as his radioman grunted and rolled over, red splashing from his head. He glanced longingly at the radio van, heard bullets striking it. He would not be able to send for reinforcements. None would be sent by the general. He had exceeded his authority, and unless he brought back the American and vital intelligence information he was in deep trouble.

A mortar shell landed near him, and a billow of damp loess dust whipped around him in a suffocating snarl. He gripped his pistol tighter and crawled toward the sergeant. He was going to order a fast run away from the Kuomintang patrol that had surprised them. He had to give up his plan to capture the man who was coming over the pass high up in the mountain behind him. A pass that was tantalizingly close. Baoji was ahead. He had to reach Baoji. There was an agent there who would shelter them and help locate the American. He raised his head and shouted the command to dash to the car and van and make a run for it.

As soon as the words were out of his mouth he was up and running, bullets whipping around him. He prayed the surprise would work. He did not notice the slip of paper that fell out of his pocket as he ran.

Carr put down the binoculars.

"The civilians down there," he said. "They've been firing automatic weapons. One of them had a knee mortar. They sure came well prepared."

"What are they doing now?" Loo's expression was worried.

"Two of them got in a car and headed north. The other three tried to get into a van, something that looks like an old bread truck at home. They were cut down. The soldiers got in their trucks and they're chasing the car." He shifted gears. "Here's our chance to get down to the road. Some of those guys back of us might be coming down. They'll never get their truck across. They'll have to go back and come across on the big pass up ahead."

He drove around another bend, expecting to find a clear access to the road below. He braked again, looking with disgust at the giant outcropping that barred his way. A sheer wall of rock lined the path on both sides for a hundred feet. There was only room for a hand-pulled or mule-drawn cart. "That does it! Damn near off this mountain and look at that! Out! Let's move!"

He wasted no time. The truck had to be abandoned. He hacked small trees to make travois poles and knotted them together with drogue-chute lines. He filled the barracks bag with all he could cram into it and tied it to the travois. He slung the binoculars and carbine over his shoulders. He roped the travois to his waist and with Loo's help got the old man up onto his back. Loo carried the .45 and a jerry-made sack containing the remaining Chinese grenades and the .45 ammunition.

Pulling the travois by the waist ropes, holding onto the legs of the old man, Carr made it through the tight passage between the tall rock sides. He heard Loo breathing heavily behind him, gasping as she stumbled or cursing lightly as wet dirt lodged itself in her sandals.

They were almost at the road when he heard Loo whisper a sharp warning. He stopped. Bent with the load of the old man riding him piggyback and the weight of the travois, he barely saw the slight movement in the thick bushes. He reached for the carbine, slowly and deliberately. The tiger crouched at the side of the trail, its head low to the ground, its huge paws braced to spring, its body hidden in the underbrush.

The .45 roared. The tiger rose, screaming thunderously, thrashing on its hind legs. The .45 roared again. Blood spurted from a hole behind the left ear of the massive head and one in the upper chest. The beast, almost upright, sprang, its lifeless body plunging out onto the trail.

Carr felt himself in the frenzied grip of Ho Ling-chi, who uttered a long squeal as the tiger fell almost at Carr's feet. Carr managed to turn. He looked into Loo's eyes. *"Ding hao!"* He squatted to let the old man off and untied the travois ropes. The old man backed away from the tiger, then unaccountably went to it and nudged it with his toe. Carr had the carbine off and ready. The tiger lay motionless, red pouring from its thick, rough, dull hair with uneven black stripes.

Carr went to Loo. She still held the automatic in both hands. He took it from her, put the hammer down, and holstered it. "Now look who's shaking," he said. He put his arm around her to comfort her. Then he led her past the dead beast, noting its huge size.

He judged it weighed 250 pounds. He took the arm of the old man and made them walk down to the place where the trail met the road. "Stay here," he said. He patrolled the battle area, carbine in hand. He went back to them, taking the travois. "There are two dead Kuomintang guys out there in the grass and rocks. Four dead civilians around that van. It looks okay except for the bullet holes in it." He undid the barracks bag, opened the door of the van's rear, and hefted it inside. He picked up the weapons. "I'll be a son of a bitch," he said to Loo, who brought the remaining items. "Where did they get automatic weapons like this?" He peered inside, then went into the van. He lifted the lid of the sturdy metal box at the far end, fastened to the rear of the cab. He stared in complete amazement at the radio transmitter/receiver. "This is American equipment," he said to Loo, standing at the open door. "How crazy can things get!" He hopped out, looking up at the thick overcast. He put the weapons in the back.

"Those guys had a radio. It was protected by a steel box. It has an antenna, an insulated wire that can be thrown up into a tree when they send or receive. Get him up on the seat. I'll see if this thing still runs. Those soldiers might come back at any moment!" He tried the engine. It refused to start. He opened the hood and tinkered with the engine. The second time it caught. "That's a real nice sound," he said. He drove down the road. "We're going north. What do those markings on the sides say?"

"It belongs to a rice combine. They go around buying crops from landowners and sell them to the army." Her voice was thin. She hadn't recovered from the suddenness of the tiger's attack.

"Rice combine, hell!" He pulled the slip of paper from his pocket. "What's on this? I found it back there."

She studied it. "Not Chinese. It's Japanese!"

"Can you read it?"

"No."

The road was fairly passable. It ran through a wide grassland area skirting the mountain range. He had recovered from the jolt of seeing the tiger. He felt his confidence returning. The van drove better than the truck they'd abandoned. "I thought it was funny how those guys in Chinese clothes were fighting. They looked like well-trained soldiers to me. They had damned good weapons. My guess is that they are Japanese fifth columnists. This van is their cover.''

''What are they doing here so far north?'' Loo was pressed against her grandfather to keep him steady on the smooth, thinly padded seat.

''Damned if I know. I don't even understand why those soldiers were chasing us. They put on a good operation. They'll try to catch us by getting over the next pass and onto this road. I shot their deserters. Why would they be chasing me?''

Loo peered around her grandfather. ''Ho Ling-chi, I told you, is a very important man in Yenan. If those men were to capture him, Tai Li's group would reward them very well. I mean nothing to them.''

Carr felt the pressure of the Moffett packet in the small of his back. Despite the wind and the cold, he felt buoyant. They were moving, and that's what he wanted. ''Ask him if he knows how we can miss the pass up there and get past Baoji and find a way to get through the blockade.'' Several minutes of soft Chinese followed.

''He's trying to remember,'' Loo said. ''So much has happened. He is still frightened of the tiger, even though it is dead. He fears its spirit. He feels disoriented. He believes there is a small turnoff road up there, far ahead, where the three tall rock formations are. He thinks he remembers it.''

Carr saw the rock spires. ''Tell him he's quite a gentleman. He hasn't complained once.''

It was the first time he'd heard her laugh. It was a pleasant sound over the noise of the van with the wind hitting it and blowing through the bullet holes. ''He's learned it does no good to complain. He is tortured over the death of his friends and he grieves for them.'' She paused. ''He is also saddened for you, that you have had to kill so many men just for us.''

''I was there, too. They would have shot me.''

''He is amazed at the things you do. He has never seen anyone like you. He fears you. He worries that the warrior you are will turn on us.''

Carr was surprised. ''That's dumb!'' They drove for a while in silence. They saw deserted, fire-burned huts and houses. They saw no people. The grasslands seemed to stretch for miles, ripped by rock formations, surrounded by the mountain range to the west.

"The Long March went this way," Loo said. "This is the Great Grasslands. Fierce battles were fought here between the Red Army and the Nationalists. My grandfather was on this part of the Long March."

"I heard about it. What was it, six thousand miles?"

"Eighteen thousand lis, yes. Many died in battle. Many died along the way, from sickness, disease, starvation. My country will never forget it. This Great Grasslands area has few people. The ones who live here are mantzu, aboriginal tribesmen, very fierce."

They were getting nearer to the rock formations. "The two fifth columnists who got away in the car—I think the fat one took a slug. He went down and got up. He had what looked like a machine pistol. If he's wounded, they'll probably head for Baoji."

"There's a small medical clinic there," Loo said after talking to her grandfather. Ho Ling-chi seemed to have recovered. Color had returned to his face. He fingered his long white chin whiskers, looking out at the countryside as the van bounced along the often deeply rutted road of loess soil. Loo leaned toward Carr. "I must ask you a question. Please do not be offended."

He turned to her. The road was clear for a mile ahead. "What?"

"When you shot—I mean, when you fought—those men, what did you feel?"

He thought about it. "Everything happened so fast. All my life I've been taught to move right in on things. I have an anger that rises very fast. It makes me move because I want to change the situation that angers me. When those men were attacking you, I reacted with anger. When the truck came after us, I was angry. I couldn't help firing at the bandits. I had thought of getting the drop on them and making them surrender, and then the fat one surprised me. There was nothing else I could do." He swallowed. "I felt fear, real fear, deep down. I saw bullets hit all of them. I couldn't believe they were dead."

"How did you become an aviator?"

"At the university I had my own plane. Dad put me through school. I worked in a radio repair shop and made enough money to buy a used single-engine Stinson. I made enough money while going to high school to buy my own ham radio operator's set. I put my own radio in the Stinson. After I graduated I went into cadets. That's our training program for pilots."

"You do so many things. You can fly an airplane!" Her dark eyes reflected her amazement. "I thought you were a radio man."

"I would have been a pilot in the Army Air Corps. I wanted to fly fighter planes. The fastest ones." He steered around a slight bend, seeing the rock spires getting closer. "I was on my final check, ready to get my wings. A tire blew on the last landing. We ground-looped and the plane caught on fire. The senior instructor was burned to death." He coughed with the bitter memory. "They washed me out. They wouldn't give me my wings. They said I was responsible for the instructor's death. They sent me to a radio school, then a radar school. I came over here a year ago. I do the navigation. Radio beams and the loran. That's long-range radar. I get them there and back."

"You were disappointed. What a terrible thing to happen."

He eyed the rock pillars. "It's something you don't forget. Ask Mr. Ho what we do now. We'll be there in a minute."

More Kuo-yu. "There is a family he knows," she said. "If they are still there. Pass the rock formations and turn right on the first road. The family is about five or six of your miles. They will feed us and we can rest there."

"Pray to Lenin that they're there!" he said.

"You know about Lenin?"

"And Karl Marx, Joe Stalin, the Politburo. Hell, back home the papers were full of stories about Russian Communists. What I don't know much about is you Red Chinese."

Her voice hardened. "All you need to know is that the Red Army fights the Japanese, while Chiang Kai-shek avoids it. He has killed many thousands of Communists. It is a passion with him. Now you Americans help him, and in that way you help to kill more of our people." Her voice had risen. "My grandfather knows, and I know, that one day all our land will be under the People's Party!" Her eyes shone with vehemence.

"Okay, okay," he said, seeking to calm her. So much for trying to get her to like him. The old man suddenly pointed to a patch of trees along the road. Carr understood and slowed the van, seeing tiny deserted farms and sad-looking homes, decaying, unattended. The residue of warfare. He turned on the road just past the rock spires. More ruined homes stood along the old path. Carr wondered at the desolation. He knew the long war in China had forced millions of Chinese to move from their land, to migrate. The sights he saw depressed him. This vast area of northern China, this part of the Great Grasslands, was barren of its people. War had chased them away.

The old man leaned forward and pointed. Carr braked to a halt before a ramshackle brick, mud, bamboo, and thatch building. "Damn it!" he said. "There's no one here. Where the hell is everybody?"

Loo said, "Get out, but be careful. Help me down. They are in hiding. This has been a war zone for many years. They heard us coming a long time ago. They survive by being able to disappear so they won't be shot by bandits or soldiers."

He helped them down, holding the carbine. They walked around the old farm. It had been cultivated. It looked inhabited. He knew Loo was right. People were there, hiding. There was a well with a greenish bucket and a dirty coiled rope at the top. From somewhere in the trees a chicken made a noise.

Loo raised her hands, and her fingers made signs that were meaningless to Carr. "What's that all about?"

"They can see us," she said. "I want them to know we are friends." She turned to him. "In this land—China, as you call it— most of the people cannot read or write. We communicate by printed ideographs, or picture signs. Or signs like the hand motions I just made." They waited. A shapeless form appeared in the dense trees, dim in the poor light under the overcast. An old man with a long chin beard, longer than Loo's grandfather's, stepped out. His arms were hidden in the crossed folds of his long, cotton-padded sleeves. His head was covered with a conical cotton hat.

Carr saw Loo's grandfather step forward in great dignity. There was a muffled Chinese greeting. The two old men approached each other slowly. The farmer peered intently, cocking his head from side to side. A smile broke on his deeply lined face, darkly weathered, and he bowed rapidly. Facing each other, the two ancients went through the ageless rituals of old friends seeing each other after a very long time.

Loo pushed a hand against Carr's arm. "I prayed to Lenin," she said solemnly, "and he answered my prayer!"

"Mine, too. Ask Father Time here where we can hide this damned van and if he has some boiled water and food for us. Ask him if any KMT soldiers are around. Ask him how we can get through the blockade and to Yenan.''

She gave him a mock British salute. ''Yes, my American emperor. But please let your bloody servant take her bloody time. In my country, these things are not rushed. We must always preserve face. You, my American emperor, are in my country and you must do as we do.''

He looked into her sparkling eyes, brilliant white surrounding ebony centers, seeing again how beautiful she was, dirt-streaked face and mud-smeared clothes notwithstanding. The weary peaked cap atop her jet-black hair looked somehow fashionable. ''You know what I think?'' he said.

She shook her head, and the small graceful movement tantalized him. ''I think,'' he said slowly, ''that if we live through this goddamned mess you'll be voted Miss People's Party.''

She showed her disdain. ''We do not have beauty contests!''

''We have in my country. You'd win there, Loo.''

They turned to see the three members of the farmer's family greeting Ho Ling-Chi, his wife and two grandsons, as they learned. Gone was the cautious formal atmosphere. They were talking excitedly, pointing unashamedly at the bullet-riddled van and at the strange, tall white man with blond hair who stood holding a carbine under the glowering China skies. It was the first time they'd seen an American in uniform. They stared at his woolen issue under the leather jacket and his leather flight helmet. They smiled at the sight.

Carr stared back. The woman was old, slightly bent. She looked as if she had arthritis. The two boys, in their teens, were dark-faced from outdoor work. They were slender but they looked capable. He thought of them playing softball in an American sandlot and wondered what they did for fun in this bleak area of China.

Ho motioned them to come with them into the home, such as it was. Carr hid the van in the trees where planes would not spot it. He joined them, smelling tea brewing, feeling the warmth of a cooking fire, listening to the Chinese voices.

Strangely, he felt at home.

Fog blanketed Myitkyina, grounding all aircraft and making ground movement dangerous.

Max Ribbands ate the hated Vienna sausages covered with despicable tomato sauce and drank the appalling coffee in the officers' mess, slapping canned butter on thick slices of day-old quartermaster bread. His stomach felt leaden. Finished with his evening meal, he groped his way to the operations Quonset hut and found Major Foxx poring over radio messages and flight-loading reports. "Bhamo's clear, for a change," Foxx said. "Everything else around here is closed down."

Ribbands pulled up a chair and sat heavily in it. "What's the latest on the OSS flight to Yenan?" He rubbed his irritated belly. "Christ! They're yelling at us to move more of Chiang's troops, move more tonnage. The Japs hit a couple of spots this afternoon around Meiktila. The B-24s out of Dum Dum are doing a big spread. They're hitting targets below this damned weather."

Henry Foxx grimaced. "OSS has been in here three times already. They got wet pants trying to get another of theirs to Yenan, but we can't clear the flight until we get better weather reports over that area. Another stinking storm. The Twentieth Bomber Command at Chengtu is down along with the Fourteenth fighters because of it."

The air-raid siren sounded. They looked at each other in disgust. They left the Quonset hut on the run with the other operations officers and by practice, rather than sight, ran to the sandbagged trench and jumped into it. They swore loudly at the unseen single Japanese bomber flying on top of the thick ground fog as it dropped its load of nuisance bombs.

"It would indeed be a lovely thing if our guys would get Pissin' Sam, that bastard!" Ribbands said, standing in the trench as the sounds of the Japanese Betty and the ack-ack faded. "The son of a bitch was really late today." They made their way back through the eddying mists to the Quonset, brushing their jungle-issue uniforms. Inside, Ribbands said, "So OSS is on hold until the weather clears at Yenan. What do the weather guys say about the storm? How long will it last?"

"Most of the night. Actually, it's hitting far below Yenan, over the same mountains our ship went down in. It will blow out sometime tomorrow. Out of Mongolia again." Foxx pointed to a report. "We've got this C-46 on heavy guard around the clock. OSS has their man pacing up and down. They got a radio message in to Chance Beard up there.''

"So the smart-asses finally had to go to radio!" Ribbands felt a large balloon of gas pushing though his intestines. "They could have done that in the first place."

Foxx looked at him quizzically. "Are you all right?"

Ribbands felt the gas coming. He looked roofward and the blast echoed in the Quonset. No one turned to him. "Now I feel better. That leaves us with Carr loose up there in the mountains with the Moffett packet." He sat down, relieved. "I wonder what that poor son of a bitch is doing in that damned storm. I'll bet the stupid ass is being chased by bandits or tribesmen and wishing the hell he'd stayed for the search-and-rescue team."

Baoji, on the Wei River
Northwest China

Lieutenant Oshima sat on the bamboo-fiber floor cushion looking into the shielded eyes of his Baoji agent, a Kempetai fellow officer.

"How did you manage to get through the blockade patrols?" the agent said, visibly impressed.

"I bribed the sick dogs. A handful of yuan and they are all agreeable. They almost licked my hand."

"It is regrettable about your men. Only you and your sergeant survived, and he has a flesh wound in his left arm." The agent made a small, sympathetic motion with his hands. "I have friends who are attending to him. He lost blood, but he is strong and will mend rapidly." A pause while the agent sought cautious words. "I am most pleased that you are here, but there is much movement of both the Kuomintang and the Communist troops. Is it wise for you to stay here?"

"I stay only long enough to rest," the lieutenant said. "I have a most important mission, one that brought me this far north into enemy territory."

"I am your servant, Lieutenant."

"We have very little time. We were trapped by a Kuomintang patrol, as I told you. We were able to outrace them and then abandoned our car because it had bullet holes in it. We hid in bushes until the patrol left. You must help me quickly. How many Chinese do you have in your network?"

"Seventeen. They are all most unhappy with those who would be their Communist masters, and with the Kuomintang as well."

The lieutenant leaned forward. "There is an American. His plane crashed in the mountains a long way from here. He was on his way to Yenan. The others with him were killed."

"Yenan!" The agent breathed the word.

"He carries extremely important military intelligence information. I must capture this man. We intercepted Chinese radio messages. He is with two Chinese. How he managed that, I do not know. But I am convinced from the way the Kuomintang patrols were chasing him that he was headed this way. He has either arrived here or he soon will. Your people must circulate and bring to you any report on an American aviator."

"What does he look like?"

The lieutenant was irritated and struggled to maintain his calm pose. "I do not know. Sufficient to say he is an American, in uniform, and he is with two Chinese. I suspect they are hill people he has paid to guide him to Yenan."

The agent thought about it. "With your permission, I will go now. You are safe in this house for at least a day. I have another house on the other side of Baoji where the sergeant is. You can be moved to it if the soldiers begin a search." He motioned to a large packet. "In that are clothes that it would be wise for you to wear. They are more in keeping with this area than what you have on now. My people are bringing you food and wine. While you rest, I will organize a probe for this American." Another pause. "What kind of a fool is he who crashes in the mountains and does not wait for the American rescue experts? Why would he attempt to travel on foot for such a long distance to Yenan? How can he hide in this area where so few of his people have come? It is impossible that he will not be seen and reported!"

The lieutenant breathed deeply. "If you had seen the wreck of that large aircraft from which he survived, you would agree that he is a man driven by the winds of insanity."

"He is insane?"

"He may well be dead. He was being chased by at least two patrols of Kuomintang. They must want him for ransom. He is crafty, very intelligent. If he escaped the patrols and made it across the pass near where we were attacked, the only northern route he can follow leads to Baoji." He wiped his palms together. "To me he is a most valuable prize. You must find him for me. But be careful. We are dealing with a most capable enemy. I don't know how he lived through that crash, or how he is moving on the ground. But he is active and cautious. He is an enemy to respect." His face was lively as he spoke. "I need to know the name of our key man in Yenan. I do not have that information."

The agent rose from his floor mat and bowed. "I will consider that request. The information is most sensitive." There was a scratching at the door. He went to the door of the single-room house, empty but for them, and opened the door a crack. He beckoned to a small boy who stood nearby. The boy handed him a covered basket. He shut the door quickly. "Your food and drink. Please rest. I will return as soon as I have things under way."

The lieutenant watched him leave. The strength he had mustered for the meeting with the Baoji agent evaporated. He sagged. The American could well be dead, the information gone. Only the delicate thought that the American was alive and in Baoji or coming to it sustained him. He looked around the barren room, at its white-washed walls, its kang with the small furnace built into the bricks for warmth. A fire glowed; tallow candles lighted its gloom. There was a single chair and an old table. The absence of windows pleased him. The door appeared to be sturdy. He stood and bolted it. He laid the Mauser next to him as he sat down again.

He was deep in enemy territory, on the trail of an elusive quarry, one he would have captured if the patrol had not come upon him. He reached for the basket. Under the cover were two bottles of Chinese wine, bread, sausages, and fruit. He ate slowly, thinking of his adversary. In his immense weariness he knew he had found the challenge he had long sought. The American, with intelligence information. Clever, strong, adaptable. A worthy quarry.

He brightened as he thought of the Japanese-born agent out rounding up his fifth-column sympathizers. They would cover the city, listening to the gossips. If the American was in Bajoi they would learn of it. News spread fast in all Chinese communities, particularly news about a strange American aviator. He could capture the man and find a way to take him to General Ishimura. A great victory! The challenge appealed to him, in his loneliness and desolation at the loss of his men, more than it ever had before. He reached for a bottle of wine.

A hunter had to be wiser than the quarry. A hunter had to be patient, more clever, more capable, more strong than the hunted.

He was the hunter. He would achieve his victory.

Carr sat on the wooden bench in the radio van, working by the beam of the flashlight held by Loo.

"How much longer will it take?" she said.

"I'll test it in the morning. I think I've got the frequencies worked out. They lettered in their own marks, but the American settings are still there."

"What will you do if it works?"

"I'll hang up the insulated antenna. It's covered with rubber. I'll see if I can get in touch with some of our guys." He looked at the sleeping mats the four men had used for bedding. The food stocked in the van had been removed to the house. He picked up one of the weapons he'd collected at the battle site. "Can you read these markings?"

She held the flashlight close. "Japanese."

He whistled as a coldness other than the brisk night air swept through him. "I don't believe in coincidences. There had to be a reason why six Japanese dressed in Chinese clothes would be on that road so close to the pass."

"I don't understand."

He took the light and played it around, studying the inside of the van. "This was a military type of operation. They sealed the radio in this steel box. That saved it from the bullets. They weren't buying rice in January. They were on an intelligence patrol. I'm guessing they were looking for me."

She was incredulous. "How would they know about you?"

"I sent a Mayday. That's our universal distress call. Just before we crashed. The Japs have a damned good radio intelligence operation. They must have picked up my key-down, gotten fixes, and came looking for the wreck."

Loo was still puzzled. "What would they gain?"

"They would know that an American plane, that late at night, and on a course northwest of Chengtu, was on a different kind of mission. They wanted to find out what the mission was."

"But the crash was far away from where they fought the Nationalists."

"Look at it this way. What would you do if you were the officer in charge of that patrol? You find the wreck. There are four bodies laid out in it. It's obvious someone survived and put them there. There's no report of a C-46 taking off from Chengtu. It's an empty plane. No cargo, no weapons, all the food and survival stuff are gone. You think it out. Here's an American on foot. Why didn't he stay with the wreck?"

Carr flexed his shoulders. "I screwed up. I never thought a Jap patrol would get to the wreck. I figured it would be a Kuomintang unit. I didn't want them to get me." He chewed on a lip. "Besides, I couldn't stay there, not with them dead."

"It was not your fault the plane crashed." Loo clearly was trying to help him, aware of his emotions.

His voice dropped. "I must have the survivor syndrome. I was shocked at the thought I had lived and they had died. I went through that in Burma and back in Texas. I just wanted to get away. I didn't want to stay with those bodies. I came to with blood dripping on me! All I thought of was getting to Yenan, like a damned fool, with the message that was the reason for the damned mission in the first place. It gave me something to hold onto."

She sat on the small stool next to him. "You still must hold onto it. Think of all you've done. You saved our lives!"

He felt a sharp pain in his stomach. "I made mistakes. I came down off the wrong side of that ridge. If I'd gone the other way, I wouldn't have met you and I'd have been on the side the Japs were. That mistake worked out all right." He patted her back. "But it was stupid of me to leave. I could have laid out ground markers for the search plane. Sent up smoke signals. I blew it!"

She leaned closer to comfort him. "What you did ended up keeping me from rape and my grandfather and me from becoming prisoners. I want you to turn your mind away from your strange 'survivor syndrome.' I have survived while my father and brother

died. I am in the same way that you are, but I look for tomorrow
and not at yesterday.''

"All right," he said. "We've been in here long enough." He
looked at her in the glow of the flashlight. "I don't know why,
Loo, but I feel I've known you all my life."

"We have been through much together in such a short time. War
does that to people. In Calcutta, I heard many stories of war from
the British. We do what we must and we accept what happens.''

He helped her down from the van and closed its rear door. They
made their way through the dark to the farmer's house. "I accept
meeting you and Ho Ling-chi," he said. "Fate can be kind and it
can be unkind. I accept that.''

By any standard, the home of the white-whiskered Tan Sen was
ugly but sturdy. Carr and Loo entered it through a heavy wooden
door that could be removed easily and turned into a kang. They
found Ho still seated at the rough wooden table, talking to Tan.

The light of an old kerosene lantern, a luxury, played on their
animated faces. Tan's aged wife and two grandsons had long since
gone to bed on their simple brick kangs, wrapped in worn padded
pukais—homemade bedding. In the mountain farm country, few
stayed up late. There was much work to be done in the morning.

In one corner of the single-room home, reed baskets held more
than a dozen sleeping brood chickens and layers. Two goats, three
small pigs, and a hungry-looking dog were quartered in a pen near
them, next to cotton sacks filled with grain and combed cotton,
ready for weaving. A hand plow, four hoes, and a pull-harrow
hung by leather straps along one wall. Spinning wheels hung from
the rafters of the unceilinged room.

Tan insisted on pouring them small cups of warm *pai-kan*, wine
served from a stoneware bottle. He went back to the table to rejoin
Ho, who seemed to have shed many years. Carr was surprised at
the energy the old man displayed in his conversation with the
farmer. "How old is your grandfather?" he said to Loo. He
learned Ho was seventy-four. He'd been born in Kunming, Yunnan province, in 1870, the year Lenin was born. He'd been thirty
when the Boxer Rebellion broke out in 1900, an anti-foreign upris-
ing in China, and had been active in the "First Revolution" in
1911 that overthrew the Manchu dynasty in central and south
China. In 1921, Ho had been involved in the first congress of the

Chinese Communist Party held at Shanghai. In 1925, he had read Mao Tse-tung's classic *Analysis of Chinese Society*. In 1936, he had joined Chairman Mao in the Long March. He had served in his younger years as a propaganda expert, then in the foreign office at Yenan, and was now on the Central Committee of the Chinese Communist Party. He had attended Pei-ta, the national university at Peking, in 1890–94, where he'd been known for his anti-Japanese activities. His former business, exporting lumber from China, had been taken over by Loo's father, Ho Li-san, until the Kuomintang had taken it away from the family.

Loo told the story of her grandfather to Carr as they sat on wooden stools. Carr glanced at his navigator's hack watch. "I feel like Gulliver in his strange travels," he said. "It's almost nine o'clock. I feel comfortable here. This is a nice family."

"That was cabbage-and-mutton soup you had," she said. "Did you like it?"

"Very good. And steamed bread and rice." He smiled. "I'll never get the hang of chopsticks."

"Mr. Tan built this house. He carried bricks from a town that used to be near here. It was destroyed by shellfire in a battle between our armies and the Kuomintang years ago. He is proud of this brick floor and that charcoal brazier they cook on."

"Where are his sons?"

"They were killed. One by the Kuomintang and the other by bandits." She sighed. "There once were more homes in this area. They were burned when the blockade was set up. The Kuomintang soldiers were brutal. They wanted the people here to support them, but many went north to join the Red Army. That brought more reprisals. This is still a war zone. The bandits roam at large. The people's militia can be almost as bad at times."

"What are they?"

"Armed peasants, for the most part. They hide their weapons during the day and go out and fight at night. Families have been tortured and killed by the Kuomintang around here for years. Tan has stayed because he grows food in the summer and weaves cotton in the winter. And because he knows how to bend with the winds."

Carr sipped the last of his wine. "This *pai-kan* tastes oily, but good."

"It is the traditional wine of our country."

"Are they speaking Kuo-yu?"

"No, Grandfather is quite a linguist. They speak pai-hua, which is our spoken language. Kuo-yu is a national tongue. What you called Mandarin before is Kuan Hua, the official language. It is still in use. It comes from the civil servants who worked in the many governments of our Middle Kingdom since the days of the Han dynasty." She laughed. "That dynasty ended in the year 220, so you know how long Kuan Hua has been spoken!"

"Why don't you Chinese call your land China?"

Her expression changed. "Only foreigners call it that. It comes from the Ch'in family, very ancient, who ruled this country centuries ago."

"What do you call it, then?"

"Chung Kuo. That means Middle Country, or Middle Kingdom. Some of the elders still call it Chung Hua Min Kuo. That means the Central Flowery People's Nation."

He felt the power of the warm wine. "Why does Mr. Tan shave his head? He's bald from his forehead to halfway down the back of his head."

"That is an old custom of the peasant people."

"How much land does he farm?"

"He has twenty-one mon. A mon is one-sixth of your acre. That is much land for a farmer, but so many have fled from here that he is able to work it with the help of his grandsons."

"He's a tough one, going through all that."

"He is also very good at making koalin objects. That is a fine porcelain clay. But to do that, he must travel to Baoji, where there are kilns he can rent."

"He sells these objects?"

"They are mostly tableware, much in need. Some are bought by merchants who ship them south to a better market."

He learned that Tan mixed white clay from the area with feld-spathic rock and lime. The result was thin, translucent, high-glazed porcelain that, fired under very high temperatures, came out in cobalt-blue and oxblood-red colors.

He learned that the Long March was called *ch'ang cheng.* Cigarettes were called *chien men.* Loo proudly reminded him that the Chinese had invented the world's first currency, block printing, the compass, gunpowder, and paper.

She told him that in northern China the vast bulk of the people had Mongol characteristics—high cheekbones and straight black hair. Chinese eyes had the distinct fold of skin over the inner angle of the eyes. While the practice was fading, there were still many Chinese women who hobbled on feet bound from birth so that they were mere stumps. "It was to keep them docile, from running away," she said. The women of the area cut their hair in short bobs, or wore it long it pigtails. No woman wore cosmetics; there were none.

Wutai meant mountains; *chiu* meant wine. To the north of Yenan there was a portion of the Great Wall of China. To the east of Yenan was the Hwang Ho, the famed Yellow River. The first Red Army had been formed in 1928. The Chinese Communist Party was trying to deal with ancient customs of corruption, thievery, terrorism, secret societies, and the foul methods of landlords and warlords. In Yenan, she told him, he would find Tibetans, Manchus, Mongols, Moslems, Kalmucks, Uigurs, Formosans, and Miao and Lolo tribesmen.

Carr placed his cup on the floor and leaned toward Loo. "Did Mr. Tan tell you how we can get through the blockade? You talked to him before you helped me at the van. What did he say?"

"He knows this area very well, naturally. He met my grandfather many years ago. As a young man he was indentured to a merchant in Sianfu. He met my grandfather, who was on a business trip there." She darted a glance at the two old men. "Later, before he came back to his ancestral farm to take over, he helped my grandfather secure a contract to take certain lumber from this district. He knew whom to bribe in the government in those days. Yes, he said we must cross the River Wei, which is most turbulent at this time of the year because of the snowstorms and the runoff. He will tell us in the morning how we must go. He has a relative—I'm not sure if it's a cousin or a nephew—who owns a barge. If we can get to the village along the Wei where the relative lives, we can get across during the night."

"Who set this blockade in the first place?"

"It is called the Shensi-Kansu-Ninghsia Border Area. Chiang Kai-shek, as I told you, hates Communists. When he couldn't kill them all and when Chairman Mao made the Long March north to

Yenan, Chiang set up the blockade to keep them penned in the north.''

Carr, feeling the wine and the insistent aching of his tired body, looked at the straw mats and *pukai* bedding laid out for them. ''What's the protocol here? I can't stay awake any longer.'' He picked up the carbine. ''What about sentry duty?''

''Not tonight. We both need our sleep. We'll take a chance on it.'' She smiled. ''Come on. I'm ready, too.''

They stretched out on the mats and covered themselves with the bedding. He placed the carbine at his side, the .45 at hers. ''In the morning, I will plan on how to make you a robe,'' she said softly.

His voice was fuzzy. ''A what?''

''I will make you the Dragon Robe of the Emperor of China.''

He fell asleep with the sound of her light laughter in his ears.

In his first dream, he strode through a mighty city, amid the sounds of bugles, drums, and gongs, to the cheers of thousands of people.

And he wore the Dragon Robe of the Emperor of China.

CHAPTER FIVE

The Combat Cargo C-46 swept skyward from the "Charlie Yoke" air base at Kunming. Wheels and flaps up, it headed toward its destination of Myitkyina, 820 miles north of Rangoon, Burma. Rolling gently in its familiar way, it began its slow western climb over the 500 miles of the Hump, a range of wild mountains, some rising up to 19,999 feet. It would follow Aluminum Alley, a corridor 50 miles wide where hundreds of airplanes had crashed in the effort to supply Chiang Kai-shek.

The January day was just starting. The craft broke through the cloud cover, with the reddish morning sunshine at its rear. It was the U.S. Air Corps' largest and heaviest twin-engine plane in service. Its wingspan was 108 feet long, it stretched 76 feet from nose to tail end, its cruising speed at 15,000 feet was 183 miles per hour, its service ceiling was 27,600 feet, and it could carry an overload of up to 50,000 pounds. It was powered by two 2,000-hp Pratt and Whitney Double Wasp eighteen-cylinder radial air-cooled engines with four-bladed constant-speed full-feathering airscrews. Its range was 1,200 miles. It could carry forty fully armed troops or thirty-three stretcher cases. It was painted olive-green. Its number was 3953.

It was not the best of airplanes. Its carburetor had a nasty habit of icing up. It was vulnerable to fires in its engine nacelles that the carbon dioxide bombs in the nacelles often could not extinguish in flight. They failed to snuff out the flames when the thin hydraulic tubes burst and the oil was ignited by the hot engines. Its crew would be on oxygen for five or six hours, as would its passengers, eleven wounded and sick Americans bound for the hospital at Myitkyina. It carried the sealed bags of the effects of thirty-six other Americans who had died in China and been buried there. The bags would go to the U.S., to be delivered to the next of kin.

Ahead lay icing conditions that the boots on the massive wings might or might not knock loose, winds sometimes up to 200 miles per hour that would blow them off course, down drafts that had been recorded of as much as 6,000 feet, temperatures fifteen degrees below zero at times, and the possibility of attack by Japanese fighters.

Forty-one minutes out of Kunming, the radio operator leaned forward, slapping his left hand to his headset, and twiddled a dial. He brought in the signal louder on the emergency frequency, which he had been monitoring between his position reports. He pressed his throat microphone under his oxygen mask. ''Sir,'' he said, ''I'm picking up a funny signal!'' With the sound strong in his ears he wrote rapidly with a pencil on the message pad on the tiny table under his transmitter/receiver unit. The swift, expert Morse code ended abruptly, and he looked at what he'd written. He tore off the paper and turned to hand the slip to the pilot.

''Any idea what this means?'' he said, using the throat mike.

The pilot read it into the intercom as the crew chief, who'd been tending to the men strapped to their stretchers in the main cargo compartment, came into the cockpit with his walk-around oxygen bottle clipped to the thigh of his flight suit.

''Tin Man and Straw Man on way to Oz with Dorothy. Wicked witch making yellow brick path perilous. Box of cookies okay. Stanley Steamer.'' The pilot's brow furrowed. ''This came in the clear?''

The radioman nodded. ''I've heard that fist before.''

The pilot turned to look at him. ''You think it's one of ours?''

''Who knows, sir?'' The radioman reached to pull an air chart from the pocket in the back of the pilot's seat. ''I got a direction reading on it.'' He unfolded the chart and found the line. ''We're about here. It came from this line, up north.''

The pilot's eyes swept the instrument panel. The plane was on George, the autopilot. He glanced at the altimeter, the airspeed indicator, the rate-of-climb indicator, the tachometer, the fuel gauges, the oil temperature gauge, and the manifold pressure gauge. Satisfied, he turned to the copilot. ''Chengtu's on that line. It could be somebody cute up there.''

The copilot shrugged and pressed his throat microphone. "Jap bombers were in that area yesterday. The Fourteenth chased them away. Maybe the Japs have got a new twist this morning."

The radioman leaned forward. "This was a bona fide American fist, sir. I'd swear to that."

"Who's this Stanley Steamer?" the pilot said. "Any of you guys know him?"

"It's an automobile," the crew chief said, his voice fuzzy in his oxygen mask. He had his mike plugged into the auxiliary intercom unit.

"This war gets crazier and crazier," the pilot said. "Now we got a car sending a silly message in the clear."

"Sir," the crew chief said, "there was a Doug Carr who went down with Nick Engels a few days ago."

"Doug Carr!" The radioman slapped his hands together, the thick flight gloves making a muffled sound. "Sure! He gave me my loran training—long-range radar for the Hump. I knew I'd heard that fist before!"

The pilot held up a hand in decision. "Send it in code to Myitkyina. One of the black-cape guys might know what it means."

The radioman dropped his two-hundred-foot trailing antenna and watched the needle rise to the proper kilocycle range. He switched on the transmitting key and began working from the code book.

The crew chief, standing behind the pilot, said, "It makes sense, sir. Search-and-rescue got the bodies of Major Holland, Captain Buchanan, Nick Engels, and some other guy off that mountain in north China where they went down. Carr was missing."

"So we heard in Kunming," the pilot said. "But how in hell did he get a radio? He went down a long way from Chengtu. If he was at the base there he wouldn't be sending a message like that. What the hell's he up to?"

Working rapidly from the code book, the radioman sent the message to Myitkyina. He asked for a check to make certain it had been received correctly. By the time the relay was finished and confirmed, he felt the creeping cold and knew they were on their second leg of their long flight over the Himalayas, the forbidding Hump. He zippered up his alpaca-lined flight jacket.

Ahead was Kanchenjunga, the third-tallest mountain in the

world, amid other ugly mountains rising to 19,000 feet. He made his regular position reports in code and on time, but he kept listening to the distress frequency, hoping Doug Carr would send another message. He wondered if the Japs had read *The Wizard of Oz,* and he tried to think of what Carr was saying in the strange transmission from the north. What mattered was that Carr was alive.

Where was he and what was he doing?

There were seven other confirmations on the Oz message.

Joe Karras, Max Ribbands, and Henry Foxx sat at the tottering table looking at the decodes of the confirmations. "Goddamn it!" Ribbands said. "What kind of horseshit is this? With all the radio traffic we've got, who the hell is pulling a dumb stunt like this?"

Karras studied the message. "Tin Man," he said. "Okay, let's say it's a guy in an airplane. Straw Man. Who sleeps on straw? A Chinese? A Japanese? Okay, an Asian. Dorothy? That means a broad. Oz? That could be anywhere. A place to get to." He rubbed his neck. "Wicked witch and yellow brick path that's perilous. Yellow peril? Chinese!"

"Box of cookies?" Foxx said. "What's in a box? Not cookies. Not in China." A thought struck him. "What if Oz means OSS? A phonetic?"

They all looked at each other. "You mean," Karras said slowly, "that this Stanley Steamer is Carr and he still has the OSS packet?"

"Makes sense," Foxx said.

"Then what he's saying is that he's on his way to OSS in Yenan with the Moffett packet," Karras said. "He's got two Chinese with him, a man and a woman." He shook his head in disbelief. "That bastard is really something! He walks away from a C-46 wreck, finds a couple of natives to guide him, and rustles up a radio to use!"

Ribbands rubbed his still-complaining belly. "Oh, shit! It's just some joker playing a game with us!"

"Remember, Max," Foxx said, "this Carr walked out of the Hump last fall. Don't sell him short."

Karras leaned back in his chair, his drawn face reflecting deeply sober thoughts. "To boot, he's doing all this in storms that have shut the place down up there. Chance Beard knows Carr is on the loose. He knows we can't get another man up there for a few more days. What worries me is that Carr could fall into enemy hands— the Kuomintang, in this case. If they find that packet, we're in the kettle.''

Ribbands stood. "What you're saying is that we'd be better off if Carr were dead?"

"Not necessarily. The Kuomintang could find his body and the packet. He's near the blockade area. Deserted villages, hill tribes, bandits. What I'd give to have a good Jesuit priest in a mission up there! We don't have a single agent or any American sympathizers within a hundred miles." Karras eyed the faded maps on the wall. "I'm damned if I know how he's moving around with those winter storms snapping at his ass. That message about Oz came from a long way northeast of where the crash site is. How did the son of a bitch make distance like that with two Chinese? Who the hell are this Straw Man and Dorothy?"

Foxx brushed a huge bug from his summer uniform, thinking of the coldness of the north and the muggy heat of Myitkyina. "Well, somehow he got a radio. The fact he sent that message so quick on the distress frequency and cut out means to me that he isn't in a position to sit around waiting for us to contact him."

Karras agreed. "He thinks he can get to Yenan. The crash must have scrambled his brains. He has something like a death wish to complete the mission."

"Oh, for chrissake!" Ribbands boomed. "The dumb bastard could have stayed and been rescued. Don't try to psych him! He's a dumb stubborn bastard who doesn't know what he's doing. He's sticking his neck in where it doesn't belong."

"Still, I've got to admire Carr," Karras said mildly. "He doesn't stand a chance of getting through that weather and terrain. Yet here he is, telling us he's on his way." He looked at his pipe on the table. "He knows his plane was sabotaged. We know it and the slopes that did it are dead and we can't brace the Tai Li people with the fact we know his agents did it. We still don't know how they found out where we were sending Moffett and why. Carr obviously has read the papers. It keeps him going."

They were silent, hearing the sounds of the operations people around them in the Quonset. Karras looked at Foxx. "Henry," he said, "can you phone over and see if radio has picked up anything new from the kid?"

Foxx picked up the phone. Nothing.

"Well," said Karras, standing and stretching, locking eyes with Ribbands, "I've got to get a shot off to Chance Beard. He'll need to know about Carr's message."

"My money is still on Carr," Foxx said, rising and rubbing the damp seat of his khaki shorts. "Anyone dumb enough to try what he's doing just might be lucky enough to make it."

Lieutenant Oshima in the last hour of the dark night had been ferreted from the tiny house on the southern outskirts of Baoji to an even smaller one on the northern side.

He wore his fresh Chinese clothes, adequately worn and patched, inconspicuous. Following the agent into the small house, he found the squat bulk of Sergeant Masumi Mutagachi stretched under a blanket on a woven straw mat on the floor, a white bandage wrapped around his fat left forearm, a look of apprehension on his broad face.

The agent closed and bolted the door. "It was necessary," he said. "The peasants who patrol at night found your car. They saw the bullet holes in it. They reported it to the military. The ones you bribed admitted that the two of you had passed through." He smiled thinly. "As Chinese merchants!"

The lieutenant eyed the room glumly. It was completely bare except for two brick and cement kangs, a bench, and a small table. It had a single window, heavily shuttered. He looked at the melting snow on his shoes. "How soon will he be able to move?" he said, pointing to the sergeant. The fat little man pushed off the blanket and stood up, clad only in his winter underwear, as if at attention, indicating without a word that he was ready.

The lieutenant changed his mind. "No, you must stay and recover. I will go to Yenan alone. They are looking for two of us. One stands a better chance of getting through."

The sergeant was alarmed. "Please," he said, "it is a very long way. The storm has passed, but it is cold. There are many soldiers on both sides of the blockade. It is most dangerous. You will need me."

"Nonsense! All I need are forged papers, one for each side of the blockade. Ammunition for my Mauser. Some food and water to carry." The lieutenant stared at the agent. "And the name of our man in Yenan."

The agent backed away. "I do not have authority to give it to you. He is in a most sensitive position."

"Give me the man's name and where to find him!" the lieutenant shouted, and the agent and the sergeant both glanced furtively at the door, wondering if the lieutenant's loud voice had been heard outside in the predawn hour.

The three stood stiffly, looking at each other. The agent shrugged. "He has several names. I will give you his Chinese name and his address." A worried pause. "You must not tell him I have done this."

"He will not know."

The agent whispered the name and address. The lieutenant nodded. "What does he look like?"

"I have only seen him once. Something of your build. He was born in Japan and raised in the Shansi province when his father was sent under our covert operations there. He always wears a felt hat."

The lieutenant motioned for them to be seated. With a mat under him to protect his haunches from the ice-cold dirt floor, he said, "First, attend to my requests. I will eat here with the sergeant and wait until nightfall. Can you provide some kind of a vehicle for me? I will need a map. The ones I have do not go but a short way past here."

The agent was thoughtful. "I know where there is a motorcycle. It is not in good condition but it runs. Can you manage it?"

"I can." The lieutenant thought for a moment of his younger days when he rode his own small motorcycle. He felt a leaden pang of homesickness, remembering Takasaki, to the west of Tokyo, where he had been born and raised, remembering his mother and father and two younger sisters still there. Remembering his older brother, at the bottom of the ocean in a ship, a cruiser, sunk by the Americans. He brought himself out of his reverie. "I will need a blanket and extra clothes to protect me from the cold. A flashlight.

The first pass should identify me as a Kuomintang businessman with the postal service. The second should say that I am a mining expert with the Red Army.''

The agent's eyes were busy, darting from the sergeant to the lieutenant. He nodded at last and stood. "It is a most dangerous journey," he said flatly. "But I will do all I can for you." He left, leaving behind the unmistakable impression he felt he was dealing with a man who would soon be dead.

The lieutenant grinned at the sergeant. "You are not lucky. You must remain here and heal while I have the enjoyment of going to Yenan."

"The American?"

"Our friend told me on the way here that no word has been spoken in Baoji about an American. That means he has skirted this city. He must use the same roads I will be on. Once I capture him, I will find a way to get him and us out of this miserable place."

The sergeant's eyes told him he, too, felt he was looking at a dead man.

Oshima laughed uproariously.

The old farmer, unable to understand an American air chart, had drawn his own crude map, using Carr's pencil and the back of the chart.

With Loo translating, Carr learned that Tan's route would take them along narrow trails used by peasants and their hand-pulled wagons to the east of Baoji. He knew the trails would be treacherous for the van, small as it was, with the snow thinly covering the ground. The line of trails trickled through rough, inhospitable hills and valleys, across streams and around rocky prominences, in a senseless pattern.

Carr rolled up the chart and stuck it in a pocket of the Chinese clothes he wore over his uniform. Tan's wife, after a whispered consultation with Tan, had rummaged in woven baskets and brought forth cotton padded pants and a jacket made years before for a customer who had not returned to claim them. They barely fit his large frame. He wore his paratrooper's boots. His feet were far too big for the Chinese shoes. On his head was a quilted conical hat with long earflaps that could be tied under his chin. Loo had darkened his face with a vegetable paste. "From a distance," she'd said, "as you drive, you must look Chinese. You stand out too much with your blond hair and pinkish-white complexion." She had smiled. "You don't look like an emperor, but if no one stares at you closely you might get by."

Carr pointed a finger at Tan. "I'd like to give him something. I have an extra knife in the bag. Do you think he'd like it?"

She frowned. "Please do not. He will lose face if you give him a gift in front of his family and my grandfather."

"Why?" Carr couldn't understand. "Look what he's done for us."

"He will see no reason for the gift. He has nothing to offer you in return. He will be forced to reject it and you both will lose face. The salt packet was for all of us."

Carr surrendered. "Tell him how much I appreciate it." He left the home, walking uncomfortably in his uniform covered by the bulky Chinese clothes. He started the van, thinking of the vast differences between his culture and that of the Chinese. He thought of the message he had sent earlier. He had pushed the insulated antenna wire through the small hole in the top of the van. One end he had plugged into the transmitter/receiver. The other, weighted, he had thrown over a tree. He'd switched on the set, with the engine running. The dials rose to the proper distress-frequency setting. He'd sent the brief message, happy with the feel of the key under his finger and the sharp sounds of the Morse code in his earphones. Someone had copied it immediately. An "RW": Roger, will comply.

He'd flipped off the switch at once. To stay on the air longer would have given the Kuomintang intercept stations a chance to get triangle coordinates of his position. He'd looked at the faded Hallicrafter markings, feeling a twinge of loneliness. How often had he sat at similar sets on the farm near Bloomington, talking in Morse code to ham operators around the world? Centuries ago. He recovered the wire and stowed it. He'd removed one of the Japanese automatic rifles and placed it with his carbine next to the steering wheel, where he now sat. He placed the chart on the small dashboard. In each pocket was a hand grenade. He wore his .45 automatic pistol in the shoulder holster under the quilted blue jacket.

The knives were strapped to his legs above the boots under the blue pants. The Gurkha knife was sheathed and stuck in his waistband. The ties of the earflaps bothered him and he knotted them together under his chin.

Loo had helped him load their things on the van—the barracks bag, water bottles, and a small porcelain bowl of cooked rice and vegetables. He'd filled the gas tank, checked the radiator for water, and loaded and placed the extra Japanese weapons next to the rear door of the van where he could reach them easily. He drove the van from the trees to the front of the Tan home, watching Ho Ling-chi bid a long farewell. Loo, the obedient girl-child, made a close-to-emotional farewell herself. Then they joined him in the cab. He drove away, looking back once to see the ancient farmer, his wife, and his grandsons standing in the clearing. He turned away, rolled up the window against the biting cold, and steered toward the first bend in the road.

They were going north, moving away from and around Baoji. He could see the dim smoke haze of the city under the cloud cover, aware of how close they were to it and glad they were some distance from it. He checked the map with Tan's and Loo's markings. They drove in silence for nearly an hour. "What did Mr. Tan say about this bridge up here?" he said at last. "Is it a big river or a small one?"

"Small. There are many streams running into the Wei. He said the bridge had been bombed months ago but has been repaired. The troops use it all of the time."

"Jolly good!"

"I told you we are in a war zone."

"By George, mate, so you did."

She glanced coolly at him. "Don't be flippish."

The van skidded often in the rutted trail, climbing steep grades and sliding fishlike down them. It was a test of endurance, holding the wheel and shifting constantly. They passed several groups of peasants and a few singles on foot. They chugged around a man leading two small mules, who hastened to get his animals off the trail and into the snow-laden bushes as he heard the van coming.

"Well, at least we're not alone on the face of the earth," he said. "They all stop and stare at us."

"They hear us and think we are soldiers," she said. "I saw some of them hiding behind trees and boulders."

"Don't blame them."

"The bridge is not far." Loo held the penciled map.

"We cross over it to get to the road that takes us to the River Wei. Then we go to the place where Mr. Tan's relative has the barge?"

She nodded, and he pressed the accelerator a bit harder, anxious to get to the bridge, to get off the long, winding, heaving trail and onto a better road. He gave a whoop. "Soldiers!" A work crew was ahead, repairing a telephone line that ran across the trail and disappeared up and over a small hill. Three men in shabby, floppy gray padded uniforms stood on the trail, rifles slung over their shoulders. Two others were on flimsy wooden ladders, working on the short telephone poles. A coil of wire lay at the base of one pole.

"Hold on!" Carr snapped. "There's room to get by them!" He saw the men turn toward the approaching van as it picked up speed. His foot bore down hard on the gas pedal and he swung the wheel sharply to the right and then left as he steered past the military truck parked slightly to one side. There were shouts, and then the van was past them. He craned his neck out the quickly rolled-down window to see them running toward the truck. He felt the sharp cold and rolled up the window.

"Jolly good show, mate," Loo said. He darted a look at her, seeing her whitened face and worried dark eyes. His knuckles were white on the steering wheel.

"They'll know we're headed toward the bridge," he said through clenched teeth. "They expected us to stop. That we didn't means we're hiding something. But I couldn't see stopping."

"You did the right thing, but how will we get away from them? They're Kuomintang!" They roared past more groups of peasants, some carrying chickens to market, others carrying reed baskets, all wearing shapeless clothing against the morning cold. They trudged slowly in the thin snow, then moved quickly to get out of the way of the racing van.

Loo saw the bridge first. "There it is!" she shouted.

There was no one on it or near it. Carr drove across it and braked to a stop. "Take it up the road!" He jumped out, holding the automatic rifle.

She slid behind the wheel. "Stay with us!"

"If I do, they'll catch us! Do what I say! Get moving." She shifted, and the van moved away. He ran to one side of the bridge and threw himself flat on his stomach, pulling the grenades from his pocket. He placed the rifle within reach in the dry, crisp snow. He pulled both pins with his teeth, clasping the grenades in his cold-reddened hands.

The Kuomintang truck, blessedly noisy, came racing up the trail toward the bridge. Carr studied the structure from his low position. It was sturdy, made of iron buttresses and stanchions, its flooring of heavy solid wood planks. He timed his first pitch and threw with his right arm, a swift overhand lob. The grenade bounced on the planking just as the truck started over the bridge. He pressed himself flat into the snow as the grenade exploded. Metal hissed over his head. He half rose and lobbed the second grenade directly at the truck. He felt for the automatic rifle and pulled back its ejector. The grenade burst as he flattened himself again. In seconds the smoke had cleared in the brisk breeze. He stood, seeing a soldier hanging halfway out of the cab's right door. The front tires of the truck were lodged deep in a hole blasted in the planking. Its top part was shattered and smoking. Bodies lay on each side.

Carr walked toward the truck, rifle ready. "You sons of bitches!" he shouted. "You and your goddamned Tai Li!" He fired at the men who moved. He fired at the motionless bodies. He fired at the truck. He stopped only when the magazine emptied. He felt he was in a dream. He stared at the red-splashed bodies and the water steaming out of the perforated radiator.

The explosions, so close, had cottoned his ears. He heard nothing but a shrill humming. He turned and began running away from the bridge, along the wider road heading to the north. He saw the van. Loo stood next to it, wide-eyed, her arms at her sides, trembling. He kept running toward her, an insane grin forming on his face, wondering how he was moving across the ground when he felt nothing at all.

Nothing at all.

* * *

They waited at the Yenan airstrip for the courier plane from Chungking, staring morosely at the heavy morning overcast which forbade the sun to reach them.

Colonel Dean McHugh, in charge of the Dixie Mission, wore his treasured Army greatcoat against the cold. He stamped his boots to warm his feet and pointed to the south with a gloved hand. "Chance, those last two storms hit pretty heavy on the other side of the Wei. Up here, all we got was wind and more cold. If Carr's alive, he's working his way up through snow. What do our weather guys say about that area?"

Chance Beard watched a group of young Red Army soldiers in a clumsy parading exercise near the crushed-rock runway. He knew their own voices did not carry that far. "It's settled down. The mountains got several feet, but the valleys were just dusted."

"Where did he find a radio? That part of the blockade area has been stripped of people. How's he managing to move around?"

"God knows."

McHugh shook his head. "I'm worried. Your message from Joe Karras about Carr and his yellow brick path is just what we don't need right now. We need a top-level guy to come in here and talk to Mao, Chou, and General Chu about the kidnap plot." He looked at the towering yellow pagoda in the distance, one of Yenan's landmarks. "If a master sergeant shows up with Moffett's papers and the Commies get him before we do, we'll be holding the wrong end of the stick."

Beard agreed. "When Dilly brought me Joe's dispatch yesterday I couldn't make up my mind to advise you to go to General Chu and tell him about the Tai Li group's kidnap plot or to wait it out."

"I'd have wrung your neck if you hadn't told me."

"So I thought about it for a couple of hours, then I came to you. We're in enough trouble here after what the Commies think General Hurley did to them. If we go to them with a story that Tai Li has agents here ready to kidnap them, they'll want some proof."

"That's what the Moffett papers were supposed to do. All very top-level." McHugh peered at the gloomy overcast, wishing for the sound of the Yenan run aircraft. From somewhere in the military compound there was a shrill sound of bugles. "We have to wait until Joe gets another man and a new set of papers to us."

"The Tai Li people are out of their minds if the story is true." Beard's voice was raspy.

McHugh glanced quickly at Beard. "You don't believe it?"

"Tai Li's no dummy. He's a smart cookie. I'm guessing it's someone under him, and he and Chiang don't know about it."

"Not likely."

"But if they pull it off, and Tai Li gets credit for it, he'd be a bigger man in Chungking. Chiang would fix him up for life."

McHugh was unimpressed. "He's already a millionaire. But he would see the glory in it. Whoever is behind it probably sees a snatch like that as helping end the war between the Kuomintang and the Red Army." He studied the melancholy sky. "Where the hell's that shuttle? We need those supplies and dispatches!"

They both turned to see a small Chinese in his winter uniform, blue, shabby, and too large, trotting toward them. He saluted and spoke in fairly good English. "Colonel McHugh, Captain Beard, Chungking radio just reported. The aircraft has been returned to the base. Something wrong with the engines. They hope it will arrive tomorrow if the weather does not worsen."

McHugh returned the salute. "Thank you, Lieutenant Feng." he said. The man smiled, saluted smartly again, and trotted back to the small brick building with the whipping wind sock and swaying radio antennas on top. "I was hoping," McHugh said, "that somehow you OSS freaks had routed the new man and papers through Chungking, that he'd be on the shuttle."

Beard was surprised. "Not through there! That's too chancy. One-oh-one is playing it through Myitkyina. You know damned well that if they can get another Combat Cargo C-46 through this weather they'll send him up the same route they sent Moffett."

"That brings us back to Carr." McHugh wheeled and began walking back to the Dixie Mission quarters in the caves dug into the loess hills of Yenan. Beard hurried to catch up. It would be another long walk, and he wasn't through talking about the kidnap plot.

"Until Joe Karras gets someone here, we have to find a way to intercept Carr," he said. "Let's get some coffee and weave something together."

"Chance," McHugh said over his shoulder, his pace picking up against the exhilarating cold, "so many things have gone wrong with the Dixie Mission that we can't expect it to go right with this Carr thing."

Beard began to breathe heavily from the exertion. He wore a Red Army winter uniform, one of those made for the Dixie Mission officers by their hosts. He envied the greatcoat McHugh was wearing. His own was being repaired and cleaned. "My gut feeling," he said, "is that we should sit down with the general and tell him what's going on."

McHugh stopped suddenly. He slapped his gloved hands together. "Something's been nagging at me ever since you told me about this stupid plot." He cocked his head, encased in a winter-issue cap with earflaps. "The Chinese have a great sense of drama. Let's take your idea and dramatize the hell out of Carr! He's on a mission to save Mao, Chou, and General Chu. A high-level officer died in the crash. This noncom survived and is fighting his way here against great odds to prevent a terrible catastrophe to the Red Army!" He grinned. "How does that grab you?"

Beard liked it. "The weather has prevented another high-level officer from getting to Yenan and the indomitable Carr is struggling heroically to carry out the mission. Yeah, very good! They'll like that!"

McHugh's grin broadened. "Come on, we'll get our coffee and lay out the scenario. The hammier we make it the easier it will be when we spring it on them." He started off again.

Beard, pounding alongside, had another thought. "We can ask the general to alert his men to help Carr get through the blockade. That's been worrying me. The poor bastard could get shot by some trigger-happy goof with a red star on his cap even if he gets through the blockade."

"It's in the scenario. It bothered me, too." Strangely, McHugh began to whistle. "Maybe we can work it out after all!"

He strode quickly, with Beard hurrying to keep up.

Lieutenant Oshima hated the motorcycle.

It had stalled four times on him. Only his expert tinkering with the balky engine kept it running. The pressing cold was bitter against his body, finding small openings in his Chinese clothes to play havoc with his chest and limbs. He had tied a thick strip of cloth over his face for protection from the searing wind. The tin of extra gasoline kept banging noisily against the side where it had been strapped on.

He drove the machine past a small group of Chinese leading mules harnessed to little wagons. He whipped it around more peasants walking in single file, cotton sacks filled with market produce and loaded on their backs. One man used a switch to guide four pigs, their eyelids sewn shut to make them docile as they went to be sold. At an intersection, he stopped to check the agent's map. From a distance he heard the sound of engines. He waited, not certain what to do. A convoy of three trucks filled with Kuomintang soldiers chugged by. One soldier waved to him and he waved back. A good omen. He swung the motorcycle and followed them, staying well back.

Several miles later the trucks pulled to one side of the road and stopped at a bridge. He slowed down, dragging his foot. A mass of peasants were busy prying a wrecked truck from a hole in the bridge. They had trampled the snow into mud. He switched off the machine and pushed it closer.

They had a large wooden beam as a lever. Six men worked at it, prying up the front of the devastated truck as dozens of others tugged at ropes to pull the truck back and off the bridge where it had blocked most of the traffic. He looked with great curiosity at the vehicle, aware for the first time that it had not simply fallen through the bridge deck but had been hit by machine-gun fire and some kind of explosive.

He pushed down the set bar of the motorcycle and walked up to where the soldiers were helping the peasants pull the shattered truck free. A knot of soldiers broke, and he saw six bodies laid together, dried maroonish blood spread across their faded gray uniforms. One officer was busy collecting the dead men's weapons and shouting orders to his men to get busy and repair the bridge. Soldiers ran to one of the convoy trucks to remove thick replacement planking. Oshima, feeling both bold and curious, approached a soldier. He spoke in Kuo-yu. "What happened?"

The soldier was young, smallish. He carried no weapon. Oshima guessed he was a driver. "Your business?"

"I am with the Ministry of Communications in the Postal and Telegraph Administration," Oshima said, affecting an air of great importance. "I am due in Sianfu this day." He decided to try his luck. "Would you like to see my papers?"

The youth shrugged. "That is for the officer. I was told to wait here."

"What happened?" Oshima persisted.

The youth eyed the milling pack around the ruined truck. "There was a telephone work crew over there." The soldier pointed to the trail to the south which joined the road that the bridge served. "A van refused to stop and the crew chased it. As they came to this bridge from that trail the bandits—everyone says it was bandits—ambushed the truck." He looked angry. "Our men did not have an opportunity to use their weapons! Some villagers saw them in the truck, chasing the van. They heard the explosions and gunfire but they were not near enough to the bridge to see what happened here. They did not see who committed this crime."

A van! Oshima's intuition was stirred. "Did they see what the van looked like?"

"Only a quick glimpse of it. By the time they hurried here it was gone." The youth's eyes flared. "The dead cannot tell us!"

Oshima decided not to trust his luck further. He was convinced, without evidence, that the van was his. He returned to the motorcycle, started it, and moved slowly through the peasants and soldiers until he was across the bridge, skirting the hole in the flooring. The officer did not notice him; he was busy shouting more orders at the men with the planking.

Oshima twisted the handle accelerator and moved off at a slow pace, not wishing to attract any undue attention to himself. Would the youth report him? When he was far enough away he increased his speed. He thought about the van. But the van had been disabled. It had been bullet-riddled. His men had been cut down trying to get into it and escape with him and Sergeant Mutagachi. The American! Somehow, his elusive quarry, with great cunning, had found the van and got it moving.

He turned his thoughts reluctantly to the area ahead. It would be many hours over this road before he arrived at the Wei River. The Baoji agent had instructed him on how he was to get across with his motorcycle. There were fishermen who for a handful of yuan would take him across during the night. He had the names of three of them. As he rode, bent forward to ease the wind pressure on his ice-cold body, racing under the low overcast, he made a decision. He would not attempt to take the American back to General Ishi-mura. The chase had gone on too long for that. The American was responsible for what had happened at the bridge. He was certain of that. Without his men, with the sergeant nursing his wound in Baoji, the odds were too high for him to bring the prisoner back.

He would capture the American. He would interrogate him in good Kempetai fashion. He would find out what the mission was all about.

Then he would put the Mauser to the man's head and pull the trigger.

They came to the river settlement on the banks of the historic Wei, Loo driving, Ho Ling-chi sitting quietly in the middle, and Carr, head still foggy from the explosions, holding the carbine and automatic rifle between his knees. It was almost four in the after-noon, and the scudding clouds were thicker than in the morning when they had driven away from the bridge.

They had not stopped, but they had passed around the porcelain bowl and eaten from it. They had been in the van for more than eight hours, seeing many more people on the road, following a Kuomintang procession of vehicles loaded with materials and sol-diers, following as if they were part of the procession, until the mil-itary trucks turned off on another dirt road. No one had paid any attention to them. The van was completely covered with mud and was indistinguishable from the other vehicles. They were out of the snow area and the road was muddy and slippery.

With the settlement in sight as they breasted a hill, Loo slowed the van to a stop and shifted into neutral. "How do you feel?" she said to Carr, leaning past her grandfather. "You have said nothing since the bridge." She peered intently into Carr's still-dazed eyes. "We are almost at the river. We have an early night. I will have to put on the headlights to see further." She got out and scraped caked mud from the headlamps.

Back behind the wheel, she spoke to her grandfather. She took the flashlight and studied Tan's map. "The encampment of boat people which we seek is to the west of the village," she said. "My grandfather was through here only once and his memory has faded. I think I can get us to the home of Mr. Tan's relative."

Carr's mind functioned, but it was a struggle. He felt it was embedded in a layer of foam rubber. His voice was thick. "If we can get there, maybe they have something to hide the van."

She shifted. "We will go there at once." She was tired from fighting the wheel and from the jarring and bumping of the van over the poorly maintained road. "Did you notice we're out of the snow?"

It seemed to be news to him. He stared dully out the window. "You're right."

Loo took the path to the west and saw a forest of masts in the gloom. She spoke to her grandfather and braked. The old man leaned forward and squinted through the dirty windshield. He pointed, talking softly. Close to the water was a cluster of decrepit shacks. "There is the one Mr. Tan described," she said. "He told my grandfather to look for a wooden star on a pole nailed to the roof. See it?" She drove the van alongside the shack with the white painted star on the pole. "Stay here," she said to Carr. "But be ready. There is danger here." She saw him lift the carbine to his lap.

She was back in minutes. "We're in luck," she said, opening the van door. "Tan's name is a charm. The relative lives here. He is out on his barge, but he will return soon. His wife, two sons, and his daughter are here. They will cover the van with reed mats. We are welcome inside, where it is warm and we can have tea." The relief in her voice was evident to Carr.

He followed her and the old man into the shack, carrying the rifles. Tallow candles flickered as the door was opened again and the children ran outside to cover the van. They returned to stare silently at the big man in bulky clothes who squatted in a corner, a rifle in each hand.

Loo removed her jacket and spoke for a long time to the thin woman who was busy making tea and warming zhou, a gruel of rice cooked with an abundance of water. She came to kneel next to Carr, listening as her grandfather left to find the communal latrine and tend to his aching bladder. "She is concerned about you," Loo said. "She wonders if you are using opium. She has some *huang chio*. It is a wine, yellow in color, that she will heat for you."

Carr avoided looking into her eyes. "I don't feel well. What's happening to me?"

"I saw something like this in a hospital in Calcutta where I was a volunteer aide last summer. I believe you are in shock. Let me get you the wine. It may help you." She stood. "What you need is rest. First the wine, then some food and boiled water. After that, sleep."

"The barge?"

"The barge will be no good to us unless you are on your feet and capable of leading us."

He understood. "Yes. You're right, Loo." His eyes met hers. "I'll do what you say. Will you see if these kids will stand sentry until the barge man gets here?"

She brought him a large cup of *huang chio* and watched him sip it. She fed him the zhou, Fukien tea, and boiled water. When he was finished, she helped him remove the padded suiting. She made him lie on a worn mat and covered him with bedding. The rifles were near at hand as his eyes closed.

Loo went to the woman, who had been darting worried glances at them, listening to the strange sounds of the English words. In Kuo-yu Loo said, "This man is a great one. He is on a mission of high importance. We have darkened his face, but you see his uniform and you are wise. You have heard us speak in another language. He is an American, an aviator. His airplane crashed in the mountains a long way south of here." She lifted her cup of steaming tea. "He is a man who flies high in the sky in a very big metal machine. He has saved our lives. Tan Sen helped us last night. We are most grateful that you and your husband will help us this night. We must cross the river in darkness, with the motor machine which your children have covered from prying eyes."

She played her trump. "We have much yuan to help you for your trouble." From the sudden interest in the woman's eyes she knew the husband would be no trouble. She arranged for the children to stand sentry outside in shifts, well bundled against the night's cold. Loo found that Tan's relative was indeed a nephew. She began to relax. A nephew was better than a cousin. The Chinese put great store in family closeness.

"The soldiers?" she said. "Do they come often?" The woman, dipping zhou for Loo, jerked her head in disgust. The patrols had been through the settlement that morning. They would not return until the next morning. Besides, this was the night of the January feast day. The troops in the area would be at their headquarters hosting important village officials from the riverbank tract.

But there was one thing, the woman said, motioning the children to stop staring at the sleeping man. There was no telling about the river patrols. They came at different times. The trick was to wait until they had passed, then pole the barge across. After a long conversation, when Loo was on her second cup of tea, the door opened suddenly. The nephew of Tan Sen entered.

Sung En-po was tall and well-built, his face weather-beaten, his hands large and callused from barge work. He was all smiles, delighted to meet friends of his uncle. He would be most happy to take them across the river. His barge was docked close by. It would hold the van, which could be driven right onto it from the dock. He would have helpers.

Loo was pleased. In contrast to the expressionless wife, who constantly brushed long wisps of hair from her face, Sung was a happy-go-lucky river man, unburdened with political nonsense or convictions. Loo asked about the other side of the Wei. Sung laughed, his big body shaking. Those on the other side were like him, freebooters who did what they could to make money, to barter, to live. With enough yuan, they would carry anyone on their shoulders to wherever anyone wanted to go.

Sung's laughter was infectious. Even Ho Ling-chi, sipping his tea, smiled. Loo told Sung about Carr. "It is your right to know. It is an aviator from America who has fought the Japanese that you are helping. We are most humble in our gratitude for your hospitality, for your help, and that you honor your uncle in this way."

They were the right words. Sung reached for a stoneware bottle of *huang chio*. "Let us drink to the Kuomintang, who are in their walled compound on this feast day," he said. "I know them. They will be on wine and opium, most of them, and they will run their patrol right up onto the bank!" He laughed loudly, and the children giggled.

Sung, ever the businessman, turned his attention to the pay he would receive. When Ho Ling-chi told him two hundred yuan, his face mirrored his great pleasure. "For that," he said, raising his cup of warm wine, ''I would swim across the Wei with you in the van and the van on my shoulders!''

From his corner, Carr suddenly snored, and the sound sent Sung into a fit of body-shaking laughter.

CHAPTER SIX

"Will these men talk?" Carr said.

He sat behind the wheel, watching Sung and four men ready the barge for the van to be driven on it. They worked without lanterns, pulling on familiar ropes and talking softly to each other in the damp cold of the winter night.

"They are smugglers," Loo said beside him, one shoulder pressed against her grandfather to keep him from falling off the seat. "Sung has paid them well."

He looked at his watch. "Almost twenty-three hundred. Eleven o'clock." He peered at the black turbulent water, the faraway-shore lanterns glistening on it. "There's almost no wind. Good! What did Sung say about the other side?"

Loo shifted to take some of the pressure off her back. "It is a feast day over there, too. Some things do not stop because of a blockade and an insane war between Chinese."

"Let's hope they're all drunk. I meant, what about the roads? We'll have to travel in the dark. Will there be Kuomintang or peasant patrols?"

"The river acts here as a blockade point. The blockade moves back and forth. There will be *pa lu*s over there."

"*Pa lu*s. Yes, I remember. Red Army soldiers." He felt alive and vigorous. He'd come out of his depression after the long sleep in Sung's shack. Still, he felt uneasy about the ambush at the bridge. Despite his physical rebound, he harbored a black thought that he'd become a killer. He knew he'd had little choice at the bridge; he had to stop the truck filled with Chinese soldiers. But what had made him fire the automatic weapon at them *after* the grenades had stopped the truck? He knew, distantly, that he was coming into a new dimension of himself, a man changed by murderous weapons. He wasn't prepared to grapple with the change. He'd seen other men, knew that jungle war had changed them. He'd been at Dum Dum air base near Calcutta and seen the B-24s landing, bodies of dead crewmen removed, the planes hosed out to remove the blood, and new crews put aboard for more missions. He'd carried weapons in India, Burma, and China. Now within a few days, he had used them. Each time he'd had a slight advantage. How long could that go on? He forced his uneasy thoughts to the river crossing.

"The people around here," he said. "They saw us drive up. The van's been next to Sung's place for hours. Some of them may go to whatever authorities there are around here, or to the KMT."

Loo was positive. "You're wrong. They'd rather jump in the Wei than betray one of their own. They're all involved in some illicit activity. They leave well enough alone. Besides, Sung is sort of a folk hero in this encampment."

He saw Sung motioning to him, a black shape against a black river beyond the rickety dock. He started the engine and moved the van. The barge dipped and righted itself as the van's front wheels reached it. The smugglers held tightly to their steadying ropes. Then the van moved on board, and Sung placed chunks of wood at its wheels and came to whisper through the open window to Loo. "He wants us out," she said. She awakened her grandfather, who got down with them, surprising Carr with his quickness. She spoke to Sung as the men pushed the barge free and jumped aboard with long push-poles to propel the barge away from the shore. "He says we are to take out of the van any small thing we want to keep," she said softly to Carr.

He was confused. "What?"

"There are wood planks over there next to the van. If we are intercepted and shot at, perhaps we will have to go into the river and use the planks to float to shore." She was solemn. "The men will have to push the van into the water to avoid being caught with it."

He understood. "Naturally. Sung would end up without his head." He looked at the distant shoreline, aware that the water was fast and turbulent despite the lack of a strong wind. The shoreline was lighted by lanterns strung out along the encampment of river shacks. In minutes, as the men poled in the shallower waters, the twinkling lights faded into the night's blackness. He was pleased that his night vision was good and his hearing had returned.

Loo came to his side, groping in the dark. "How do you feel?" she whispered. "You slept six hours and you ate again."

"I'm scared stiff. I'm afraid our luck is going to run out." Her nearness to him was comforting. He couldn't see her face, but he could smell the Fukien tea on her breath. Her British accent had lessened; her softly spoken words had more Chinese singsong to them. In the darkness he sought her gloved hand. "Loo, I have to tell you. I went crazy back there. I shot at dead men! I'm beginning to believe your grandfather sees more in me than I do. I don't understand me. I'm doing things I never thought I would do."

Her hand tightened in his grasp. "You did what you had to do. It is true. You are a warrior. You Americans believe in democracy and the rights of other people. But you are not in America. You are in a war. You do what other strong men do. You fight." She moved closer to him, and he resisted the impulse to put his arms around her and hold her tightly to him. "And you worry too much. There is no such thing as luck. It is fate. See, we're halfway across."

Sung and the smugglers had switched to long poles with flat blades at the end, which they were using to oar the lurching barge. The oarlocks were heavily greased. The blades dipped and pushed almost noiselessly against the strong current. Carr pointed suddenly, releasing her hand. "What's that!" he whispered. Sung had seen the dark shape on the water and was standing motionlessly at his pole. The other men froze into position.

"A fisherman's boat," Loo said into his ear.

The two craft came close together, and Carr's finger tightened on the trigger of Moffett's pistol. Sung, recognizing the outline of the fisherman's boat, bent to his long oar, and the barge moved again toward the shore. The men worked their poles, keeping an eye on the nearby craft.

"There's a motorcycle on that boat," Carr whispered to Loo. He had a glimpse of a man's dark shape standing by the cycle. Two other shapes were at the end of the boat, working the large scull oar. Then the barge and the boat swung away from each other. Blackness claimed the smaller shape, which pushed ahead toward the riverbank.

Loo went to Sung. He couldn't hear their voices. She shuffled back to him across the rough flooring of the barge. He released his grip on the pistol and stuck it into his pocket. "Sung says many fishermen take individuals or small parties across at night. Both ways." She laughed lightly. "In the way of war, each side is concerned only with keeping people from entering, not so much those who want to leave. Besides, the Kuomintang and the Red Army trade with each other."

"You're kidding!"

"It is well known that even the Japanese come out at night on their fronts to trade with Chinese soldiers and peasants. Right in the middle of battlefields. They have bazaars that are set up after dark and taken down before the first morning light. Then the fighting starts again."

A soft sound from Sung startled them. He gave an order, and the men began working their oars feverishly. From the east there was a glint of light. Loo followed Carr's gaze. "A patrol boat!" The distant sound of its heavy engine came to them across the water. Carr watched the light growing brighter. The dark shoreline came closer. He thought of the carbine and automatic rifle in the van, of the grenades and other weapons stored by the rear door. He brought out the pistol with its silencer. One well-placed shot would put out that searchlight.

The barge scraped over something in the river, then was free. The shore was a few yards away. Sung and the men grunted as they grabbed the push-poles to work the barge in the shallow water. The barge came alongside a ramshackle dock, and men standing on it were throwing ropes to the smugglers. Not a word was spoken. Carr wondered who the men were who obviously were waiting for them.

The moment the barge was secured, more ropes were tied to the van. Loo jumped behind the wheel to steer as the van was pulled onto the dock, then up the dock into the cover of a thicket of low trees. Ho Ling-chi, helped by Sung, hobbled along the dock and disappeared into the trees, followed quickly by the smugglers and the shore help.

The sound of the patrol boat was loud, a rasping, chugging noise that filled the night air. The searchlight played straight ahead. Carr lay down on the barge, holding the pistol across the heavy wooden end of the boat. The Moffett packet scraped against his shoulder blades, reminding him for the hundredth time of his ultimate goal. The patrol boat went by. Carr saw four soldiers, rifles slung across their backs, lounging against the small lighted cabin. A machine gun was mounted on the bow. Then the sound faded and the light disappeared as the craft went around a slight bend in the river.

Carr rose and ran along the dock, seeing for the first time the fisherman's boat tied up on the other side. The one that had carried the motorcycle and its rider. Loo and her grandfather waited in the cab of the van. Sung and the small group of men stood near the open door, talking softly to Loo. Carr pushed through them and got behind the wheel. "Sung said the men here report it has been a busy night," Loo said in a normal voice. "Four boats have come across, and two left from this side."

"What about that boat back at the dock?"

"One passenger and a motorcycle."

Carr started the engine. "Tell Sung we appreciate what he's done."

"I have. He and the others will wait here until nearly dawn. Then they will return home." She laughed. "I think he hopes to pick up a passenger or two who will pay him to get to the side we have left."

"Does he know anything about troop movements around here?" Carr waved to the men, barely able to see them in the dark. Without headlights, he steered the van along the narrow path that ended at the dock.

"There are always patrols. Sometimes the Kuomintang comes here. Sometimes the *pa lu*s come through. It is very disorganized, this blockade."

Feeling an immense sense of relief, Carr strained to see through the streaked windshield. He silently cursed the blackness of the night, aware it was well past two o'clock, but he knew the cloud cover that blocked the distant moon was a blessing. Well away from the river the road widened and became more easy to follow. The van picked up speed, and he blew out a gust of air. He thought of the map Sung had drawn for Loo, knowing that in a short time they would come to a better road leading to Yenan.

He jerked the wheel suddenly to avoid a low-hanging branch and heard a loud thump in the rear of the van.

"What was that?" Loo said, startled.

He stopped the van and reached for the carbine. "I'll take a look." He opened the door and got out. There was little he could see in the blackness. The narrow road was lined with short trees with stout, reaching branches, listless in the stillness of the night. He examined the back of the van on both sides, thinking that a long branch might have whacked against the van.

As he rounded the back of the van to get back into the cab, the rear door slammed open and two bodies hurtled at him. The carbine was knocked from his hand, and in his shock he realized two of the smugglers had entered the van as they had driven away. The stench of fish and brackish river water was overwhelming. One smuggler grappled with him while the other rolled free and raised a thick wooden club.

Carr's frantic hands reached the knives at his ankles. He kicked in a mighty convulsion, feeling his paratrooper boots go into the man's belly. The man flew backward in an arc, screaming in pain. The smuggler with the club rushed at Carr, squirming to get onto his feet. The club struck the ground an inch from his head, bringing the man within striking distance of the knife in Carr's right hand. The knife went upward, slicing into the smuggler's exposed chest.

Then Carr pushed himself free of the man's body, away from the piercing sound of death in his ear. He lunged at the other smuggler, who was on his knees, bent in extreme pain, head almost to the ground. The second knife went into the man's back, below the shoulders. The body tumbled sideways and was still.

Carr unzippered his leather jacket and pulled the .45 free of the shoulder holster. Weapon thrust forward, he approached the back of the van. The door was swinging loosely. There was no one inside. Unsteadily, he replaced the automatic, seeing Loo peering from around the side of the van.

She said nothing, staring at the motionless forms in the dirt of the road. Unable to speak, he motioned her to go back. She moved quickly, and he heard the cab door shut. He retrieved his knives, wiping them on the smugglers' garments and then replacing them in their sheaths in his ankles. He picked up the carbine and wiped the dirt from it. With one hand he pulled the bodies into the trees well away from the road.

The shock faded. He stood for a moment, listening. He heard

nothing in the darkness of the night. He got back into the cab, avoiding Ho Ling-chi's gaze. Before he shifted, he said to Loo, "Two of those guys who helped Sung got into the back. I think they wanted to hijack the van." He had difficulty controlling his voice. It cracked. "If they'd had guns it would have been all over." Another thought came to him, and he snapped his mouth shut to keep from saying it aloud. The men more likely had been after Loo! They had planned to kill him, kill Ho Ling-chi, and have Loo. He leaned back, exhausted, and shifted, driving away.

They cleared the heavily treed area and entered into an open plain. The small road met a larger one, the one Carr was looking for. He drove in silence for a long time until Loo spoke. "I saw your knives in those men back there. They got into the van back at the river, didn't they?"

"They scared the hell out of me!"

"I heard the screaming and I thought something had happened to you." She leaned past her grandfather, and Carr could see her in the dim light within the cab. "I was afraid something had killed you."

The sincerity in her voice forced him out of his depression. "Damn it, Loo," he said, "they jumped at me from the door."

Her words were reassuring. "Once again, you did what you had to do. You have very quick instincts. Don't blame yourself."

"Do I have blood on me?" It concerned him. He had seen too much blood in too few days. She found the flashlight and turned it on him.

"Some on your arms. I'll wash it off later." She turned off the light, but not before he had seen Ho Ling-chi's fascinated gaze on the dark red spots on his sleeves.

He turned his attention to driving, a weird mixture of feelings running through him. Suddenly he tensed, fighting a rising sense of foreboding. He bent to peer cautiously through the windshield.

"What's the matter?" she said.

"I'm all out of tune. My worry bug just bit me again."

"Listen," she said from her corner of the cab, "if you're going to wear the Dragon Robe of the Emperor of China you've got to stop worrying." She paused. "I know what must be going through your mind. I was so frightened when I heard the screams. Then I saw you standing there." Another pause. "I am most grateful that you killed those smugglers. You know what they would have done to me and to my grandfather.''

Carr sighed. *She knew.*

''You've been through so much danger since your plane crashed,'' she went on. ''You must not worry. You must not feel it is all your fault. It is your instinct to survive. It is your instinct to protect us from harm.'' She pointed ahead. ''We are getting close to the Red Army. By the time it is light we will be with them.''

He fought down his nervousness. ''We're still a long way from Yenan.''

''Yes, and we're also a long way from the cave where you saved us from disaster.''

Her comforting words soothed him. He tried not to think of the feel of his knives going into the smugglers, the sight of his bullets hitting the soldiers, the bandits, the knife flashing through the air at Ku the Miserable. He released his tight grip on the steering wheel. The van seemed to pick up speed. They passed a large clump of tall rock formations. They did not see the man behind them, lying flat on the ground next to the motorcycle on its side next to him.

Lieutenant Oshima raised his head as the van passed and watched it disappear into the darkness. There had been just enough light for him to see it. He righted the detested motorcycle and sat astride it for a long time, thinking. In that brief glimpse he had seen the bullet holes in the mud-covered side of the van. The sound of the engine had been all too familiar to him. He was confused by the strange turn of events—seeing the shape of the van on the barge in the river, seeing it go past the rock formations which concealed him. He pulled his clothes around him to ward off the chill, knowing it was useless. The van would have to stay on this main road. Was the American aviator driving the van? Had someone else found it? What was it doing on this road?

He started the motorcycle and moved off slowly, giving himself more time to think. He came to the conclusion that the American, the quarry he sought, had indeed found the van and somehow had brought it this far. He had been wise not to attempt to ambush the van in the dark, he thought. He could not see those who sat in the cab. They could all be well armed against his Mauser. He reached for the map the agent had drawn for him, stopping the machine suddenly and risking the flashlight cupped in cold-seeped hands under leather-and-woolen gloves.

He sought a way to leave the main road and get ahead of the van so that he could see it more clearly in daylight. The map indicated he could take a number of foot trails paralleling the road. If he made good time, he could return to the road and wait for the van. That settled it. He clicked off the light, refolded the map, put them both away, and turned his attention to the task of finding where the first foot trail left the road, giving him a route to bypass the van. His resolve strengthened as he found the trail. He fought the bucking machine, skidding often in the damp loess dirt. His night sight saved him from running into objects near the trail despite the lack of goggles to keep the biting cold from his eyes. His plan appealed to him. In the morning light he would find his quarry. He began to laugh, thinking of the look on the agent's face in Baoji. He and Mutagachi both thought he was mad. They thought he was going to a certain death. The cold beat against the wrapping around his face and almost froze his hands, despite his gloves, to the handlebars.

His luck was holding! He was near a great victory!

He was going to win!

They made a stop after driving some distance to allow the old man to attend to his bladder.

Carr, carbine in hand, the automatic rifle in the cab, listened nervously as he stood near the van. Loo came out of the bushes. "Too much tea," she said. She noticed his taut posture. "Why are you standing like that?"

He held up a warning hand, head cocked. Then he said, "There's a motorcycle over to the east. The wind is from that direction. It carries the sound in the cold."

Ho Ling-chi appeared, and they helped him up into the cab. "It must be the same motorcycle the fisherman brought over," she said.

"There can't be too many of them around here. Not at night. It bothers me."

"Why? It's just someone going the same direction we are."

"Get in." He slid behind the wheel and sat for a moment. "Why isn't he on this road? Why is he off to one side on a foot trail? You saw the map. There are no other main roads around here. He has some purpose in avoiding this road.''

"Perhaps he is going to Yenan, just as we are."

"I'm thinking it has something to do with us. Anyone else going to Yenan would be on this road. He got across ahead of us. That gave him plenty of lead time. Yet there he is out there in the dark riding on a damned foot trail.''

She was impatient. "Why do we sit here?"

He started the van and drove off. "It has something to do with this van, Loo. The Japanese had it. Two of them got away after that fight with the KMT." He was silent for a minute. "Ever since that crash, things have been crazy. Nothing makes sense."

"You mean you think one of the Japanese is riding that motorcy- cle?" She laughed, a bright sound in the cab.

"That's exactly what I think. If it were a Chinese on business on this side of the blockade, there'd be no need for him to be off on this road and over there in rough country without his headlight on.''

"We don't have our headlights on."

He reached impulsively for the light switch and his hand stopped. "I'll be damned! Look at that!"

He, Loo, and her grandfather stared at the unusual sight. The cloud cover had broken. The weak moon, far to the horizon, cast a hazy light on the road ahead. Suddenly, there were dark hills and towering mountains around them.

"Things are improving," he said. "No snow, and now the clouds are giving up." With the better light, he found the dirt road easier to drive on. "What's the name of the town ahead?" he said after a long, silent spell of driving.

"Binxian." She spoke to her grandfather, who seemed happy to talk. His voice rose in pitch and he gestured. She turned to Carr. "There is a Red Army garrison there. Or there was when he came through here on his way to Hanzhong to meet me. The soldiers move around, so one never knows."

With the greatly improved vision ahead, Carr felt a familiar wonderment at nature. It had been days since he'd seen so far ahead. It was like a miracle to see the snowcapped mountains and rounded hills stretching for miles into the distance. They'd gone past villages, asleep along their lanes leading to the single main road, a few night lanterns here and there, the sound of barking dogs. He realized that the low, gloomy overcast had depressed him.

He sat back, enjoying the driving now that he could see the road in the thin moonlight. The van sped around a series of bends in the road and over a range of hills, then down through cuts amid small forests. Coming around a wide bend, he suddenly braked the van, nearly throwing them all against the front of the cab. Flashes of light burst from both sides of the road before them.

"Gunfire!" he said sharply, turning off the ignition. He opened the door and leaned out to hear better. The sounds of rifle fire came to him. "Jesus Christ!" he muttered. "It's four in the morning and there's a battle going on!"

Loo put a hand on his, and he knew by the motion that she was alarmed. "What will we do?" she said. "They're shooting across the road!"

"We wait." They sat in the cold, missing the small heater in the cab that had kept them reasonably warm, watching the flashes, hearing the echoes of the rifle fire. The flashes to the left faded out. Then the flashes to the right. "One side is in retreat," he said. "God help us if whoever is doing the shooting decides to come down the road this way."

"Could it be the Kuomintang this far north?" Loo said, talking aloud to herself.

"Who knows? I guess there were at least twenty men on the west side and thirty on the east. I can't tell how far away they are from us, but they seemed to be shooting at long range. No mortars, no machine guns, no artillery. Rifles."

She was still distressed. "It doesn't make sense. This is supposed to be *pa lu* territory. The town is not far away."

Carr turned on the ignition. "Let's make a run for it. You stay down and tell your grandfather to stay down, too." The van raced along, rocking in the ruts of the road. Over the noise of the engine he heard Loo talking to the old man. She said to Carr, "He thinks maybe it was the *tu fei*s, bandits, and that the soldiers were fighting them."

"Bandits! I thought the Red Army had cleared them out of here."

"They do whatever they want to do, even here. But there are fewer of the bands all the time."

They reached the area where the fighting had taken place. Carr slowed down when he saw several dark figures in the road. He reached for the flashlight and the automatic rifle, which he had taken pains to reload. "Take it," he said. "We either back up or we find out if we can get through. I don't want to back up." Rifle at ready, he swung down from the cab and walked slowly toward the shapes. In a moment he saw them clearly; one soldier, carrying a rifle, was helping another to walk. He felt Loo at his side and turned to her angrily. "Get back!" he ordered. "These guys are armed!"

"And you speak no Chinese!" she said harshly. The limping soldier fell. Carr, a few yards away, saw that it was a *pa lu* with a red star on his shapeless cap. The soldier with him raised his rifle. Loo spoke quickly. Surprised, the soldier lowered the weapon and said something to Loo in a high-pitched voice. "His comrade is wounded," she said to Carr. "He asks if we can help."

"Get the first-aid stuff." Carr placed his rifle on the ground. Hands held outward, he went to the wounded soldier. He flicked on the flashlight. A bright red splash covered the right shoulder of the dirty blue uniform. He studied the face of the body lying on the road. A youngster, no more than sixteen or seventeen.

He looked up at the youth's buddy, realizing with a slight shock that he, too, was a very young soldier. Loo came running to them, followed by Ho Ling-chi. He heard their voices as he opened the first-aid items. He pulled open the young soldier's jacket and saw the ugly shoulder wound in the beam of light. He wiped the blood away with a piece of gauze. "Flesh wound," he said to no one in particular. "He's lost a lot of blood." He sprinkled sulfa on the raw wound and pressed cotton against the long gash. Then he taped a thick patch of gauze on top of the cotton. He stood. "Tell him he's lucky. If we can get him to a hospital to make sure there's no infection, he should live." Loo spoke excitedly to the two youths. The wounded one, eyes wide with pain, moaned softly. His companion, squatting near him, put a hand on his brow and said something.

"What did he say?" Carr asked.

"He said he is among friends, that everything will be all right."

"Ask him what the hell went on."

More Kuo-yu. "*Tu feis*—bandits—as my grandfather guessed," she said, kneeling next to the wounded soldier. "They raided a small village near here to get food. The garrison is lightly manned now, but after some of the villagers escaped and ran into Binxian a patrol was sent out. They've been fighting the bandits since late last night."

"Where did the bandits go?"

"He said they fled back into the hills, to the west. Other *pa lu*s are chasing them in the night."

Carr looked at the lightening sky to the east. "Bring up the van. We'll take these two into town. The kid needs medical attention right away." He picked up his rifle. Loo hurried to bring the van to them. Carr, with the help of the other youth, loaded the wounded one into the back of the van. They started off, stopping three times when they came to other soldiers on foot on the road. Loo talked to them and they lowered their rifles and then climbed into the van.

Binxian was a small town. They reached it as the moonlight faded and the first light of the morning sun gave definition to the land around it. They were met by armed soldiers, who stared at the mud-caked, bullet-riddled van loaded with soldiers. They spoke in disbelief to Loo and her grandfather. An officer astride a thin horse led them into the town and to the stark, crude-looking garrison post at its center.

They were surrounded by *pa lu*s, talking excitedly and gesturing at the van and its occupants. The officer on horse proceeded to a building where there was great activity. It was a primitive type of hospital. "Stay behind the wheel," Loo said to Carr. "Let us handle this. We don't want them to get a good look at you until we have this thing in order. Don't say anything!"

She left the cab, guiding her grandfather through the milling crowd, some of them holding lanterns, even though the early morning light was pushing back the darkness. Carr looked down at the inquisitive faces of the Red Army soldiers gathered around the van. They were speaking to him, and all he could do was shake his head and point to his throat. He knew there was no danger. He felt relaxed and at home. He studied the soldiers, most of them slight and young, in their shapeless winter uniforms. He looked at their caps with the red stars, their old rifles, and their shoes, which looked like rough copies of tennis shoes. These were the Communist soldiers that Chiang Kai-shek despised and feared! They wore two red bars as insignia.

A bugle sounded in the distance, and the soldiers ran from the van. Carr opened the door to see what the commotion was about. In the near distance there were torches held by soldiers approaching on horseback. With a last triumphant blast of the bugle the horsemen, three in all, surrounded by happy shouting *pa lu*s, led three captured bandits into the compound. Carr had no trouble understanding. The disheveled, dirt-smeared bandits had been caught after a long chase. Their hands were bound tightly behind their backs.

He turned to see the officer striding toward the group, shouting orders. The men obeyed, making way for him and standing in a rough semblance of attention. The officer stood before the captives, glaring angrily at them. He pointed to a small brick building and snapped another command. Soldiers ran to the bandits and dragged them by the ropes around their necks to the building, where they were thrown rudely inside. The door was bolted from the outside. There were no windows in the building, and Carr knew it served as sort of a jail. He looked down from the cab to see Loo.

"Come," she said. "There is a telegraph line here. They are sending a message to Yenan."

"What message?"

"That Ho Ling-chi will arrive there tomorrow. That Master Sergeant Douglas Carr of the United States Air Corps is escorting him!" The smile on her face in the fresh morning light was bewitching. "You and your worry bug! We made it, mate!"

Carr pointed to the officer who was talking to a group of soldiers. "Ask him if I can send a message to my own people."

Loo was surprised. "Now?"

"I want them to know I'm alive, damn it!"

Loo talked to the officer, who strode over to the van and peered intently at Carr. Carr, realizing he wore Chinese clothes, got down from the cab and removed them. He used his soiled olive-green handkerchief to wipe the vegetable paste from his face. He removed the conical cap and put on his garrison cap. The officer blinked at the strange uniform and nodded to Loo. Carr motioned to the officer to follow. With Loo interpreting, he threw the insulated antenna over a nearby tree, selected the frequency, started the engine, and, with the officer looking on curiously, sent his message.

"Myitkyina. This is Tin Man. Straw Man and Dorothy alive and well. Near the end of the yellow brick road. Will be in Oz to see the Wizard tomorrow. Please instruct. Over."

Almost immediately he received a reply. "Hold."

He pressed the earphones closer. He waited. The crisp instructions came in the clear. "Tin Man, Myitkyina. Congratulations. Take your chance, but shave your beard for ceremony at Oz. Little Miss Muppet anxious to see you. Out."

Carr switched off the set. He knew that "Muppet" referred to Moffett. He turned to Loo and the officer. He had no idea what rank the man held. "Tell him I'm to meet someone named Chance Beard at Yenan. Tell him that in addition to escorting Ho Ling-chi, I am bringing an important message to the Red Army leaders in Yenan."

Loo was intrigued. "You wrote nothing down! How do you understand those radio signals?" She had heard the sharp Morse code from his ear set.

"It wasn't in cipher code. I don't have a cryptography code book, one that is usable today, anyway. I can translate in my head when it's sent as well as that one."

The officer said something. Loo turned to Carr. "He wants to know if all Americans wear whatever it was you had on your face!" She laughed, and told the officer it was a disguise to help the American get through the blockade. The man's intent face broke into a smile. He spoke what seemed to be three sentences. Loo said, "He knows what you have done to bring Ho Ling-chi back to the People's Party and the Red Army, and to help the *pa lus*. He says you have done a great service to Chairman Mao. He would like you to join him in a morning meal with my grandfather and me. He will have some ceremonial tea."

Carr stuck out a hand to shake with the officer. "Tell him he's got a deal. But first, I have to find a latrine!"

Lieutenant Oshima found himself surrounded by soldiers as he straightened up from pouring the last of the tin of gasoline into the motorcycle.

He froze in place as the silent men advanced ominously toward him in the shadow of the early morning light. Where had they come from? Why were they hidden on this lonely trail instead of patrolling on the main road farther away? He thought of the rifle fire he had heard in the dark hours before. It was an ugly moment before he could talk to them. He told them he had identification. Slowly he removed the forged papers from his pocket, gauging his chances of pulling out the Mauser. There were five of them. The odds were too great. Their cocked rifles were leveled at him.

The papers were passed around. From the expressions on their faces he realized none of them could read. He breathed easier and his confidence soared. He adopted the official pose. He was a mining expert called suddenly to Yenan. He had heard the rifle fire and had taken a detour to avoid the battle in order to get to Yenan on schedule.

They asked if he had seen any of the bandits. So they had been fighting bandits! He said no, he hadn't. They walked around the small motorcycle, seeing that it carried no weapons. His dress was that of an official, suitably aged and worn. He spoke pai-hua, even though there was a slight strangeness to his tone and mannerisms. They relaxed and shouldered their rifles, offering advice on the trails and road to Yenan. He took the papers from the last man to receive them and put them back in his pocket.

"You are brave men," he said. "We are fortunate to have you protecting us. I am only a humble man working in the mines for the glory of the Red Army, but I am proud that I serve with you even in this small way." They were the right words. The men all smiled. He sat on the motorcycle and kicked it into life. *"Ta-tao Kuomintang!"* he said loudly. Down with the Kuomintang! That did it. They waved and he roared off, not bothering to look back at them. It no longer felt cold. He was warmed by the small victory, this escape from the Red Army soldiers. He was invincible!

His luck was holding!

Chance Beard was awake when Fraser Dillon brought in the signals from Myitkyina.

He used the code book. "Carr reported in. Close to you. Expect him tomorrow. Report at 0915 hours on Mao's reaction this news relative your meeting with General Chu yesterday. One-oh-one will hold on second flight depending on your session with Mao today. Place Carr in protective custody if possible. Find out about man and woman with him. Details of his travel priority importance. Do not expose Carr to Mao or others until you have debriefed him. New details indicate not Himmler but subordinate on snatch plot. Working on this to clear. Karras.''

Beard looked up from his writing. "Maybe it wasn't Tai Li. Some slopehead under him.'' He whistled slightly. "Dilly, we got our hands full. I'm glad Colonel McHugh met with me, Mao, and Chou En-lai yesterday. It makes it easier to get Carr into our hands so we can find out what the hell he's been up to.''

"I don't believe that guy!'' Dillon leaned against the cold white-washed wall of the cave room in the loess hillside. "What he's done is impossible.''

"He's still with two Chinese, a man and a woman. If he's close enough to get here tomorrow that means he found a vehicle to move around in. How did he get through the blockade?''

Dillon's face mirrored his thoughtfulness. "Just as a devil's advocate, what if it isn't Carr?''

Beard looked at him through squinting eyes. "What makes you say that?''

"What if it's Moffett playing like he's Carr to throw off the radio intercepts?''

Beard shook his head. "He's using a radio, damn it! Moffett, from all I know about him, couldn't use a Morse key if his life depended on it.''

Dillon shrugged. "Just an idea. I have trouble accepting a master sergeant doing what he's supposed to have done. It's more in the style of a well-trained OSS agent.''

Beard stood, reaching for his greatcoat. "What we have here,'' he said slowly, "is a damned good pilot who should have been an officer. He got screwed in Texas. He's got a fire in his ass over what he feels was an injustice. He walked out of Burma and, by God, he's showin' us that he's walkin' out of China. That tells me he thinks he's somethin' special, a guy tryin' to prove he's one of the best. He's proven it to me. We better be damned well prepared to handle him before we parade him in front of Chairman Mao, Ambassador Chou En-lai, and General Chu Teh.''

"Because of the kidnap plot?''

"Because he's a damned sharp kid, this Carr. He's bringin' in the Moffett papers. The top Commies here know about it because we told them yesterday. Now we've got to stage a real show for them. It better come off good, or sure as hell this mission will get kicked out of Yenan!"

Dillon followed him down the narrow entrance to the cave door.

The officer's name was Lieutenant Ting Teh-neng.

With Ho Ling-chi opting to skip the breakfast and sleep in a nearby barracks, Carr sat with Ting and Loo at a scarred wooden table, on uneasy benches, eating a meal of rice, boiled eggs, and sausages, and drinking hot tea. There was a bowl of apples on the table, the first Carr had seen in a long time. Ting explained the garrison status. Men had been pulled out several days before to fill a gap in the blockade made by another Red Army group that had been shifted. Then the bandits had struck the night before at the small village, setting fire to a number of buildings and raising hell in general. He had sent all the men he could spare to fight the bandits. The three who had been captured would be taken back to that same village in the afternoon.

"Ask him what will happen to them."

Loo did. "They will be turned over to the villagers, who will hang them in the square."

Carr accepted the Oriental way of justice. "How does he plan to get us to Yenan?" He looked forward to a bath and the removal of the packet, which had worn a raw spot on his back. And he was anxious to get moving.

Loo translated. "My grandfather will ride in the one good truck they have here. You and I will follow in the van. We will have soldiers with us." Her face was solemn. "The lieutenant suggests we bathe in the troop's quarters, because it is too cold to use the river near here. Our clothes will be cleaned while we sleep. We will leave after we have slept a few hours. He has patrols out and he awaits their reports. They will return soon, and he will organize our movement to Yenan."

Carr understood. Ready as he was to move on, he knew he was on an emotional high, having made it through the blockade. He realized they had gone through the night without much sleep. A bath, some sleep, and clean clothes were necessary. "Tell him this," he said. "There are men in our military and political organizations who understand the Red Army. There are others of our leaders who do not understand. The decision was made back in the United States to support Chiang Kai-shek and the Kuomintang. We have a military observer mission in Yenan, as he knows. That mission has been looking for ways to turn things around and see if the United States can give military and political aid to the great Chairman Mao." He paused, and Loo spoke in Kuo-yu.

"Tell him that I am one man," Carr went on. "And my voice is small against those who support the generalissimo. But when I reach Yenan I mean to make my voice heard as loudly as possible. The Kuomintang sabotaged my aircraft, and four fine men died because of it. The Kuomintang and their deserters tried to capture us." He gave Loo a chance to translate.

"I have come to hate the Kuomintang. I may be in serious trouble with my commanding officer for even trying to reach Yenan. I will probably be in trouble after my superiors in Yenan hear me speak. But I have compared the Kuomintang with the Red Army and I am on the side of the Red Army, even though I am not a Communist, nor will ever be one. I feel your cause is just even though it is a highly controversial issue with the leaders of my country."

He listened to Loo's Chinese, watching the expression on the lieutenant's face. The officer was slightly built, perhaps thirty or thirty-five years old. His face was darkened by many days in the sun. He wore his hair closely cropped. His uniform was clean, but patched and worn at the elbows. He smelled only slightly of the horse he had ridden. The clear dark eyes remained locked with his as Loo talked. Then Ting nodded. His voice was low for a Chinese, a bit less staccato.

"The lieutenant understands," Loo said. "You are the first American aviator he has seen. He has not been to Yenan to see your comrades there. He has seen American missionaries. Once, when he was a boy, he studied for a short time at an American Christian school in Hunan province, where he was born." She reached for her tea to take a quick sip.

"He has heard of your General Hurley, who went to Yenan. He knows of the breakdown in the negotiations. He says it is all the fault of the Kuomintang. They will never allow the Red Army to have its just recognition or for the People's Party to be accepted into a combined government. He is astonished at what you have done. He knows the leaders in Yenan will be grateful that you have brought Ho Ling-chi back safely.''

Carr jerked his head toward her. "What about you?''

Her face was sober. "Girls in this land do not count. I told you that.''

He laughed, breaking the somber mood of the discussion. "You count with me!''

Her face changed. "Perhaps that is all that counts.''

A nagging thought surfaced. "Ask him if he has any reports of a man on a motorcycle.''

Loo spoke, and Ting nodded. "He said that just before we came here a patrol came back in from the east. They stopped such a man.''

"He was Chinese?''

Loo asked. "Yes, he had papers that identified him as a mining expert. He was on his way to Yenan.''

Carr studied the teacup in his hands. "Tell him I think the man is Japanese, that he is following us.''

Loo looked at him curiously. "That is still in your mind? You have no proof.''

"Ask him to send a message to Yenan to detain this man. I want to have a look at him. There were two Japanese back there. I saw them. One was stocky and the other was thinner. If it is one or the other I will know. I want to see that man.'' His voice rose and he straightened on the bench, feeling the familiar giddiness from his tired condition.

Loo spoke again to Ting. The officer called, and a soldier came quickly and bent at his side, listening to the instructions. "It has been done,'' Loo said. "They will alert all of the posts between here and Yenan and Yenan itself to hold this man and bring him to you.''

Carr sagged. "Okay. Thank him for the breakfast. Tell him I am honored to drink ceremonial tea with him. Tell him I believe he is a fine officer. Tell him I would be honored to serve with him.'' He blinked. "Tell him I am ready for a bath and a shave.'' He rubbed the bristles on his face. "Then a bed!''

The bathtub was a large cement vat in which soldiers poured

steaming pitchers of hot water. The soap felt as if it were taking off
his skin, and it smelled terrible. He lay in the water after shaving,
feeling every part of his body aching. He looked up at the heavily
thatched roof and thought of Loo's naked body. Near him was his
dirty barracks bag, in which he had placed the Moffett packet,
Moffett's pistol and silencer, the grenades, ammunition, knives,
and the .45. He had roped the carbine and Japanese weapons to it
and tied the top securely.

He closed his eyes. He had known Loo all of his life. He wanted
to know her the rest of his life. It seemed as if she and her grandfather were his family. He tried to think of home, of Bloomington, of
the girls he had known there. Nothing came through. He was Chinese, running scared through the hills, mountains, and Great
Grasslands and valleys of this desolate northern country.

He was asleep. The laughing soldiers lifted him from the tub,
dried him, wrapped him in blankets, and laid him on a Chinese-
type cot in the barracks. They placed his heavy bag at his side.
Two remained to guard over him. They fingered his long blond
hair, talking in whispers about the strange American. When other
soldiers came in, they lifted the blanket and pointed at the American's Burma suntan, the white skin where the khaki shorts had covered him from the sun, and the stout muscles that ran thoughout his
body.

In his dream, Carr was surrounded by bitter-eyed Chans in a jungle clearing. They approached with long-handled swords raised.
The one who came closest held a bloody sword. His teeth were
bared.

Standing unarmed in the clearing, hearing the war cries of the vi-
cious jungle men, he watched the man come closer.

He looked into the man's eyes and knew.

The sword was upraised and the man was shouting at him.

In Japanese.

CHAPTER SEVEN

The Binxian garrison's political officer, proud of the great honor, sat stiffly in the cab of the shabby truck with Ho Ling-chi and a struggling young driver as the vehicle skidded and bounced in the rutted road leading to Yenan. Four young soldiers squatted in the stake bed, holding on desperately to keep from being tossed over the end.

Carr and Loo, accompanied by two *pa lu*s sitting in the van, it's rear door tied open despite the cold, followed a short distance behind. In two hours, the truck stopped on a crest of a massive hill for an en route rest. Carr, feeling refreshed and renewed in his cleaned woolen uniform, got out to stretch his legs. They'd crossed a river and were on the road to Huangling and then to Yenan. Loo, wearing a clean set of padded cotton winter clothes and a peaked army cap, joined him. She'd napped beside him, curled on the hard seat.

"Know something?" he said. "You're beautiful!" In the bright afternoon sun, her complexion was perfect. "Your eyes have the whitest white and the darkest pupils I've ever seen. You'd look great in one of those slit dresses I saw Chinese women wearing in Calcutta."

"That's called a cheongsam—very seductive," she said. "It shows much of the legs."

"You've got great legs. You've got great everything."

"Thank you." She smiled knowingly. "That's because I'm the only girl around here."

"Nuts! It's because you're you. I think you're terrific."

"Did you know that Chinese men are erotically stimulated by women's feet and if their throats and necks are long?"

"Listen, you're a little powerhouse of stimulation, Loo. I've seen a lot of Chinese girls. None of them turned me on the way you do.''

"Turn you on? What does that mean?"

"Like a bulb. I glow and heat up when I'm near you."

She giggled. "You Americans!" She seemed embarrassed and turned to look down the road. She pointed. The road northward was choked with peasants moving over the next hill, a marching line that stretched for at least a mile. They had come from an intersecting trail to reach the road. Carr got the binoculars to study the mass of people moving slowly away from them. "I see a couple of soldiers in front. It's no army, just peasants." He turned to Loo. "What's it all about?"

She took the binoculars. Looking through them she said, "I've heard of this. I believe it is a village on the move. Some of them have carts with their possessions. Others carry what they can on their backs. There are children and dogs. I see some pigs. Cages of chickens. The old ones are lagging in the rear."

"A village? Where are they going?"

"It has happened often. On the Kuomintang side of the blockade the soldiers mistreat the people. They confiscate what they want at gunpoint. Many times the soldiers are not paid and they do not have food. They rob the villagers for food and take whatever appeals to them." She handed him the binoculars. "Wherever it was, they have left their village, crossed through the blockade somehow, and are joining Chairman Mao on this side."

"Where will they go?"

"The *pa lu*s will help them set up a new village, help build shelters for them. They will be given land to work. Some of the young men will join the Red Army. Others will take up their crafts again."

The political officer who had been standing in the road with the driver waved and indicated they could proceed. They drove ahead slowly, the peasants moving to one side reluctantly to make room for them. Carr saw the many faces of China staring up at him. Some pointed with interest at his non-Chinese face. All of them wore dirty clothes. Many had rags wrapped around their hands in place of gloves. Some were barefoot in the cold. An old man, withered and frail, rode piggyback on a young man's back. Carr estimated there were more than a thousand in the mass.

"Can't the army help them now?" Carr said in irritation. "They look half dead. Hungry. Tired. God, they must have been on the move for days. See those over there? They're bleeding at the feet. Why don't we stop and do something?"

Loo held up a warning hand. "It would be a mistake. If you gave even one of them a piece of food or a bandage the others would besiege you. We would never get past them."

"It's a damned shame!"

"All of this land has been uprooted by the war with the Japanese," she said, "and by the war between the Kuomintang and the Red Army." Bitterness was in every word. "Millions of people have died. Starved to death. Shot, bayoneted. Their homes burned. Women raped and slaughtered. Men taken in rope gangs to become soldiers. The land laid to waste."

They cleared the last of the villagers, spread out along the road coursing over a rolling range of hills. To the west, a long line of snow-crested mountains loomed in the distance. The area between was filled with small forests of trees and a great number of rock formations and scrub bushes. The sky was clear, its blue a beautiful shade.

Carr saw that the road was better. It had been repaired. There were bomb craters alongside the road, recently filled.

"You said you talked to Lieutenant Ting after I had my bath," he said. He laughed, a strange sound in his own ears. "They must have dug me out of that tub to put me to bed. I don't remember anything. Did he say anything about the fighting up here?"

"There is always fighting. The Kuomintang has airplanes. The Red Army does not have them. The enemy can come here and bomb as they please. My grandfather said they bomb bridges and any Red Army troop concentrations they can find."

"They've done that recently. Those craters look new. This road has been patched."

"My grandfather said many of the Kuomintang pilots have been trained by you Americans. They fly your B-25 bombers and your P-40 and P-51 fighters. They do much damage."

"I met some of them in Texas," he said. "There was a story—I heard it last year—about some Nationalist bomber crews. The story was they would fly up here, land, sell their planes to the Communists, have money put in bank accounts in San Francisco, then walk out and say they were shot down.''

She sniffed in disdain. "I doubt it. The Red Army does not have that kind of money. Who would fly the bombers?''

"Aren't there any Russians up here? I heard that, too. Some of them could be pilots.''

"My grandfather says he knows of only one Russian in Yenan. He is with Tass, the newspaper service. He is supposed to be with the MVD.''

"The Russian secret police.''

"To keep an eye on us. The Red Army has received no war supplies from the Russians.'' She sounded disgusted. "In fact, the Russians have given supplies to the Kuomintang, just as you Americans do.''

He glanced at her sharply. "Blame someone else, not me! I didn't give them a damned thing! You know we've got a mission in Yenan, trying to find ways we can help the Red Army. We want to beat the hell out of the Japs, and we're up to our ears in this stupid thing between the Red Army and Chiang Kai-shek!''

Loo stiffened. "Lieutenant Ting told me many things this morning after you left and before I had my bath in the women's quarters. The Nationalists have been unbelievably cruel. They are corrupt all the way through!'' Her words came in a torrent. "There were many efforts since 1937 when the Japanese invaded our country to convince Chiang to allow the Red Army to join in unified fighting against the invaders. He would have none of it. He has great armies all along the blockade line to keep our people penned in. He has only one aim, to kill all Communists and to govern this land as a great emperor!''

"Some of our guys call him Shanker Jack,'' Carr said. "He wins no popularity contest with us.''

Her dark eyes glistened. "My brother, Ch'en, and my father, they are dead because of this man. Your friends in the plane that crashed, they are dead because of him. They sabotaged your flight. They are evil men, all of them!''

Carr kept his eyes on the winding road ahead. It snaked up and down the hills, with the mountains bordering the west. "I don't understand. If the Red Army is so great, why do they allow themselves to be blockaded in here? Why don't they take on the Nationalists and beat the hell out of them?''

She glared at him. ''Listen! Chiang is able to mass his armies against us because you Americans equip him. Bombers! Fighters! Artillery! He could not win a single battle with us if he did not have all this war equipment from you!''

Carr sighed, working the steering wheel to keep the van from sliding as they went around another of the many bends in the road. He thought of the two soldiers bouncing in the back of the van. ''Well, where the hell do your guys get their weapons?''

''They make some, but a great amount of it has been captured from the Nationalists and the Japanese. The Red Army has received nothing from the foreigners who side with Chiang.''

''My feeling, from what I've seen of the Red Army, is that they'd whip the Nationalists if they were equal in military strength.''

He saw her relax, lowering her shoulders and unclasping her hands. ''Sometimes you are a difficult person,'' she said.

He grinned. ''Look. I'm just a guy sent over here to do a job. In less than a week I've made some insane mistakes. I should have stayed with the wreck. I'd be out by now. I'd never shot at anyone in my life until I met you and Ho Ling-chi. Now I'm running around this damned miserable north China wondering what the hell is going to happen next. If that makes me difficult I apologize.''

She regarded the carbine and automatic rifle at his knee, the .45 in his shoulder holster, and the bulge of the two grenades in his pocket. ''Yes, if you had stayed, you would be in Chentu, or even back in Myitkyina. But the weather was so bad. How could you be certain?'' She put a small hand on his arm. ''I said before, if you had not done what you did, I would be dead and my grandfather would be paraded in Chungking and then beheaded.''

He grunted. ''Don't pay any attention to me, Loo. All this has been so strange. I've done things I never knew I could do. All the training I had was for radio and radar, and flying. The fighting part of it was something I never thought would happen to me.'' He coughed. ''Now I'm a lousy ambusher, a killer.''

The van bounced heavily, and she withdrew her hand to steady herself. She stared moodily at the sunlit countryside. ''You still do not know yourself. You are stronger and cleverer than you realize.

No one has to train you in survival. Your instincts have saved you, and they saved us.''

Carr pointed. Far ahead there was another large group clogging the road. For a change, the road was fairly straight, running through a narrow valley. Alongside the road were the familiar patches of trees, bushes, and rock formations. The road scooped down into the loess soil here and there so that the van was almost fender-deep in the cuts.

Loo studied the shapes. "Soldiers," she said, lowering the binoculars. "Probably coming to escort the villagers back there." In a few more minutes they were close enough to see the Red Army banner at the front. The banner had the rayed sun and the hammer and sickle. The soldiers were on foot. Some pulled a convoy of four large-wheeled carts. "They must have food and water for the people in those carts. Medical supplies."

From behind them there were shouts. "What's that?" Carr said. The soldiers in the rear of the van were thumping the sides and shrieking. Carr braked to a stop. He was out, holding the automatic rifle, seeing the *pa lu*s running for cover in the nearby trees. "Get out!" he shouted at Loo. "Run away! Get down and stay down!" He grabbed her as she reached the ground and half lifted, half pushed her away from the van to the cover of a stand of small trees. He saw that the Red Army truck with her grandfather was still rolling along the road.

The bomber came in low. He saw the bomb bay doors open, saw the unmistakable silhouette of a B-25. Then the short stick of bombs falling, coming down toward the road. The earth erupted in a mass of thundering sound. He was on the ground behind a tree, Loo almost hidden under his covering body. As the great roar faded, echoing in the hills, he raised himself. The van stood untouched, dust and smoke swirling around it. The truck with Ho Ling-chi and the political officer had left the road and was perched nose up at a sharp angle atop a rock formation.

"Stay here!" he commanded, unable to hear his own voice in ears deafened by the bomb blasts. He began running toward the truck, glancing often to watch the circling bomber. He saw the bright white twelve points of the blue China star emblem of the Nationalist army on its fuselage and below its wings. He knew that it would come back on a strafing run. He chose a point and threw himself on the ground, face up, as the bomber swooped around and leveled off for its second run. He saw the twin machine guns in its nose.

He raised the rifle, flipping the lever to full fire. The flashes of the nose gun started. He waited, judging the bomber's speed and altitude. It came in about one hundred feet over the ground. He pressed the trigger, spraying the bullets ahead of the approaching bomber. He saw them strike the plane's belly and wings as it roared past. Rolling, he saw the machine gunners raking the truck, lead whipping against it and spraying loess dust into the air around it. The soldiers were still running for cover, some leaping into the smoking craters. Others stood firing their rifles uselessly at the plane.

The bomber pulled up steeply, banked, and began another long circle. Carr cursed himself for not having another clip with him. The automatic rifle was now useless. The bomber made a complete circle, rising to several thousand feet. "You son of a bitch!" Carr shouted at it. He stood, trying to see if there were any movements around the truck. He saw bodies lying in the road and alongside it. The carts were overturned, and one was on fire. He looked again at the bomber. Something was coming from one of its wings, a long ghostlike spray. The bomber banked and headed south, its engine noise dying out quickly in the cold afternoon air.

He walked back to Loo, sitting with her back against the tree where he had left her. The two pa lus, searching the sky, came cautiously from their cover. He stood over her, holding the empty automatic rifle, hot in his hand. "I hit the bastard," he said. "I think they're leaking fuel." He stared at the sky to the south. "They'll head for home, wherever that is, but they may radio for some of their other bombers." He helped her up. She was trembling.

"Tell me something," he said. She looked at him dazedly. "I know there's a Nationalist net. A system of telephone, telegraph, and radio to warn about Japanese planes and troop movements. Does the Red Army have a net like that up here?"

She nodded.

"Then goddamn it!" he shouted. "Why the hell don't they use it?"

She turned and walked through the tall grass and large rocks toward the van. He followed. "Somebody on this side must have seen that bomber," he said to her back. "Why weren't we warned?"

She stopped and whirled on him. "Because we do not have enough radios!" Her voice was a screech. She pointed up the road. "Those men do not have a radio with them. But our people knew about that bomber and a warning had been given." She halted, near tears. "You are the one with the radio." She jerked a finger toward the van. "But you do not understand Chinese, so what use was it?"

Her watery eyes brought him out of his agitated state. "Oh, hell, Loo," he said, taking her arm. "I was foolish. I thought we were on the safe side of the blockade. You're right. We're in a war zone. I won't forget it again." She blinked, and tears rolled down her ivory cheeks.

"We must move the van and see if we can help those who are wounded," she said. She swallowed. "And find my grandfather."

They stopped at the truck which was surrounded by soldiers. Ho Ling-chi was stretched out on a thick grassy spot, with the political officer kneeling over him. Ho, in his clean padded blue suit, seemed like an old rag doll. Loo ran to him. Carr stood, snapping a fresh clip into the automatic rifle, looking with sober eyes at the wounded. He counted sixteen men down. He listened to the singsong Chinese.

Loo got to her feet. "He is only tired from the exertion of running away from the truck," she said, relieved. "He wishes to remain quiet for a while until his headache leaves and he can rise."

Carr got the medical supplies and helped Loo dress the many wounds. She gave bandages, tape, and disinfectant to some of the soldiers, and they ran to administer to other wounded soldiers. Seven men were carried to be laid together, their lifeless and blood-soaked bodies about the same size.

Carr looked down at them. All but one were young boys. The seventh was older, perhaps forty. He heard the cacophony of Chinese voices around him and felt as if he were standing back at the wrecked C-46 staring at the bodies of Major Holland, Captain Buchanan, Nick Engels, and Ambrose Moffett amid the horror of the twisted metal. He felt Loo tugging at his sleeve. "Are you all right?" she said anxiously. "You have such a strange look on your face."

He shook himself free of the vision. "We've lost time because of this. Is there anything else we can do here?"

The *pa lus* had regrouped. The bodies of the dead men were loaded on the truck's stake bed, the wounded into the back of the van. "Grandfather is ready," she said, "and we are to go on to Huangling. There another escort is waiting." She indicated a man standing next to the political officer. "That one is in command of this group. He is to meet the villagers and take them, not to Huangling, but to Hangchen, which is further to the east. There they will be taken care of."

They arrived in Huangling to the sound of bugles, drums, and cymbals. Carr, trailing behind Ho Ling-chi, was introduced to the town's officials and to the military officers. He was shown their radio post, which they displayed proudly. With Loo interpreting, he asked if the B-25 had been spotted and put on the net. He was assured it had been, as had a number of other Nationalist air sorties across the Wei River. Loo explained, as she had before, that the shortage of radios with batteries had placed the soldiers sent to meet the villagers in the dangerous position of not being in the net. An effort was being made, they said, to send a radio truck to join the detachment to prevent a reoccurrence of the attack they had experienced.

Carr asked about the man on the motorcycle. They said the message had been received and all patrol units had been alerted, but no one had reported seeing the man.

The wounded had been taken to a field hospital just outside the town, and the dead had been carted away for burial. They sat in a large communal hall and ate a meal, then made their polite farewells and were on their way again in the bright afternoon sun in the cold sky. Shadows ran before the van as it negotiated the deeply scooped loess road.

"Why do they call them coolies?" Carr said as he drove.

"I don't know. I heard that term in Calcutta. I'll have to ask my grandfather."

"The ones that build the runways," he said, "they run in front of the planes that take off. I was told in Kunming that the Chinese believe an evil dragon follows them, that if they run in front of our planes the propellers will kill the dragon."

"I've seen photographs of the people building your runways.

They break the rocks into small pieces, and big machines are pulled over the pieces to make the landing strips. Yes, it is a belief in my country that an evil dragon follows you.''

He searched the countryside, seeing only the small cloud of loess dust from the truck ahead of them. ''I can't get my own dragon out of my mind.''

''The one on the motorcycle? He is your dragon?''

''I know he's following me. I still have the strangest feeling that he's Japanese.'' He glanced at her. ''Do you think I'm crazy?''

''It's your instincts at work. You have put mysterious pieces together and they form your dragon. Who is to say the man is not Japanese posing now as Chinese? We found that slip of paper. You have the Japanese weapons. Even the one next to your leg.'' She punched him playfully. ''I trust your instincts. They have gotten us this far. Yenan is getting closer all the time. We will make it!''

He took his eyes off the road long enough to study her. She had cleaned the dirt from her clothes. She sat, small but upright, close to him, her hands tucked into the long, loose sleeves for warmth. Her long black hair was tucked up under the peaked cap with the red star on the front. Her smooth ivory complexion was pinked by the nipping cold that flowed through the cab despite the small heater. Her jet-black pupils, surrounded by pure white, were bewitching. ''I've wondered why they allow us to be together so much,'' he said. ''What does that mean to you?''

''In this country, women are protected from foreigners.'' Her voice was suddenly low, and he strained to hear it over the noise of the engine. ''But you escort Ho Ling-chi. You have saved his life. Thus, you are not a foreigner who brings evil ways but one who brings friendship. One who displays bravery.'' She met his eyes. ''Women are not valued highly in Chung Kuo, the Middle Kingdom. But I speak your language. I am your official interpreter.''

He thought about that. ''What happens when we get to Yenan? Will they still let you be with me?''

She shrugged. ''I do not know. I will speak to my grandfather. Perhaps he can arrange it. They have men there who speak English. They may decide that one of them will interpret for you. Besides, you have your own people there. Some of them speak our national tongue."

"What I have to say may sound dumb to you," he said, moving the van around still another wide bend in the wake of the military truck. He glimpsed the armed soldiers sitting in the back of it. Two others sat in the back of the van, replacing the ones from the Binxian garrison. "In my country, there is a word we use in a very special way. The word is *love*. What do you call it here?"

She cocked her head toward him. "Here it is called *fa-sheng lien-ai*."

"Back home, in Bloomington, I was in love with a girl."

Loo turned away.

"I took her on dates before I went into the Air Corps. I've written her letters. I have her picture back in my tent at Myitkyina. I haven't see her for a very long time. I'm like most of the other guys. We stay faithful when we're away."

"You do not go to prostitutes?" She continued to look the other way.

"Some guys do. Kunming and Chungking are loaded with those girls. The places are called 'Slit Alley.' I've never been interested in them."

"You think of your loved one at home. Is that why?"

He grunted. "I did. This is what I wanted to say. I can't even recall right now what she looks like."

She turned back in curiosity. "Why? How could you forget so soon?"

"Because all I think of is you, Loo."

They rode in silence, looking at the mountains in the sunlight, at the many hills studded with scrub trees and wild bushes.

"You must not think of me," she said in a small voice.

"You have someone?" he blurted out.

She shook her head. "The English officers in Calcutta tried to make me theirs. The Chinese men there tried as well. No, I do not have a man."

He felt better and straightened. "I wondered if I had competition. I have to come out and say it, Loo. I want to be with you. I want to find out if there is a way we can stay together."

Her eyes studied him intently as she bent forward to see his face. "I don't understand."

"It's easy. I've never met anyone like you. While you're Chinese, you speak as if you're from London. You're tough and full of energy. You have life in you that makes the girls back home look like stuffed dolls."

"It is because we have been together during very difficult times. When we part, you will forget me."

He braked the van, hearing the sudden shouts of the soldiers in the cabin. He drove slowly, allowing the truck ahead to lengthen the distance between them. "Listen to me, Loo. When I say I think of you, I think of you as I've thought of no one else. You're very special to me."

"Is it because you saw me without clothes, when the Kuomintang deserters were going to rape me?" She blushed. "I am much ashamed of that!"

He held up a hand. "Don't be! Yes, I'll admit I liked seeing all of you. You have a terrific body." He turned to smile at her. "It's what's in your body that counts with me." He laughed. "Here I am in China and I fantasize about making love to you!" He pressed the gas pedal, and the van picked up speed. "We've been on the run so much. I wish there could be a quiet time when we could just be together. We've so much to talk about."

"Since you're being honest, so will I. I fantasize about you."

"I'll be damned!" He couldn't believe it.

"Do you believe our fantasies can become realities?"

"Hell, Loo, I never thought we'd get this far. If we get to Yenan, all things are possible. There must be a way we can cope with our cultural differences and be together without causing an international incident. I want you to get to know me better. I want you to see that my love for you is real and that I want you to love me."

"You say you love me. Is it real or is it fantasy?"

He let out a deep breath. "People go through life making decisions. Some good, some bad. One of the most difficult decisions to make is who to love. You made that decision for me."

"How could I?"

"Because you are Loo, because I find you so very lovely, so very desirable, and because I think I would make one damned fine husband for you."

Her voice was a tiny whisper. "You wish to marry me?"

He reached to take her hand. "I don't want to let you get away. I want you with me for the rest of my life."

Her other hand tightened on his. "We are so different! Our ways are so different!" She laughed and then went into a high giggle. "What the bloody hell," she said in a cockney accent, "why not, mate?"

He laughed with her. "Why not?"

"I know of women who have married foreigners. It is hard on them. Our people do not encourage it." She giggled again. "I can see Grandfather's face!"

The thought sobered him. "Yeah. I'm not one of his favorites."

"You are wrong! He thinks very highly of you!"

"Come on, Loo. He's hardly looked at me. He's never said a word to me."

"You do not understand him. He is embarrassed because he cannot speak to you directly. He feels he has lost face with you because he communicates to you through me, a girl. That upsets his sense of pride and dignity. He knows he lives because of you. He is a very proud, stubborn old man who has had a life filled with great difficulties and sorrows. My grandmother died many years ago from typhoid. He raised my father and would not take another wife. The Kuomintang tried to get him but he chose to serve Chairman Mao and he lost his business and endured many hardships. He has been most kind to me. It was dangerous for him to come to meet me to help bury my father at our ancestral village. Old as he is, he came. That should tell you something about his courage."

"But he doesn't like Americans because we support Chiang. Do you think he'll stand in our way?"

"Even proud, stubborn old men can be talked to if it's done in the proper way. We will have to plan our method so that he can find nothing to object to."

He gripped her hand more tightly. "That's the ticket. We need to talk things over and get our act in shape."

"It is not an act!"

"That's an American expression. It means to plan things so we don't get in trouble."

Her smile was radiant. "When you saw me first, at that cave, I was frightened by you. You looked so fearsome. You shot those men, and I thought you were going to shoot us.''

"And I thought you were a little girl. You are small, but there are girls back home who would give anything to have your body. It's unbelievable.''

"Never in my wildest dreams did I imagine I would be with a big American with blond hair, with blue eyes, who carries so many weapons, who can do as many things as you do.''

"The whole thing's weird, but it comes down to something simple. I love you and I want to have you with me.''

She moved closer to him. "I want to find out more about love. I don't think I see it as you do. You must explain it to me.''

"Loo, love is when you want to share your life with someone. To be with that person as much as possible. We're in a war, and that puts strange pressures on people. But this war won't last forever. You know the Japanese are at the end of their rope. It's just a matter of time before the Allies beat the Germans in Europe. We'll beat the Japs here. Hell, we've got B-29s that are bombing their homeland right now.''

"You seem to look into the future. What do you see for us in the future?''

"Another decision. Whether we'll stay in your country or whether we'll go to mine.''

Her brightness faded. "Your parents! What would they think of me? Surely they want you to marry an American girl.''

He laughed again. "Damn it, Loo! There are Chinese families living in Bloomington. They're in Chicago, where there's a Chinatown. San Francisco has a large population of Chinese. They're all over the place, and many of them have married Americans with Irish, German, Polish, what have you, backgrounds.''

"But they were born there.''

"Not all of them.''

She was reassured. "Then I wouldn't be an oddity there.''

"My mom and dad will love you, believe me. You'd fit right in after you got used to the place.''

"As you have fitted into this place. That's the other side of the coin. Could you live in this country with me?''

"Sure," he said. "A week ago I'd have said no. But these days with you have changed all that. I can find some kind of work here when the war's over. I can fly any kind of a plane. I can operate a radio system. I can be a small-time ambassador. We'll have to see what we can work out. If we go to the States, I'll have a big farm to run and there's a chance I can expand it by taking options on some adjoining spreads. The people who own them are elderly. I've talked to them. If that worked out, we'd have a real nice thing going there.''

She squeezed his hand. "I must tell you a secret. I saw movies in Calcutta. Men and women kissed each other. My secret, I have never been kissed." He braked the van slowly and put it in park. He was glad the van had a wall between the cab and the rear cabin. He put his right arm around her and with his left hand tilted her face up. He kissed her. He kissed her again, thrilling at the touch of her full red lips. It was the thumping in the back that forced him to let her go and start the van moving again. He hadn't wanted the *pa lus* to embarrass her by coming around and seeing them kissing.

"Wow!" he said, kicking the gas pedal. "Your lips are like sweet velvet. They taste like strawberries." Her closeness warmed him, and he felt exhilarated. "Damn it, Loo! We've just got to find a way to work this out. The hell with fantasy. I want you!''

"Are you of a religion?" she said.

He was surprised. "Presbyterian. I'll have to tell you about that. What are you?''

"Grandfather used to be a believer of Confucius. But when he joined Chairman Mao he longer followed that faith. I am of no religion. Not Buddha, not Catholic, not Protestant, Taoist, Christian, Moslem, not anything. I saw the religions in India, but I was not attracted to them. My father did not believe in the great prophets, nor did my brother.''

"We'll cross that bridge later," he said. The truck ahead was slowing. He saw the reason; another truck coming from the north. The two vehicles stopped a short distance apart. Carr brought up the van and cut the engine. He reached for the carbine.

"No," Loo said, "it is a Red Army officer."

They left the cab, hearing the confused voices of the soldiers getting out of the rear of the van. Ho Ling-chi was engaged in the ritual of greeting an important person and being greeted in kind. He stood with the officer in the space between the two trucks. Six armed men fanned out from the Red Army truck, looking carefully at the countryside. They squinted at Carr in his strange uniform. Ho motioned to Carr and Loo to join him. He spoke to Loo. She said, "This is Colonel Wu of the intelligence section. He has come to meet my grandfather and you." From the tone of her voice he knew she was warning him. Intelligence section? He accepted that. It made sense.

"Tell the colonel I must meet with an American known as Chance Beard."

She translated. "He said Captain Beard and Colonel McHugh are waiting for you in Yenan. He has taken it upon himself to come first to talk to you."

"What does he want? Tell him I'm interested in knowing if the Red Army has found that man on the motorcycle."

She did. "He said all of the patrols and stations are alerted. The man was seen and is being followed. They believe they can intercept him over there, to the northeast."

Carr breathed heavily. There was something in the colonel's face he didn't like. The man was a foot shorter than he, wearing a gray padded cotton uniform with a holstered pistol at his side. His jacket had four pockets, a symbol of his rank. Carr listened to the exchange in Chinese. He felt uneasy, on edge.

The warning was still in Loo's voice. "He said he knows you are here on an important mission. General Chu Teh told him to watch for you and to take you to your comrades. He received the telegraph messages from Binxian and Huangling. He has been waiting on this road for some time. He would like to know what your mission is."

"Tell him that I cannot talk to him about that. I must get to Captain Beard first." So Beard was a captain. Who was Colonel McHugh? The piece fell in place. McHugh would be the one in charge of the Dixie Mission. Carr stood still, aware of the Moffett packet, which he had placed inside his shirt at the front, away from the raw spot on his back. He met the officer's eyes, knowing the man was tough and used to command.

"He says you do not understand. He is in charge of intelligence. It is his duty to interrogate you before you go further." There was a sharp edge to Loo's words. She looked at him anxiously.

Carr didn't budge. "Tell the colonel that I am under the direction of my commanding officer at Myitkyina. I have orders to go directly to Captain Beard. If he prevents that, it will be a breach between his army and the United States Air Corps.''

More translation. Colonel Wu's eyes never left Carr's. Hell, thought Carr, this is kid stuff. No one can stare me down. He relaxed, seeing from the corner of his eye the taut posture of Ho Ling-chi. I've come this far with Moffett's packet. I'll get the rest of the way.

Loo said, ''He is most unhappy with your attitude. He says you are in Red Army territory. He insists that you tell him what your mission is.''

Carr moved until he was two feet away from the smaller man. ''Tell Colonel Wu that I understand military commands as well as he does. Tell him he can't insist on anything. I am escorting Ho Ling-chi to Yenan. I am expected by the American Military Observer Mission at Yenan. Tell him that if I talk to anyone before I see Colonel McHugh and Captain Beard it will be Chairman Mao himself.''

Loo was shocked and showed it. ''Tell him,'' Carr ordered, and she did.

Colonel Wu's expression hardened with her words. He turned abruptly and strode stiff-legged back to his truck. He gave no order, but the soldiers piled back into it. The driver backed up, and made a turn, and the vehicle moved quickly in the direction of Yenan.

''Were you wise to say that?'' Loo said.

''Tell your grandfather and the others to load up. We're going on into Yenan.'' He jumped up into the van and started the tired engine, driving away. ''Goddamn, that makes me mad!''

Loo shrank back at the heatedness of his voice. ''Why are you so angry? Your face is that of a hunting hawk!''

''That son of a bitch thought he could bluff me with a show of power! Who the hell does he think he is!'' He felt his control slipping, irritation rising to the danger point. ''Miserable bastard!'' He pounded the wheel with his clenched right fist, sending Loo further back into the seat in startled fascination. ''I didn't come down off that stinking mountain and come through all the goddamned messes we've been in just to tell that cruddy bastard what Moffett's mission was all about!''

''Please don't be so angry,'' she said, pleading.

"Intelligence officer!" he almost shouted. "My orders are to get to Chance Beard, not to Colonel Wu!" He pounded his fist against the wheel again. "Does he have any idea of what we had to do to get this far? Does he think I'm going to curtsy to him and say hell, yes, kind sir, here's what four guys died for and thank you for asking!"

"Please," she said, putting a hand on his arm. "He was just doing what he thought was right."

Carr turned to glare at her. The sight of her frightened face jarred him out of his anger. He let out a deep breath. "Oh, hell, Loo, I'm sorry." He unclenched his fist and drove carefully as he felt himself calming down. "I can see why he's so nosy. He's probably picked up my messages to Myitkyina and theirs to me and wonders what the hell is going on. Our people in Yenan obviously haven't told him. They know I'm coming and he knows, but they haven't told him. If he's what he says he is, you'd think he'd be the first to know."

"Your face was dark and fierce," she said, bending forward to see him better. "Now color is returning to it. That is better."

"I'm okay. Just flipped my lid a little." He brushed a hand across his face. "I've been living with this secrecy thing too long. All this time I've felt like I was carrying the biggest secret in the world with me."

"You'll be with your people very soon."

The anger hadn't left him completely, and he fought back a quick surge of temper. "It makes me wonder what kind of a game my people are playing." He stared at the road ahead. "With all the time that's been lost, why the hell haven't they told the Red Army about the kidnap plot?"

It was several seconds before it sank in. Loo sat up straight. "What kidnap plot?"

Carr raised his head toward the roof of the cab. "Oh, Jesus Christ!"

"You said kidnap plot," she persisted. "Who in Yenan is to be kidnapped?"

Carr shook his head in disgust. "That slipped out." He looked at her. "Boy, I sure do some dumb things."

"You are in an angry state," she said, moving closer to him in an effort to help him calm down. "Is that what your mission was all about, to prevent a kidnapping?"

"I've already opened my big mouth." His words were wrapped in self-disgust. "Loo, this is a top-secret mission for our people. The Kuomintang has a plot to kidnap Chairman Mao, Ambassador Chou En-lai, and General Chu Teh."

Her dark eyes looked into his. "But how do they think they can get away with that?"

Loess dust from the trucks ahead swept over the van, adding more dirt to an already filthy windshield. "Our intelligence people in Chungking found out about it. We have an organization called the OSS. Office of Strategic Services. They have a group called Detachment 101. The people in 101 at Myitkyina decided to handle it from there rather than from Chungking, where their intelligence operation might have been uncovered. They didn't want General Tai Li and his people to know they'd found out about the plot. So they sent Moffett in our plane to inform Chairman Mao about it."

"Wasn't that complicated?" Loo was intrigued. "Couldn't they just have sent a radio message?"

"The KMT might have intercepted it and broken the code. The Tai Li men at Myitkyina must have heard some loose talk. The cabin fuel tanks were a giveaway to a long flight to Yenan. They put the explosive on our plane to prevent Moffett from getting to Yenan. Our people must have caught them, or my people in their message to me would have told me the deal was blown. Instead, they told me to go ahead. In other words, that they felt Tai Li still did not know about Moffett's mission and that I was to complete it by getting the papers to Yenan."

She slumped back against the seat. "You said you had a message. I couldn't understand what was so important that it would make you try to complete it by getting the papers to Yenan."

"The weather held up everything," he said. "Now that it's clear up here my people had two choices. They could send someone else or use me, since I'm almost there. I want to get into Yenan and give these damn papers to Chance Beard. I guess he's the OSS guy there. After that, it's his problem."

"But what if you'd been killed or captured?"

"They wouldn't have known about it for a long time. When I radioed them, it must have shook them up. But they went along with me instead of telling me to stay put until they got to me. They probably had a backup flight ready to come in as soon as the weather improved, which it has.''

"Now I understand more things about you," she said. She peered out the side window. The sun was low to the west. Darkness would come in another hour or less. The truck ahead was picking up speed, racing down a straight path. "Yenan!" she cried. "I can see the top of the yellow pagoda!"

Two horsemen rode out of a patch of trees to intercept the van. Carr slowed, stopping in the deeply rutted road. The horsemen spurred their mounts toward them, waving hands and shouting. The two trucks had disappeared into the city. He heard the nearest one yell, "Master Sergeant Carr! Where are you?"

Carr stepped down from the cab. He unsnapped the strap of his .45 holster. "Over here!"

They reined up in front of him. He looked at their American faces. "I'm Master Sergeant Douglas Carr," he said. He looked at their Red Army uniforms, puzzled. Everything about them was distinctly American. "Who are you?"

They slid from their horses, small, spare mounts that were fitted with Mongol-looking saddles and rope reins. The larger of the two walked toward him. "I'm Captain Chance Beard. This is Lieutenant Fraser Dillon, our signals officer."

Carr saluted, feeling awkward. They snapped off salutes, looking just as embarrassed. "We borrowed the horses for some exercise," Beard said. "We saw Colonel Wu start off on this road. We figured he would try to intercept you."

"He did, sir."

"Tell him anything?" There was a sharpness to his question.

"No, sir. Nor will I tell you anything until you show me your officer's I.D.'s."

Beard's face broke into a grin. He reached into a pocket for a billfold. Dillon followed suit. They held out their identity cards. Carr produced his own. Everyone relaxed. Carr took the Moffett packet from his shirt and handed it to Beard. "I've got the personal effects of Major James Holland, Captain Rollo Buchanan, Lieutenant Colonel Ambrose Moffett, and Staff Sergeant Nick Engels in the van. I want to turn them over to you." It was then he noticed the two *pa lu*s standing behind him, totally confused. They hadn't understood a word.

Beard looked at the packet and glanced at Loo. To Carr he said, "Is this Dorothy? Which one is Straw Man?"

Carr said, "This is Miss Ho. Her name is Liu-ch'ao. You missed Straw Man. That's her grandfather, Ho Ling-chi. He was in that truck up ahead. He's a member of the Central Committee of the Communist Party of China." He motioned to the *pa lu*s. "These are guards from Huangling."

Beard snapped the packet against a palm. "I've heard of Mr. Ho. How the hell did you connect up with him after your C-46 went down?"

"It's a long story, sir."

"Dilly," Beard said, "you drive the van. I'm going to ride in with the sergeant and hear his story." He turned to Carr. "Ever been on a horse, son?"

"Yes, sir. Raised on a farm."

"So was I."

Carr went to Loo. His voice was low so that the others would not hear. "Yenan," he said, looking at her face and marveling at its beauty. "We're almost there! I'll go with Captain Beard." He paused. "I want to kiss you. I can't do that here." His voice was a whisper. "They can't keep me away from you! I love you. Just remember what I said. We'll find a way to work it out."

She nodded. "I knew the moment would come when we would part." There was a small break in her voice. "I don't want to lose you. It frightens me."

"You won't lose me and I won't lose you." He smiled. "I'm glad this damned thing is almost over. When it is, we can get our act together."

She smiled in turn. "Yes, let's get our act together!"

He turned and mounted the horse.

"Head 'em off at the pass," Chance Beard said, kicking his horse. "Come on, Sergeant, let's ride!"

The sun was behind the mountains when they rode in, with Carr talking nonstop, describing what had happened before and after the crash, and with Loo and her grandfather. Chance Beard kept repeating, "I'll be a son of a bitch!" Carr saw the van and the military truck. Loo and her grandfather were not in sight. Soldiers led by Lieutenant Dillon came to take the snorting mounts.

Beard put a hand on Carr's shoulder. "Come on, we've got to get cleaned up. Then you're going to meet Chairman Mao."

It was Carr's turn. "I'll be a son of a bitch!"

He stared at what he could see of Yenan. His legs felt weak. Night lights were coming on all over the place.

Yenan!

He had made it!

He remembered some of the Chinese Loo had taught him at Tan's house. *"Tao la!"* he said. "We have arrived!"

Suddenly he shuddered. Fraser Dillon looked at him. "Are you all right, Sergeant? Something just passed over your face."

Carr swallowed. "I've been trying to get here for days. Now that I'm in Yenan, I just got bit by my worry bug." He shook his head as the worrisome feeling rose within him. "It's not over yet, is it?"

"It's just starting, Sergeant," Chance Beard said. "It's just starting."

CHAPTER EIGHT

Lieutenant Oshima crouched in the darkness, listening to the sounds of the patrol searching for him.

He saw their swinging lanterns as they followed the track he had left in the loess dust of the overgrown wagon trail. He was certain the villagers where he'd slept the night before had told the army about him and word had been sent ahead. He was tired, hungry, cold, and worried about the small amount of gasoline left in the motorcycle's tank. He was at least forty miles from Yenan, and close to discovery and capture.

He thought of the daylight bombing he'd witnessed from a safe distance and the electrifying sight of the American standing at the van. The view had erased the small lingering doubt. The quarry's uniform was evidence that this man was the one who had lived through the C-46 crash, the man who carried valuable secret information to Yenan. The presence of the Red Army soldiers had made it impossible for the American to be intercepted, interrogated, and killed.

Oshima forced his thoughts away from the American and concentrated on the patrol. He was concealed in a clump of bushes a few feet away from the trail, the Mauser gripped in his hand. Anger filled him. He had to get to Yenan! He had to find the American and force the information out of him! He would have been in the city hours ago if he had not been hampered by so many army patrols, wasting precious gasoline on roundabout paths to get away from them. Now this night patrol was hard on his heels.

The lanterns came closer. On an impulse of sheer curiosity, he stood to see how many men were in the patrol. He counted four. In their lights he could see they had their rifles slung carelessly over their shoulders. He breathed easier. He would have a few seconds of surprise. He moved slowly, cautiously, through the bushes toward them, aware that they were more concerned with looking down at his tire marks in the spray of light than to the sides of the trail. He was behind a small tree when they came abreast of him. He had the advantage. He took it.

He aimed the Mauser, and it bucked in his hand as he fired. He saw three of the men go down. The fourth turned and ran back along the trail, still carrying a lantern, trying to get his rifle into place. A shot of electric emotion ran through Oshima. He raced back to his motorcycle, tripping several times in the bushes. He pumped the machine into life and drove down the dark trail away from the ambush. The soldiers were on foot. Perhaps there was a vehicle further back from which they operated. It might have a radio.

His luck was holding! He bent forward in sheer pleasure. The dim-witted Chinese had made it so easy for him. He would go as far as the machine would take him. He would get into Yenan and find the agent. He imagined the look on General Ishimura's fat face when he reported to him that he, Lieutenant Renya Oshima, had penetrated into the stronghold of the Chinese Red Army! The trail turned again, and by the light of the rising moon he found that it led to the main road. He turned onto it, happy to be away from the many low branches that whipped against him relentlessly as he rode. With the faint light from the moon it became easier to see and he drove recklessly until the motorcycle sputtered, then stopped. He shoved it off the road into a ditch. He saw the lights of Yenan as he crested a long hill and he began to walk faster. As he did, he reloaded the Mauser, aware that he might meet sentries who would challenge him.

In a half hour he was not challenged. Only one truck came along the road. Seeing its headlights, he lay flat on the ground until it had passed. He walked into the city, mingling with the people who were on its streets. With the Baoji agent's map clearly in his mind he made his way through the narrow streets, poorly lighted with lanterns and a few electric bulbs. He used the map's landmarks and found the address.

He knocked on the door of the small building which was huddled with similar buildings in an area adjacent to the Red Army training grounds. The door opened, and a spray of light silhouetted the person looking out.

The man wore a felt hat.

The Myitkyina air base was busy in the early evening hours. C-46s took off or landed on the lighted strip with only several minutes between them. Captain Joe Karras saw the C-47 land and followed it to the parking ramp in his jeep. He greeted colonel Carleton "Chick" Gregory, commanding officer of OSS 101 Detachment, coming down the short ladder. Gregory, a hearty, stout, balding, sunburned native of Oklahoma, exuded energy and authority. His every action exhibited his go-ahead drive. He jumped into the jeep next to Karras. "Got your flash, Joe," he said. "So the kid made it."

Karras drove toward the OSS headquarters, seeing the last of the Nepalese workers strung out along the road in his headlights. "Chance used the code we hid in the Moffett packet," Karras said. "I hate secret ink, but it worked. He radioed the whole story." Karras went over it in detail, reporting every fact that Chance Beard had radioed to him. They stopped before the building and went in.

"Incredible," Gregory said, throwing his small bag on the table. "So Straw Man was Ho Ling-chi and Dorothy was his granddaughter. Amazing!" His smile made his face, with its bulbous nose and thick graying eyebrows, look younger. "We've got to luck out once in a while." He opened the bag and pulled a bottle of Scotch from it. He fetched two glasses from a drawer and poured the whiskey into them, handing one to Karras. They toasted each other.

"Joe," he said, arching his thick back to rid it of an ache gained from sitting in a jump seat in the Gooney Bird during the flight to and from Calcutta, "we spent the day going over all our operations. The Yenan thing was the jewel, of course. After all the bullshit, the consensus was to go with Carr if he made it. That was Chance Beard's suggestion. We took it." He sipped the Scotch. "He's there and the Commies know about the snatch plot. Now it's up to them. We've done our part."

Karras waited until the colonel pulled up a chair and sat down, then did the same. "What we don't know is how it is supposed to be done. Carr says he's been followed by a Jap on a motorcycle. Either he's suffering something from the crash or he's got another angle to the case. There are several possibilities. One is the Kuomintang people in Yenan from their postal and telephone service. The other is that there are a lot of Jap prisoners up there and some of them could be working with the KMT to kidnap Mao, Chou, and General Chu.''

"Well, Chance can cover that with Colonel Wu. Wu's a smart cookie. He'll pull the place apart looking for the conspirators.'' Gregory reached for the bottle and refilled their glasses. "If our ink code holds up, the KMT won't know why Carr is in Yenan.''

"A matter of time,'' Karras said. "It's the best code we've got. It would take them days to break it. That gives Chance some lead time to work with Wu.''

Gregory was thoughtful. "This Carr. When I read your report, I wondered about the kid. He'll meet Mao and the others tonight. That's a heavy load to put on him, but hell, we're all carrying heavy loads. He's pissed off at the Air Corps for washing him out. I agree with you, he got a raw deal. He walked out of the Hump and he's walked out of northern China. He's turned that anger into being highly aggressive. I like that. Let's think about what we can do for him.''

Karras raised his glass. "He deserves something.''

Gregory reached in the bag and brought out a sheaf of papers with a rubber band around them. "Okay, let's get down to work. I met an Indian professor at Hastings Mill. Working for us in New Delhi. Told me some things about Myitkyina I didn't know.'' He waved a stubby-fingered hand around the room. "This used to be the showplace of Burma for the British. The railroad comes up here from Rangoon. You know that. But did you know there used to be gold mines around here? Salt mines? I've been here a long time and never knew that. Or that this used to be the capital of an old Shan State called Wainghaw.''

"I'll be damned.''

"He told me the Irrawaddy River is formed by the confluence of the Mali and the Nmai—Kachin names.'' Gregory sorted the papers. "So much for history, Joe. Here's the drill for 101 Detachment.''

They pulled their chairs closer and began the laborious process of command of intelligence operations in the China, Burma, and India theater of war. A war little understood by Americans who saw relatively few dispatches about it, who knew little about the Hump and the dangerous flights over it in unarmed cargo planes, who knew nothing of the intrigue between the political and military entities, or of the deaths of the fliers who wore the shoulder patch, shield-shaped, that bore the Star of India, the Sun of China, and the red and white stripes of the United States.

Yenan, Shensi Province
Red Army Headquarters

The debriefing had been hurried.

They were not in a relaxed state. The radio message had been sent by Fraser Dillon to Joe Karras in Myitkyina after the secret code had been raised from the back of the Moffett background paper. "We've got another fifteen minutes, Sergeant," Colonel McHugh said. "Is there anything else?"

Seated in the cave dwelling assigned to the colonel, Carr said, "I want the girl assigned to me as an interpreter."

"Why? We have interpreters."

"Sir, I couldn't have gotten here without her help. She and her grandfather couldn't have gotten here without mine. We work well together. If you're going to put this thing across to the Commies, you've got to keep us together."

"That's up to them."

"Sir, it will help if you speak up."

McHugh's eyebrows rose slightly. He looked at Carr, seeing a young man, well-built, blond hair freshly cut, tanned face newly shaved, dressed in woolen issue, blue eyes serious and determined. Then he smiled, knowing this was not the usual enlisted man. "Okay, I'll speak up."

Dillon came through the tunnel leading into the room. "Red radio reported three *pa lu*s shot about forty miles south of here. One dead, two wounded. One survivor reported hearing a motorcycle start up after the ambush in the dark. Another patrol found the motorcycle about three miles out of Yenan on the main road.''

"Jesus Christ," Chance Beard said. He'd been sprawled on the kang. "You were right about the guy on a motorcycle.''

"That means he's here in Yenan," Carr said.

McHugh rose from his chair. "You still think he's Japanese?"

"He was in the car that was with the van," Carr said. "The radio in the van had Jap markings on it. I picked up a piece of paper with Jap writing on it. The weapons are Jap."

"A lot of Commies have captured Jap weapons.''

"This was on the other side of the blockade," Carr insisted. "The place was loaded with KMT regulars and deserters. How many captured Jap weapons do they have?"

"A good point," McHugh agreed, looking at his watch. "Let's say he's a Jap. What the hell is he doing following you to Yenan?"

"I told you that, sir. I believe he and his men got to the C-46. I saw two men take off after the fight with the KMT patrol, like I said. In a car. One of them had to be the leader. He's the one on the motorcycle. He has to be in the Kempetai for him to follow me to Yenan. He wants to find out why I left the crash and came here. He's after intelligence information.'' Carr paused after the outburst. "That's why I want him captured. Colonel Wu will find out he has phony papers to get through the blockade.''

"You got through without papers," McHugh said.

"I wasn't stopped by a Red Army patrol that was shown papers. I was with Mr. Ho. His friends and smugglers helped us." Carr realized his voice had risen argumentatively. He didn't care.

McHugh looked at Beard and Dillon. "You men have any ideas?"

Beard said, "There are Jap prisoners here. Maybe some of them are Kempetai deliberately put here. He may try to use them. Another idea is that he's in on this kidnap thing and will work with Tai Li's agents here to carry it off."

Dillon had been waiting for a chance to get a word in. "This guy on the motorcycle," he said, "stayed at a small village last night. Told them he was a mining expert with the Reds. Like Carr said, he had papers and flashed them."

McHugh moved to the tunnel. "Well, they know he's here.

They'll be looking for him." He looked at Carr. "Are you ready, son? Know what you've got to do?"

"Yes, sir."

McHugh smiled. "Okay, show time. Let's not keep the chairman waiting."

Yang Ju-tung had removed his felt hat.

"Your story is preposterous," he said to Renya Oshima. "Why do you come here and jeopardize what we have built?"

"I jeopardize nothing!" Oshima said hotly. "I bring you word that this American carries important intelligence information. We must find out what it is and inform General Ishimura."

"You say you work with Ishimura. I work for General Tashiro of the Kempetai."

"You must believe me!"

Yang sat cross-legged on the floor mat, facing Oshima. Tallow candles flickered in the room, well furnished by Chinese standards. The room, with its kang and simple wooden furniture, led to a shop at the rear, narrow and filled with an array of metalworking machines dimly lighted by a small lantern hung from the ceiling.

Yang was dark-skinned, thin, and angular. He looked every inch a Chinese. His Japanese, when he spoke, was tinctured with Chinese expressions. His dark eyes were intense. His hair, cut Chinese-style, was plastered with perspiration to his forehead. "I believe you. Your papers carry the mark of our man in Baoji. Another mark indicates he did not want to inform you of my name but you forced him to. That was rashness on your part, as a fellow officer of the Kempetai. You have told me enough of your background and of General Ishimura that I believe that much is true." His voice was sarcastic. "But I also believe I am with a madman who has blundered into Yenan on an impossible mission."

At the word *madman*, Oshima smiled. "Sergeant Mutagachi and the Baoji agent felt the same way," he said. "I have not made you understand. This American survived an incredible wreck. He is one the gods favor. I should have had my hands on him often, but always I was prevented. I cannot stop until I find out why he has come to Yenan."

Yang reached for a bottle of wine and filled their empty cups. The remains of a simple meal were evident in the plates near the straw mats on which they sat. "The Communists will know about the men you shot south of here," Yang said. "They will find your motorcycle. They will know you are in Yenan. You must remain hidden here."

"I will capture the American and kill him!" Oshima said.

Yang looked at him contemptuously. "Let me tell you what you will do if you wish to remain alive. You will stay here. You have come at the worst time possible. A great project is under way, and I won't allow you to interfere with it."

"What project?" Oshima was immediately interested.

"I will not tell you. If you are captured by the Communists you would inform them of it under torture."

"I demand to know."

"You demand nothing. You are out of your Kempetai jurisdiction. General Tashiro would have my head—if we get out of here as we plan." Yang leaned forward, harshness on his face. "Let me tell you something, Oshima-san. My father came to China many years ago. I was a baby. He changed his name and took Chinese ways. He did that under the orders of our government. You are in the Kempetai. You know that many other patriotic men did the same, under the original plan for the conquest of China."

Oshima nodded. "I worked with such families in the south."

"Then you know how difficult it has been for us. My father was assigned to stay with the Communists. He did well. He set up this metal shop and he was trusted. He sent many valuable secrets to General Tashiro." Yang's voice faltered. "My honored father died three weeks ago. He was the strongest part of this great project. Now that he is gone, it is up to me to complete it."

"Why can't you tell me about it? Let me help."

Yang stared for a long time into Oshima's eyes. "My family is related to Lieutenant General Fujika Honda."

Oshima was surprised. "Our Thirty-third Army? The Northern Combat Command in Burma?" He remembered Ishimura saying he was related to General Honda. He decided to remain silent about it. He did not believe this steel-eyed man was related to the great Honda.

"I cannot bring disgrace to my family's name. You are the only person in Yenan who knows my real name. The Communist secret police believe it is Nakahira and then Yang, but it is Honda."

"They know you are of Japanese birth?"

"Of course, but my father established such a splendid cover for his Kempetai work here that they never penetrated his operations." Yang drew himself up. "They trust me as they trusted him."

"What will you do about the American?"

"I have men working with me here. Some are Japanese pretending to be Chinese. Some are Chinese who secretly want to bring down the Communists. That is why you must remain hidden. If you are caught and found to be Japanese, our entire cell will be destroyed." Yang smiled sourly. "You don't want that to happen, do you?"

"If I cannot be of use to you in your project, then I must find some way to capture the American and learn why he is here." Oshima knew he was pressing hard, but he felt compelled to.

Yang studied his wine cup. "It is dangerous for me to tell you this. I have to either kill you or swear you to Kempetai secrecy."

Oshima brightened. His face in the candlelight failed to show the exhaustion he felt. "I swear on my officer's oath!"

Yang sighed, making the decision. "The war is not going well for us. The Americans are growing stronger. They are in the Philippines. Our navy and our armies have suffered defeats. Our homeland is being bombed daily. Our project is to set the Nationalists against the Communists in great battles to create more opportunities for us to hold what we have in China and so that we can remove some of our armies to defend our islands."

Oshima's brightness faded. "How can this be done in Yenan?"

"Your oath of secrecy."

"My oath!"

"We have structured this project to appear as if it were the work of General Tai Li's secret police. If it goes as we plan, the Americans who are here in what they call the Dixie Mission will also appear to be involved."

Oshima's eyes glistened. "Very clever!"

"Within a very short time, Oshima-san, we will kidnap Mao, Chou, and General Chu. We will take them to Chungking, where they will be turned over to Chiang Kai-shek." Yang's voice was a whisper, an electrifying flow of words to Oshima.

He was stunned. "Unbelievable! That would create a greater

civil war in China. Chinese armies against Chinese armies! A fire greater than ever before! Splendid!''

Yang held up a warning hand. "But it must be done so that the Kempetai's involvement in it is never known. It must appear to be Tai Li's plot, not ours. If we are successful, we will remove a great amount of pressure against our armies. Some of our forces can be withdrawn to protect our islands.''

Oshima was agitated. "How do you plan to do this? To get them out of here and to Chungking? Such daring! Fantastic!''

Yang's voice rose in sharpness. "You know too much already. You will remain here. If you leave, either I or one of my men will kill you on sight. Do you understand that?''

Oshima could barely control himself. "I will do nothing that would endanger the project! It is such a thing as I have dreamed of!'' He stopped. "The American! Could he be here on a mission to warn the Communists about it?''

Yang lifted the wine bottle, found it empty, and reached for another one. He poured the wine into the little warmer. "You fool,'' he said. "Of course. Our people in Chungking leaked a story about the kidnap plot to the American OSS agents there. Deliberately.'' His eyes shone in the light. "The story was that a top-level officer in Tai Li's intelligence group was behind it. We wanted the OSS to alert their man here, a Captain Chance Beard, that the Nationalists were plotting to kidnap the Communist leaders.''

Oshima was entranced. "So that after it happened, the blame would all be on Chiang Kai-shek!'' He shook his head. "But now the Communists know about it!''

"We want them to know. Such news will cause them great alarm. They will be looking in every corner. But we know them well. I have a man in their radio center. I know of most of their messages, sent and received. We have a plan that will work no matter how they guard their leaders.''

"You have thought even of that!'' Oshima was awed.

"Exactly. You see now why the Kempetai is the best intelligence service in the world. It puts the Americans in a very difficult position, since they supply Chiang with so much war equipment. It will damage, if not destroy, the Americans' efforts to work with the Red Army.''

"So the American was on a very important mission! I was right!" Oshima felt a surge of elation.

"It was not the American you followed. The OSS man who was sent to do that died in the crash you saw. A low-level person brought the information. He was the one you followed. We learned of this just a short time ago. We thought they would use their radio, but they sent the OSS man in the plane instead." Yang's face became a mask of ruthlessness. "You should have left well enough alone. You are here, and if you obey I will keep you alive. It is possible that you can help us when we are ready to leave."

Oshima was almost begging. "Anything!"

"You can kill the American you followed and as many other Americans as you can. This will make it look as if the Communists wreaked terrible revenge on the Dixie Mission. It will create a massive disturbance between the American military leaders and the Red Army they court."

Oshima pointed to his Mauser lying near the mat. "All you have to do is tell me when and where."

His spirits were soaring. He thought of General Ishimura. He looked into the hawklike face of his host and knew that his quarry had led him into an amazing labyrinth of secret operations. And he, Renya Oshima, was part of it!

They entered a gray brick building, one of two that housed the Chinese Communist Party in Yenan.

Carr found himself in a small auditorium. He followed McHugh and Beard down the center aisle to where Loo was standing with three Red Army officers wearing faded gray uniforms. He saw the sharp expectancy in their faces. He introduced Loo to McHugh and Beard and she introduced them to the three men. They were official interpreters. Loo appeared nervous. "It is still strange seeing American uniforms here," she said. She pointed to the ribbons on the chests of McHugh and Beard. "You both have been in the military for a long time."

McHugh, meeting her for the first time, was visibly impressed. "Captain Beard told me you were beautiful," he said. "Now I see that for myself. Sergeant Carr has told us of your adventures. Did you really kill that tiger?"

She flushed. "I don't like to think of it!"

Beard leaned down to her. "The man on the motorcycle. Do you think he was Japanese?"

Her dark eyes took him in. "Yes."

Carr said, "Did you tell that to the people here?"

"Yes. I was informed about the ambush of the patrol and about the motorcycle being found." She looked up at him quickly. "At first I did not take you seriously. Now I believe you were right."

Beard was relieved. "Thank you. If he is Japanese, it's important to find out why he's here. We look forward to our hosts findin' him."

There was a stir by the entrance. They turned to see a burly man in a Red Army uniform entering. He appeared to be in his sixties. He had a pug nose, and he exhibited great energy. He strode toward them, nodding to McHugh and Beard.

Loo said, "Master Sergeant Carr, this is General Chu Teh, commander in chief of the Red armies." In Chinese, she introduced Carr to the general. They shook hands. Carr realized this solid man was very strong.

Another group came down the aisle. Carr recognized Chou Enlai, ambassador to the Kuomintang. He remembered what Beard had told him. Chou's party name was Shao Shan, which meant Small Mountain. Chou sported thick black eyebrows over intense luminous eyes. His uniform was a simple gray affair, but he stood erect and filled it with charm and vibrancy. Carr shook hands with him and was immediately captivated by the delicately framed diplomat.

Two more men joined them. "You have met Colonel Wu," Loo said smoothly. "And this is Captain Yang, who is also in the intelligence section." Carr looked at the man, seeing the dark skin and penetrating eyes. The captain was not in uniform. He wore civilian clothes, and a felt hat.

Chairman Mao Tse-tung chose that moment to make his entrance. He shuffled down the aisle with the rolling gait of a well-fed bear. His short husky body was topped with a fairly round head on which the hairline was receding. Carr saw that there was a tiny mole on his chin. He appeared to be in his early fifties. He spoke in a thick Hunan province accent. His drab woolen suit of light brown color was buttoned at the neck.

Loo said, "The chairman welcomes you to Yenan. He has spoken to my grandfather and knows of your travels. He regrets that my distinguished grandfather is tired and has gone to bed to recover from the long trip. He is most anxious to hear the message you have brought from Myitkyina, and he regrets deeply the deaths of your comrades on your flight.''

Behind the chairman were two other men. Carr was introduced to General Lin Piao, commander of the 115th Division, a small, thin man of correct military bearing, and General Yeh Chien-ying, chief of staff.

The chairman made a gesture, and everyone was seated. McHugh took the Moffett packet from his pocket. Carr noticed an American enlisted man in the back of the auditorium and guessed the man was an interpreter who could be called to duty if McHugh and Beard needed him. Both men spoke fairly good Chinese, but regional accents could complicate discussions. Carr stole a glance at Captain Yang, seated with Colonel Wu. The felt hat had been removed. Something about the man bothered him. Is this man another evil dragon? he thought. I'm getting paranoid. I see danger everywhere. He turned back to McHugh.

McHugh read the English papers, then gave the Chinese copies to General Chu. There was a long period while the interpreters helped with the reading of the documents.

Chairman Mao lighted a cigarette. From his stained fingers, Carr knew Mao was a chain smoker. He spoke and Loo translated. ''The chairman asks how certain is your American intelligence that there is a plot to kidnap us?''

McHugh said, ''Certain enough to send the late Lieutenant Colonel Ambrose Moffett to Yenan in person to inform you of it.''

Mao: ''And the plane was sabotaged by Tai Li's men and crashed. The brave comrade sergeant brought this information.''

McHugh: ''That is true.''

Mao: ''Why did not your people use the radio?''

McHugh: ''They felt it was safer to send a high-level officer than to trust the radio. The message is long and could have been intercepted and deciphered. They did not want to take a chance that Tai Li would find out that they knew about the plot. Also, after the crash, they were prepared to send another officer, but the weather made it impossible. They learned that Sergeant Carr had survived and had these papers. They instructed him to bring them to Yenan.''

Carr felt Mao's clear eyes on him.

Mao: "The plot is a childish one. We are secure here in Shensi. We go as we please without guards. Why have they not tried this before?"

McHugh: "They have two aims, Chairman Mao. One is to take you, Ambassador Chou, and General Chu to Chungking. The other is to make it appear that we of the American Military Observer Group were part of it."

Mao: "Yet you have no evidence of how they intend to carry out this ridiculous plan?"

McHugh: "Our people in Chungking have learned that the order did not come from General Tai Li but from one of those very high in his secret police. No, we do not know how they intend to accomplish it. That is what concerns us. Obviously, they have people in place here. These people should be uncovered. To do it, they would have to have an airplane or some vehicles at their disposal."

Mao: "We are a little short of airplanes and motor vehicles." Laughter.

McHugh: "Sergeant Carr has another element, one not mentioned in the papers he brought." After the translation, Carr felt their eyes on him. He sat relaxed, arms folded. "He was followed by a man on a motorcycle. Your patrols have encountered this man. He shot three brave soldiers, killing one of them. I understand the motorcycle has been found a short distance from here."

Wu (interceding): "He is being sought."

McHugh: "If that man turns out to be a secret agent of the Japanese Kempetai, it would throw another light on the plot."

Mao: "What is your thinking?"

McHugh: "Intelligence is a very tricky thing. Let us take this line. Let us suppose the Kempetai has penetrated into General Tai Li's operations in Chungking. Let us think of what the Japanese would gain if you were kidnapped and turned over to the generalissimo."

Mao: "Go on, please."

McHugh: "The civil war would burst into greater flames. The Red Army would not stand for such humiliation of you. The war between the Chinese armies would be calamitous. Who would gain

the most? The Japanese, at a time when our Pacific Fleet is growing stronger, achieving great victories. A time when the Japanese
homeland is being firebombed and devastated by our B-29s. A time
when they are retreating in Burma. A time when they need their
armies to defend Japan itself.''

Mao: ''Let us suppose that, indeed, the Kempetai is involved.
How could your people be a party to this?''

McHugh: ''As I said, intelligence can be tricky. Perhaps our
people in Chungking were misled cleverly. If, on the other hand,
the Kuomintang is solely involved, what do they stand to gain? A
great escalation of the war with the Red armies. They have fought
three great campaigns against you in four years and have not won.
How could they win a new campaign against the Red armies ignited by the tremendous fire of your being a prisoner in Chungking?''

Mao put out the cigarette and lit another one. He looked calmly
at his Red Army officers, then at McHugh.

Mao: ''You have brought me the puzzle but not the solution. We
do not know who actually is behind this sudden tempest. The Kuomintang? The Kempetai?'' A slow smile. ''But we are grateful for
the warning. General Chu will place Yenan on a full alert. Colonel
Wu has men out at this moment looking for the one who came by
motorcycle. Now he will have men searching for those who plot
against us.'' A pause. ''I would ask the young comrade sergeant
several questions.''

McHugh: ''Certainly. He is most honored, Chairman Mao.''

Mao: ''My treasured friend, Ho Ling-chi, has told me of your
exploits. You did not know who he was nor his importance to me,
yet you brought him here. You had this important message to
bring. Why did you take the care to bring an old man and his granddaughter to Yenan? You shared your food with them. You carried
him on your back. You fought to prevent their capture when you
could have abandoned them. Why?''

Carr (sitting upright): ''Chairman Mao, I looked at my dead
comrades and I saw the sabotage that caused their deaths. By any
sane measure I should have stayed at the wreck for rescue. In my
heart, I felt a terrible hatred for the Kuomintang, for the agents in
Myitkyina who had destroyed my plane and four brave men. I read
those papers. I was determined to get to Yenan, to complete the

mission. I knew the weather would make it difficult for another man to be flown in. I felt it was my responsibility to bring the information here.''

Mao: "Such a long distance, in winter storms."

Carr: "I felt that if I could get the packet to Yenan it would give meaning to the deaths of those with whom I flew."

Mao: "Yet, while you were obsessed with this mission, you aided an old man and a young girl. You brought them over the mountains and through the blockade."

Carr: "Chairman Mao, to me Mr. Ho is not an old man. I would have helped him no matter what his station. I have a grandfather of my own at home. He fought in the Spanish-American War. Mr. Ho reminded me of my grandfather, a man of dignity, a man of stature. I knew he was not a simple peasant, but that made no difference to me. I know the suffering he has faced with the deaths of his son and grandson. I felt privileged to be with him because he gave me some of his strength. He never complained. He bore the hardships like a great man would."

Mao: "He thinks highly of you. He is amazed at what you did to keep him alive. He is most grateful."

Carr: "Chairman Mao, it is I who am grateful to Mr. Ho. It was his friends, Mr. Tan and Mr. Tan's nephew, Mr. Sung, who risked so much to help us. I would not be alive if it had not been for all Mr. Ho did."

The chairman put his hands on the chair arms as if to rise. Carr went on quickly, drawing startled looks from everyone. "Mr. Chairman, please forgive me." He heard Loo translating. "I promised myself that if I made it to Yenan I would say what is very strong in my mind." He hurried on. "I have come to see the Kuomintang for what they are. I have come to respect the Chinese people whom they blockade up here. I know the purpose of our Military Observer Mission in Yenan. I feel very strongly that the United States should support Chairman Mao in what he is trying to do for China."

The thick hush in the auditorium lasted for a half minute. The chairman's eyes were steady on Carr's. Then he spoke. "If your leaders could see what you have seen, Comrade Sergeant, and only a few of them do, then our country would be blessed with greater fortune. We do appreciate what your mission has been trying to do here. It remains to be seen whether the results are favorable to your country and to ours.''

The chairman stood. Everyone followed suit. The session was ended. The dignitaries filed from the auditorium, filled now with Chinese voices. Carr stood with McHugh and Beard, watching. "Did I say anything wrong?" he asked.

"You did fine, Sergeant," McHugh answered.

Carr turned to Loo. "What do you think? I left you out of it deliberately."

Her eyes shone with happiness and relief. "Imagine! Chairman Mao!" Her laughter was light, reducing her tension. "It went very well. There was no need to mention me. They do not regard me as being important."

"What happens now?" Carr said to McHugh. He followed the officers up the aisle behind the departing Chinese.

"Now it's up to them to grab the guy who was following you," McHugh said, "and to prevent the snatch."

Carr turned to Loo, right behind him. "He's going to ask that you be assigned to me as my interpreter. When will I see you again?"

"Tomorrow. I believe Colonel Wu will want to talk to you first thing in the morning."

Carr saw Wu standing at the door. Then Wu was gone and Carr caught a glimpse of the man in the felt hat staring at him through the small crowd clustered at the doorway of the auditorium.

He felt a chill. *He knew.*

The man in the felt hat had been measuring him for death.

CHAPTER NINE

Colonel Wu had changed.

Gone was the stiff military posture, the air of confrontation, replaced with amiable hospitality. He sat across the mess table from Carr and Loo as they ate boiled eggs, toasted brown wheat buns, pears, and great-sized figs, and sipped tea. Despite his relaxed state, they watched him carefully. He wore the gold star, the Red Army's highest decoration.

Outside the cave-quarters guesthouse the approaching sun announced itself with its first creeping rays. The echoes of bugles bounced from the many hills in and around Yenan. There were sounds of excitement and the bustle of troop movements. The morning air was exhilarating.

Wu poured more tea, smiling broadly, playing the role of host to perfection. "There was much discussion at the party headquarters after your meeting with Chairman Mao," he said in Chinese, Loo turning it into English. "We have heard many fantastic war stories, but yours certainly is one of the most interesting."

Carr remained silent, waiting. The change in the officer bothered him. Obviously, the meeting with Mao had worked on Wu. If there were any hard feelings they had not risen to the surface.

"We are left with a serious problem," Wu said. "How to find the men who are to carry out the plot." Wu's face was shiny but well-complexioned. His hands looked strong. His movements were precise, his military bearing impeccable.

Carr shifted uneasily, suspecting the man of putting on a show for the benefit of Loo more than for him. He felt a twinge of jealousy.

"Let me give you a summary, Sergeant," Wu went on. "We

have been behind this blockade since 1936. That is more than eight years. Yet, we have six hundred thousand men under arms and we have more than a million *ming ping*. These are armed militia who farm during the day and fight at our side at night. We have more than ninety million people under our control. Compare that with the one hundred and thirty million Americans in your country today.''

Carr lifted his cup, glad to see that his hand did not shake from lack of sleep. He had spent the hours of the night talking to McHugh, Beard, and Dillon and the others of the Dixie Mission. He was buoyed by the realization that he was in Yenan and felt a deep excitement. His survivor syndrome had faded.

''Your country has fifteen men here as military observers,'' Wu said. He paced his sentences to allow Loo to interpret for Carr. ''They have tried to find ways in which the United States and the Red Army can work together. Your General Stilwell, before he was relieved, was most concerned that these ways be found. But your General Hurley was unable to bring us together with the Kuomintang because the generalissimo fears to have a Communist influence in the government and fears the movement of the Red armies across the land.''

Carr said, ''How long have you been fighting Chiang?''

''He was the commandant of the Whampoa Military Academy in 1924,'' Wu said, seeming to peer backward in time. ''In those days, Ambassador Chou En-lai was his political director. There were many who favored Communism. You must remember that the Chinese Communist Party was formed in 1921. It is called 'Kungch'antang.' Chiang had a strong liaison with the men of the party then, but in 1927 he broke with his Communist friends. Ambassador Chou, later that year, organized the workers in Shanghai. It was beautifully done, a revolution against the warlords. Chiang displayed his underhanded tactics there. He used armed gangsters who pretended to be workers. These cutthroats murdered many Communists in Shanghai. The first Red Army was organized the next year, in 1928.''

Wu waited for Loo to complete the translation. ''Then Chiang set up his own government. He called it the Nationalist Party. This was also in 1928, at Nanking. It was a counterrevolution against the Communists. He surrounded himself with right-wing Kuomintang officials. He spent years killing Communists. He set up the first blockade in 1933. Perhaps you have heard of the Long March?''

When Loo reached this part of the translation, Carr nodded. ''It is well-known in the Western world,'' he said. ''I read about it in college.''

Wu smiled. ''The next year, Chairman Mao broke out of that blockade in Hunan province and began the Long March. It covered eighteen thousand li, or six thousand miles, moving to the west and then to the northwest, until Yenan was established as our capital in 1937. Yenan, by the way, is the former capital of the old Soviet districts in our land.''

Carr said, ''Then you've been fighting him since 1927, for eighteen years. When did the Japanese invade?''

''In 1932 they attacked Shanghai, and the Red Army declared war on Japan. That was the year your President Roosevelt was elected, right? But it was in 1937 and 1938 that the dwarf people really invaded in force.''

''Why are the Japanese so cruel?'' Carr said when Loo made the translation. ''In Burma, they tied British prisoners to trees and used them for bayonet practice.''

''They are sadistic monkey people. Ruthless, and very bold as militarists. They torture and kill our people. They loot homes, burn them, destroy all they can. They gang-rape our women. They shoot people and cut out their bowels and throw them in the street. They throw dead bodies in the rivers. They tie peasants to carts and use them as mules. They bring their own whores with them.''

Carr felt uneasy. ''In all that time, it's a shame that the Red armies and the Kuomintang armies could not join together to defeat those bastards!''

Wu nodded, looking at Loo as she spoke Chinese. ''Chiang has hoarded much of the war supplies your government has given him. To use against us. Even our Russian friends have given us nothing. But they have given to Chiang. You are right, it is a shame and difficult to understand. It is the Red Army that has inflicted the worst damage on the Japanese, not the Kuomintang.'' Wu looked around the guesthouse mess hall. There were Chinese sitting at other tables, paying no attention to them. ''Chairman Mao wanted a true coalition government. He was ready to surrender the command of the Red Army a short time ago when your General Hurley was here. He wanted only to have the Communist Party to participate in the government and that there be a freedom of assembly, movement, and speech. Chiang wanted complete authority. He said it was a sacred trust from Dr. Sun Yat-sen, the founder of our modern nation. A heavenly mandate! Chairman Mao could not accept our land being governed by one man.''

"It seems nothing can be done to break down that hard-nosed jerk,'' Carr said. "Our mission here has not been successful, from what I was told last night by our people.''

Wu agreed. "We have given your mission much information about the Japanese. Your people study the weather and have learned much about the People's Liberation Army that you call the Red Army, and the Chinese Communist Party. But you are right. Nothing substantial. They proposed giving us one hundred thousand pistols for our people's militia, and we need rifles, field guns, tanks, bazookas, heavy equipment. They suggested that we help them if American forces landed in our country, and Chairman Mao said again that he would place himself under your general's command if that happened. Nothing came of it. It was scotched in Chungking and Washington.''

Carr waited for Loo to end her translation. "I heard last night that our OSS had a plan to bring in some of their men to equip and train about twenty-five thousand of your soldiers in guerrilla warfare.''

"Yes, that was suggested. One idea was to bring in your United States airborne troops for demolition operations and to lead our *pa lu*s in greater guerrilla warfare. The other was to have your OSS experts do it.'' Wu shook his head in disgust. "Both plans, just last week, were torn up. There is much conflict between General Hurley and General Wedemeyer, who replaced General Stilwell as commander of your CBI forces.'' His eyes were a touch sullen. "Now General Hurley is accusing your mission here of helping to ruin his opportunity to unite Chairman Mao with the generalissimo.''

Loo hurried the translation. "Colonel McHugh told me that General Hurley is now totally on the side of Chiang Kai-shek,'' Carr said. "He also said that Chairman Mao and Ambassador

Chou offered to go to Washington to meet with President Roosevelt, and that General Hurley wrecked that plan.''

Wu lifted his hands, palms up. "You see how we have been trying? Everything we have tried has been rebuffed." He smiled thinly. "What would you Americans do if Japan had invaded you and occupied your costal areas? You have an American army that believes in Communism blockaded in your Rocky Mountains by another American army that believes in dictatorship. That army has two million soldiers in it and about eight hundred thousand are in the blockade area to keep six hundred thousand Communists bottled up."

Loo's voice rose slightly as she translated the words into English. Carr said, "It would be a tragedy for the United States, as it is for China."

"China? You call it that, yes. Chung Kuo, the Middle Kingdom, has suffered for centuries from dynasties. It has suffered from warlords and greedy landlords. From invasion by foreign nations. Its people have been oppressed. Opium has been inflicted on them by the British. You Americans know little of this kind of oppression, nothing of the opium disease. It is difficult for you to understand what is going on here in the Middle Kingdom, even though a few of you are here to see it for yourself. Your leaders have shown they do not understand the situation here."

"What you're saying," Carr said, "is that American idealism and policies won't work in this country."

"No foreign government understands the situation here. They support Chiang Kai-shek because they believe, wrongly, that he is the real leader of the people. He is a strong man, yes, but his government is corrupt all the way through. He is too weak to govern and too strong to overthrow. He does not have the support of the people. Only the bankers and foreign investors. The chairman calls Chiang a 'turtle egg.' ''

"So how will it turn out?" Carr felt it was all too much for him to understand as well.

"First, remember that we are not Russian Communists. Chairman Mao has established his own brand of Marxism and Leninism. He has seen what capitalism has done to this country. He does not trust capitalism. He sees all but Chinese as being barbarians. Your American leaders profess to see us as agrarian reformers, as little more than bandits. If this is true, how have we existed? Why have we grown so large in numbers?''

Wu's face was sober. ''We know that you Americans tried to reform the Kuomintang last year. You made an intense effort to force them into more democratic ways. With no results. Yet you Americans tried. That is something.'' He waited for Loo to catch up. ''Your Brigadier General Claire Chennault, who came to this land with his American Volunteer Group, those called the 'Flying Tigers,' who is commander of the United States–China Air Task Force—he has fought the Japanese in a masterful way. Your men here in the Dixie Mission, they represent your Air Corps, Medical Corps, Signal Corps, and Infantry. They are good men and they are trying hard to find ways to help us.''

Wu sighed. ''The Kuomintang is dying. It is incapacitated. It is only a matter of time before all of this land unites behind Chairman Mao. It will be a better nation when that happens.''

''I feel foolish,'' Carr replied. ''I know so little about your country. I know American correspondents have been here in Yenan. Some of them have taken your side. Others have been in favor of Chiang. Because we're not Communists and have so little information about the Chinese Communist Party, it is difficult for us to see things clearly.'' Carr chose his words carefully. He knew that he was being subjected to a propaganda pitch. He would have received the same thing from some top official of the Kuomintang if the situation had been reversed. Still, he had not read much about China before he came to the CBI, and had known almost nothing about the Chinese Communists. Sitting in their capital, he did feel foolish knowing only scraps of information about them. They had existed. They had grown. He didn't know all the reasons why. He knew they had squeezed landlords, according to McHugh, and were not all rosy pink with honesty and uprightness. But they were there, a massive force to be dealt with.

Wu stood, looking at his watch, an old clamp-lid railroad type that he pulled from his uniform pocket. ''Don't blame yourself. We do not understand the United States, either. Or the United Kingdom, or France, or Italy. We have difficulty with Germany and Russia as well. I must go. I enjoyed having breakfast with you. I have asked your attractive interpreter here to take you on a visit through Yenan.''

Carr stood, feeling relief after sitting so long. "The man on the motorcycle?"

Loo translated.

"Ah, yes, that one. The fact he has disappeared, gone underground so quickly, is clear evidence he has someone here who will help him. That bolsters your story that he may be Japanese. There are Japanese among us who pretend to be Chinese. We know who they are and we search among them."

Carr gambled. "Your man, Captain Yang?"

Wu stiffened slightly. "What about him?"

"I have a strange feeling about him. It is in the way he stares at me."

Wu said nothing, looking long and hard into Carr's eyes. He turned and left the guesthouse.

"Was that wise?" Loo said. "You seem determined to rub him the wrong way."

Carr shrugged. "I got this thing about the Japanese, I guess." He looked at her. She was standing next to him, arms folded, looking irritated.

"Japanese!" Her voice was high and harsh. Several of the seated Chinese turned to look at her, unable to understand her English. "Do you know what they did in Nanking? I heard the story last night. It was in 1937. The Japanese, led by a General Hasimoto, slaughtered more than a quarter of a million of our people! They raped, killed, and hacked apart more than twenty thousand young girls and women! They took men out into the country, made them dig ditches, and machine-gunned them into the ditches! They went into a hospital and gang-raped the nurses! They used the patients for bayonet practice!" Her eyes glistened.

Carr put a hand on her shoulder and immediately withdrew it, aware for the first time that others in the guesthouse were looking at them. He knew there must be no public display of his love for her. He fought back the desire to take her in his arms. She was so upset. "The bastards are paying for it," he said. "Their Grand Fleet has been destroyed. Our B-29s are pounding them from here and from the Philippines."

He followed her out. The weather was clear and a bit warmer, but he still zippered his flight jacket against the morning chill. Not far away, under the bright blue sky, he saw the yellow Tang pagoda. They walked through Yenan. There were groups of pack animals with red tassels hanging from their heads. Ruddy-faced peasants in their thickly padded clothes bustled around. The slight breeze swept up the light tan loess dust into large, thick, choking puffs. Propaganda posters were everywhere.

"Over there," Loo said, "is the army headquarters." It was an ancient-looking place in the distance, bordering the Yen River. Gardens surrounded it. Carr and Loo walked along, looking into the stalls, looking at peasants doing their silk weaving and cotton spinning. An American weather balloon was rising, and they watched it float up into the bright sky.

"Chairman Mao is a chain smoker," Loo said as they walked, threading their way through the peasants and soldiers who stared curiously at Carr's uniform. Some of the peasants wore shapeless, brindled homespun garments. The men had sun-bronzed faces. All the women wore pants. Carr could not recall seeing a Chinese woman wearing a skirt. A few men went by, wearing long sheepskin coats. "He has his own tobacco garden," she said. "And loves pepper. He even has it baked into his bread."

Carr saw many men whose heads were shaved in the peasant style, halfway back from the forehead. He saw that Yenan sat in a bowl of sprawling hills, with solid walls that reached to their tops. He spotted machine guns in the high fortifications. Loo told him the Great Wall lay about 130 miles to the north, that Mongol cavalry hordes had ridden through Yenan on their way to sack Sianfu to the south. She pointed out hundreds of cave homes, with their black lacquered doors and rice-paper windows. They were *yaofang,* cave dwellings.

Peasants with shoulder poles went by him. There were many mule carts and a few rickshas and many wheelbarrows, some filled with passengers. When curious people spoke to Loo about him, she answered, *"Me kue shih peng yo,"* which she told him meant "The American is a friend." She pointed out soldiers of the 18th Group Army and the famed 8th Route Army. They all wore the rubber-soled canvas-cloth shoes. Some were buying sausages drying in the air.

One group of men marched by them with a guard. Loo said they were Japanese prisoners. They wore the Red uniforms. They walked by a row of open-faced buildings where the stink from hides drying in the open air made them wince. He learned that fine woolen garments were made in the area, that even some of the members of the General Committee made them.

They reminisced about Calcutta, talking about the Jain Temple, the Victoria Memorial, Eden Gardens on the Strand with its Burmese pagoda and green foliage, the forty-five acres of the Zoo Garden, and old Fort Henry on the Hooghly River.

He found that she was five foot two and weighed exactly one hundred pounds. They walked close together, and as he listened to her voice he knew his love for her was growing with each step.

They passed the Lenin Club, decorated with the hammer-and-sickle flags. Loo told him the radio broadcasters in China were all women, that the old silk route had gone through Yenan, that educated Chinese men seldom did manual labor, that the area in its seasons grew wheat, highland barley, millet, oilseeds, melons, corn, silk, flax, and cotton, that camels and sheep provided wool for clothing, that the country people were called *lao-pai-hsing*.

Many of the peasants, turning to look closely at him, had motioned to the leather patch sewn on the back of his A2 jacket. He smiled, knowing that in various Asian dialects it said, "This is an American friend. He is helping fight the Japanese. Help him in any way you can." Most of the American servicemen in the CBI theater wore the patch to help them if they parachuted from stricken airplanes and landed among natives. The patch was to serve as a ransom note, along with a "blood chit" they carried in a pocket which spelled out how the ransom was to be paid if the natives returned the American unharmed.

He looked at the animated, pleasant faces, all so alike and so unalike at the same time. He felt at ease among the Chinese, so different from when he had been among them in Chungking, Kunming, and other southern China cities and villages. He knew he was changing concepts and perceptions, and enjoyed the feeling. He looked with interest at a long line of tufted camels from the desert. "Everyone looks healthy," he said. "I haven't seen any starving people yet." They arrived at a hilltop where he could see the still-green fields beyond the buildings and the deep gulches and arroyos between the brown hills. "They must be able to get enough food around here."

"The *pa lu*s are all farmers," she said. "They help in the fields.

Food is not a serious problem, although we always need more of it. What we need are big guns, more trucks, airplanes with bombs, the kind of equipment that has been given to the Nationalists.'' They passed what looked like an outdoor stage.

"I won't argue," he said. "That's what our mission was trying to do. General Stilwell wanted to bring the Red Army under his command. Look where it got him. Recalled.''

"Chairman Mao will find a way to win this war.''

Carr swung his eyes to her, seeing her ivory complexion turned pinkish by the January cold. She had her hands thrust deep into the pockets of the padded blue jacket, which hung over the padded pants. She wore the peaked cap with the red star on it. "Colonel McHugh told me about Chairman Mao," he said. "We talked for hours after that meeting. I understand Mao was born in 1893 in Hunan province. That makes him fifty-two years old. He attended a police school, worked in a soap factory, took a law course for a while, but educated himself by reading at a library in the province.''

"Oh, he graduated from a provincial normal school," Loo said. "In 1918, he went to Peking and was an assistant librarian there for about a half year. Then he went back to Hunan. He organized a group who opposed the Japanese, mostly students, workers, and merchants. He even had his own newspaper. But the Hunan governor got mad at him, and he went back to Peking. In 1923, I think it was, he was elected to the Central Committee of the Chinese Communist Party. Did you know his first wife was murdered by the Nationalists? And that the governor of Sinkiang ordered his two brothers to be executed?''

Carr had not known those facts. They had made a circuitous sweep of Yenan and stood near the pagoda. "Look," he said, "I'm wearing thin with all this politics. Hell, I don't understand the politics back home.'' He moved closer to her. "Let's get back to us. How are we going to work this out?''

"I did not sleep last night.'' Her voice was very low. "I worried about us.''

"Can't we just talk to your grandfather?''

"No!'' She moved a few feet away from him. "They took him to the hospital this morning. They say he might have pneumonia. He does not feel well.'' She looked around with darting glances.

"We cannot do anything now. You know he admires you and respects you. Chairman Mao himself told you that. But you are an American. Your country supports Chiang Kai-shek. Grandfather is a rock-hard Communist and will never approve my marriage to you!" She was almost shouting the last words.

"Hey," he said, uneasy. "I know you said they frown on Chinese women marrying foreigners. I was hoping he'd see things different, now that we got to Yenan."

"Now that we are here, do you see things differently?" She looked at him with eyes that held a serious expression.

"Damn it, Loo! I haven't changed. I meant what I said. I love you and I want to marry you!"

Her expression softened. "I worried about that all last night." She smiled. "Perhaps it was a letdown after the meeting with Chairman Mao."

"I've been worried, too. Here's what I've come up with. Can you talk your grandfather into sending you back to the university at Calcutta?"

She thought about that. "We can see each other from time to time, then when the war is over we can be together?"

"That's the point. You know they're fighting to open the Burma–Ledo Road. When that happens, more American supplies will get through. Who knows, maybe my government will find a way to work with the Red Army. All things are possible. But if you're here in Yenan and I'm in Myitkyina or some damn place in south China, we'll have a hell of a time getting together. It would be much better if you were in Calcutta."

They turned at the sound of running feet. Carr saw an enlisted man, a corporal, coming toward them. "Sergeant Carr!" the youth said, breathing hard. "I'm Corporal Broward. They want you back at the Dixie headquarters right away!"

They hurried back with him. Carr said, "I saw you last night at the back of the auditorium. You an interpreter?"

"Sure. But I work with Lieutenant Dillon in radio ops."

"How come you speak Chinese?"

"My mother is Chinese. My dad was in the Marines. Stationed at Peking. That's where they met. He put in his twenty and my kid sister and they live in San Francisco."

"What's up?"

"Radio really came alive, Sergeant. The Nationalists are moving troops along the blockade area." They reached the hill-cave headquarters, noting the frantic sounds of bugles in the army area and the sight of soldiers running in different directions. It was obvious the Red Army was on an alert.

Captain Beard greeted them. "It's started," he said. "The oldest trick in the world. A diversion. Come on in." He led them into the large cave room where the mission had its headquarters. Pointing to a map on the whitewashed wall, he said, "The Nationalists are bombin' Red Army installations along this front. They're movin' their blockade troops and bringin' up others."

"A diversion?" Carr said. "The idea is to stir up the Communists so their agents here can carry out the kidnap plot?"

"That could be it, Sergeant."

"What are they doing here to protect the chairman and the others?"

"That's their business. We're stayin' out of it." Beard looked at Loo. "I wanted you both back here out of sight. We're goin' to hunker down and mind our business. We don't want those snatch guys pullin' us into this."

"What do you want me to do?"

"We've got a lot of our own radio traffic to handle. I want you to go with Corporal Broward. You can help Lieutenant Dillon with the radio work. Christ! We don't have enough men here to run a proper military establishment." He motioned for them to sit on the rough wooden benches. The room was extremely primitive. One map on the wall detailed the Japanese "Ichigo" offense, started the previous year to eliminate the U.S. air bases in central and southern China, an offense that had shown how weak the Nationalists forces were in protecting them. Many of the bases had been blown up by Americans before they fell into Japanese hands. There were silhouettes of Japanese war planes, Franks, Nates, Oscars, Bettys, and the Zero-Sen Type OO, know as the "Zero." Sidearms hung on pegs driven into the wall. Beard sat down heavily. "We've got big troubles everywhere," he said. "Take the Burma–Ledo Road. The Chinese started it in 1937. It was to be the Yunnan–Burma Highway from Kunming in China to Lashio in Burma, where it would connect with the railroad that runs south to Rangoon.

"The Burma Road runs seven hundred and seventeen miles.
You've been over it many times, Sergeant. It crosses the Salween,
Mekong, and Yangpi rivers. It opened in about 1939. The British
closed it a few years later when the war started. Of course, the Japs
have done what they could to keep it closed, to prevent Chiang
from gettin' war supplies after they occupied all of his ports."

Carr looked at the map that showed the Burma–Ledo Road area.
"With it closed, we had to start the air flights over the Hump.
We've lost hundreds of airplanes and men over that Hump between
Burma and India and China. Is something big going on at the
road?"

Beard was solemn. "Dispatches say the Chinese Y force is
movin' in on the Salween front in southwestern China. The Chinese Ninth Division is fightin' at the town of Wanting on the road.
That's right on the China-Burma border. If they take it, the Burma–
Ledo Road will be open."

"Hey, that's great," Carr said. "It would mean the lessening of
the dangerous Hump flights for our guys."

"The Chinese Thirty-eighth Division with armor and artillery is
movin' in to help the Y Force. If they can do that, they will link the
Ledo Road to the Burma Road and we've got another ballgame."

"You said big troubles?" Carr noticed that Loo was listening intently to Beard.

"Japanese forces are attackin' the area around Swatow. That's
above Hong Kong. Apparently they want to reopen the Hankow-
Canton Railroad. They're movin' against the Siuchan and our
Fourteenth Air Corps base at Namyung and the one at Kanchow. In
November, as you know, we had to blow up our base at Kweilin
when the Japs advanced on it under the Ichigo campaign. We lost
our fields at Lingling, Hengyang, and Liuchow."

Carr had heard most of this. "With all the big Jap attacks," he
said, "why is Chiang Kai-shek moving his armies against the
Communists? Why the hell doesn't he throw them at the Japs?" He
felt his hatred of the KMT flare up.

"I'll ask him when I see him," Beard said easily. "Right now,
we're in heavy radio traffic with our people in Chungking,
Kunming, Myitkyina, Hastings Mill and you name it."

"Do you believe in this kidnap plot?"

Beard looked at Carr steadily and then at Loo, who sat at Carr's side. "I believe there's a chance they'll try it. Dean and I both feel that the Kempetai is really behind it. The Japs are the ones who would benefit most." He grinned at Loo. "There's an old American expression, always look for the buck. In any confidence game, and war is the biggest con game of all, particularly in intelligence, you have to look for who gets the buck and who loses it. If they could pull off the snatch, the Japs would get the buck. It would keep the Chinese fightin' the Chinese and make it a hell of a lot easier for them."

Carr agreed. "I still want to see that guy on the motorcycle. If he's Chinese, then I'm a dumb ass. If he's Jap, then he's part of the plot."

"Colonel Wu was in a while ago. He believes your story. He's got a house-to-house search goin'."

"So he said at breakfast." Carr thought of the officer, then decided that he had been overly sensitive about the man's good looks, Chinese-style, in the presence of Loo.

"Wu is a smart cookie," Beard said. "He told me Chiang has lost two hundred and fifty thousand men in the last few months. When Chiang's armies lose, the Japs move in and the Commies follow to organize underground guerrilla resistance to the Japs and to Chiang." Beard tugged at an ear. "On one hand the Commies are brilliant. They're winnin' people and Chiang is losin' them. On the other hand, the Commies have no air force and don't understand one. They don't know how to use artillery. Their radio setups are patchwork nets of captured Japanese and KMT units. They steal telephone wire from the Japs and string it up for themselves. They don't have scoutin' parties and patrols for intelligence work, not like the Western countries have. They get their information from the village people, and believe me, they know what's goin' on every moment in the Jap and KMT areas. It's unbelievable!"

Carr voiced a question that had been at the front of his mind. "Sir, you figure they're going to come out on top?"

A faint shrug. "Who knows? Nobody thought the Russian revolution would last. They thought Marx and Lenin were crazy. Yet there's Russia, red as all hell. I'll only say that the Commies have a better grip on what the people want. Chiang is powerful as long as his armies support him. If the Japs withdraw, and eventually they'll have to, I don't know who will take over. I lean toward the Commies."

Carr liked Beard. No rank was being pulled. There was no posturing in front of Loo. The man was a competent professional, a credit to the OSS operation. "The Jap Grand Fleet was knocked out in October at Leyte Gulf," he said. "MacArthur is in the Philippines. The Japs are being ground down."

Beard looked up at the maps. "There are still a hell of a lot of them in China, Burma, Thailand, Indochina, those Pacific islands out there. The war is far from over."

Carr went to another level. "When we walked around Yenan Loo showed me the schools they've got here. Political schools, military schools, one for doctors, one for nurses. This K'ang-Ta University here had three thousand students."

Beard glanced casually at Loo. "Yeah, they're gettin' ready for the takeover. They're good at gettin' money. They put the heavy squeeze on landlords and the rich Chinese. In some ways they're as brutal as the Kuomintang."

"The rich must be made to pay," Loo said, her eyes smoldering under narrowed lids. "For too long they have impoverished our people!"

Beard laughed. "I knew that would get a rise out of you, Miss Ho," he said. "I wasn't being snotty. Just a statement of fact. I don't know any rich Chinese, anyway. You're right. They got rich by squattin' on the little people."

She couldn't stay irritated. She liked Beard, too. "Look," Beard said, "what Chairman Mao is doin' is gatherin' all the resources he can get, from the landlords, the warlords, what's left of them, and the rich intelligentsia. He's tryin' to root out what Confucius started and change two thousand years of the way you Chinese do business. He wants to start a new China. It's like I said, I'm leanin' to the feeling that eventually he'll pull it off."

"He will," she stated flatly.

"That's what makes me so sick," Beard said. "The United States should be on top of this great movement. If China changes, we ought to be able to change with it. God, this China is big! It has great resources. There are oil fields north of here. Minerals, coal. We're blowin' our best chance to make an alliance with the Chinese Communists, one that would pay off for decades to come."

Carr fidgeted on his bench. "After General Hurley was unable to bring about a truce between Mao and Chiang, and after your mission here has been so unproductive because of General Stilwell's recall and the fight between General Hurley and General Wedemeyer, the prospects don't look good."

Beard got up, stretching his arms roofward. "They sure as hell don't. Colonel Wu and the others have given me some strong hints. The chairman now feels that he's got to go it alone. How can he trust the United States when they turn down his offer to go to Washington and meet with President Roosevelt? When he looks at the fiasco of General Hurley tryin' to bring Yenan and Chungking together to fight the Japs. He doesn't trust the Russians, either. He knows they'd try to take China away from him."

Carr and Loo stood. They had opend their jackets in the warmth of the cave headquarters room. He found it difficult not to stare at her breasts pushing strongly against the shirt she wore under the jacket. If Beard had noticed, he'd hidden his reaction very well. "I don't blame the chairman," Carr said. "The British brought opium into China. All the foreign nations have taken chunks of this land. Loo told me this morning that Russia grabbed Siberia and part of Central Asia about a hundred years ago. France took Vietnam back in 1885. Then the British took Burma that same year and Japan took Korea in 1895." He looked at Loo. "Am I right on those dates?"

"Yes. Chairman Mao does not trust white men anymore. They have done nothing to help the people of the Middle Kingdom." Her words were matter-of-fact, uncolored with emotion.

"If Mao wins," Carr said, "look at how he can push the white man around. There are four hundred and fifty million people here. We have a hundred and thirty million in the United States. Russia has two hundred million. He'll outman us. Can't they see that in Washington?"

Beard smiled. "I forget you're not long out of college. Give or take a few million, you're right. China is bound to come out of this different than when Japan invaded it. That's why the U.S. supported Chiang. First to keep the Japs from takin' China and second to have China as its friend when the Japs are kicked out."

"Well," Carr said, "here it is, January 1945. We've been at

war with Japan since December 7, 1941. We've been backing Chiang, but Mao is winning China."

Someone came through the tunnel. It was Fraser Dillon. "Sir," he said. Seeing Loo and deciding to be formal, he saluted, a rare thing with the Dixie Mission. "Two things. The courier plane is coming early tomorrow morning. The weather between here and Chungking is improving and they got the Gooney Bird fixed up." He moved toward Beard. "The second is this message from Captain Karras at Myitkyina."

Beard took the coded dispatch. "Stand down," he said, "until I get this deciphered." He pulled the code book from a pocket and sat at the sawhorse desk. In a few minutes he had it unscrambled. He read the penciled notes. "Oh, sweet Jesus!" he said. They waited. He looked up at them. "The Yoke Force and the Chinese Ninth have taken Wanting from the Japs. The first truck convoy made it through from Myitkyina to Kunming. The Burma Road is open!"

Carr slapped his hands together. "Hey, great!" Loo grabbed his arm in happiness. Dillon smiled broadly.

"Remember this date," Beard said. "January 20, 1945—that's when the road was opened. Now the Hump flights can be helped by the Red Ball truck express." He looked at Carr. "Somethin' here for you. Your commandin' officer has named you for a temporary field promotion. Your orders are comin' on the courier plane. You are now a second lieutenant in the U.S. Army Air Corps!"

They shook Carr's hand, seeing his unbelieving expression. "That is wonderful!" Loo said at his side. She did a little shuffle of joy.

"They better send some bars along," Beard said. "We don't have any extra ones here."

"Yes, we do," Dillon said. "I saved my old ones when I made first. I think I know where they are." He left and returned in minutes. Beard pinned them on Carr's collar. "Not much of a ceremony," he said with a salute, which Carr returned in embarrassment, "but it will have to do. Colonel McHugh really should do it, but why wait? I said we're not a proper military establishment."

There was another sound in the tunnel. Corporal Broward came in, out of breath. "Sir," he said, "Chinese net is exploding. The

Nats are really moving in. Heavy bombing all along the block-ade." He glanced quickly at Carr. "They got a description of the guy on the motorcycle from a village south of here and a patrol that stopped him earlier."

"Wu has it?" Beard said.

"He sure has, sir. It's being circulated to the patrols doing the house-to-house search."

Beard pointed a finger at Carr. "Lieutenant, it's almost noon. Time for a celebration lunch on your promotion. Then you can join Dilly and Corporal Broward in the radio room." He grinned in pleasure. "And we wouldn't think of openin' a bottle of Chinese wine to celebrate unless your interpreter was with us."

On the way to the guesthouse, Beard drew Carr back as the others walked on ahead. "Now that you're an officer, even a tem-porary one, I can first-name you. Have you got somethin' goin' with this girl, Doug?"

Carr squinted. "Damn! Does it show that much?"

"Every time you look at her." Beard plodded along next to Carr, looking often at the hurried troop movements going on around them. "What the hell happened to the two of you in those mountains?"

Carr decided on honesty. "We fell in love. If we can pull it off, we're going to be married."

Beard whistled softly. "You know the problem with these Reds up here?"

"We both know it."

"Ho Ling-chi sits on the Central Committee of the Chinese Communist Party. There's a wad of the party Politburo here in Yenan for meetings. You'll have to be damned careful. Where are her folks?"

Carr told him about Ho Li-san and Ch'en. He remembered what Loo had said about her mother. "She died about eight years ago. They didn't know it, but she had heart trouble. She died in her sleep one night."

"So she's all alone except for her grandfather?" Beard looked at Loo striding ahead of them. "She's beautiful. But gettin' hitched to a Chinese woman carries its problems, Doug. I'm sure you know that. You'll have a hassle with our people to boot."

"I know." Carr watched Loo, pleased with her upright posture despite the shapeless garments she wore. He thought of her at the cave, naked on the straw mat. He thought of her lips when she'd kissed him, the touch of her hand on his.

"If I have to shoot my way out of here with her, I will," he said grimly.

Beard grunted as he stubbed a toe on a rock sticking out of the thick loess dust in which they walked. "There goes your field promotion, Doug. Take it easy."

"Just an expression. I want the promotion. I won't mess it up. I only mean I intend to find a way to get her out of Yenan and marry her when this damned war is over."

Beard brightened. "That's better. I know how I felt when I first met my Helen. I couldn't eat or sleep for weeks. From what I've seen of your Loo, she's worth the trouble you'll have to go through."

A worrisome question struggled up through Carr's mind. "I almost forgot. The things I brought from the wreck. What will you do with them?"

Beard was surprised. "Damn, I should have told you. They'll go back to Chungking on the Gooney Bird tomorrow. The personal effects will then go to Myitkyina to be put with what they left there. Then everythin' goes back to their folks in the States."

"Thanks," Carr said. "That makes me feel better."

They entered the guesthouse behind Loo, Corporal Broward, and Lieutenant Dillon. Most of the other members of the American Military Observer Group, the Dixie Mission, were waiting for them. Wine bottles were on the table, ready for the celebration.

"Word sure gets around," Beard said, reaching for a bottle. He opened it and poured it into glasses. "Here's to you, Lieutenant Carr, and whatever lies ahead for you and yours." He winked at Carr.

Carr grinned at Loo and the others.

"I'll drink to that!"

Renya Oshima had remained hidden in a secret room dug under the floor of Yang's building. During the long day he had tried to keep his emotions in check as he listened to the Chinese workers in the metal shop over his head. The machines ran constantly, giving him a headache. Dust filtered down through unseen cracks, making his breathing difficult. A small pipe leading to a concealed place outside the building gave him just enough air.

He had fruit and bread, which he ate in disgust and washed down with a jar of boiled water. The underground room, dug into the rich loess soil, had only a sawhorse bed covered with a straw mat. His flashlight, which Yang had warned him to use sparingly, was his only light. While he had been able to nap from time to time, the enforced stay in the little room was painful to him.

When the machines stopped, he heard the shuffle of feet on the wooden floor above. The workday was over. Despite the January cold, the room was warm. He had removed most of his clothes. He swept the thin layer of dust from his arms and head. It seemed an eternity until the trapdoor of the hidden room was pulled up and Yang, wearing the felt hat, peered down at him. He helped Yang replace the door after a ladder was lowered to him. He put on his clothes in the sudden chill of the workshop. He smoothed dirt over the trapdoor to reconceal it.

"What do they do with those machines?" Oshima said. "The noise all day long was deafening!"

"We repair rifles for the army," Yang said, leading the way to the living quarters. "Parts for trucks, although they have few here. Parts for generators. They allow us to have electricity for the machines. Parts for radios, machine guns, that sort of thing. Whatever needs drilling, boring, machining, shearing, cutting, soldering, or welding. We are one of a dozen units that do this work. It is essential. That is one of the reasons I have such a high security clearance." Yang's teeth showed as he smiled. "This shop was my father's cover. Now it is mine. That's one. The other is that I serve Colonel Wu in military intelligence."

Oshima was shaken. Military intelligence? He looked at Yang with new respect. The man was enormously capable. He watched as Yang fetched two wine bottles from a dilapidated cabinet with a padlock, into which he put a key. "Where are we now?" he asked.

"We are very near the end, my friend," Yang said. "The name of Honda will be brightened by what we do here in the next few hours."

Oshima took the cup, waiting for the wine to be heated over a small burner, which Yang had lit with a match. "I want to know everything." He still did not believe the man was a Honda.

When the wine was warm Yang filled their cups. "Not sake, my friend, but it will do. A toast to Emperor Hirohito!" They drank to that. "A toast to my father's friend, Lieutenant General Takahashi, commander of our forces in Central China."

They drank to Takahashi. "Why to him?" Oshima asked.

"It was his good word that prompted General Tashiro to place me in the Kempetai, to work with my father here."

"But if you are related to General Honda, why was that necessary?"

Yang glowered over the edge of his raised cup. "My father was placed here to watch the Communists. I was raised in China. There were those in Tokyo who questioned my loyalty because I have not been in Japan since I was three years old. With the help of General Takahashi, long before he became a general, I was secretly trained by Kempetai agents in China. Oh, we had difficulty finding ways for my study, but we arranged it. And a good word from him made it possible for me to become part of General Tashiro's Kempetai operations up here."

Oshima sipped his wine. He sat down, as did Yang, on a mat, cross-legged. He faced Yang. "Your family will be most honored." He guessed Yang was in his middle thirties.

"And your family will be honored by our exploits here," Yang said, showing teeth. "Let us talk, and then I will fix us a warm meal. I have thought about you all day. The fact that you made it here annoyed me at first. You left a trail a blind man could follow. All of Yenan is looking for you. But I see possibilities in your help."

"I will do what you command."

"Yes, kill the Americans. That will please me very much."

"Specifically, the one I followed here."

"Especially him. I was at a meeting last night. They treat that miserable American cur as if he were a hero. He is in the company of the granddaughter of Ho Ling-chi. She serves him as an interpreter. He is a very important man in Yenan. Even more outrageous, the fool received a field promotion. He was a master sergeant in their Air Corps. Now he is a second lieutenant."

That disappointed Oshima. "The son of a prostitute!"

"Now for the situation." Yang leaned forward. "You know they search for you. They will not look here because I am of the secret police myself. No one knows about that room below. My father and I dug it out ourselves, after my mother died five years ago. We have concealed others there.''

"How do you plan to carry out the kidnapping of the Communist leaders?'' Oshima said. ''What is the timing? How am I to get near the Americans without being caught? How do you plan for us to escape with the leaders?''

Yang's teeth showed again. They were long and very white. ''In the morning, very early, a courier plane arrives from the American base at Chungking. It will bring supplies and dispatches for the Americans. Then it will return.'' He paused for effect.

Oshima thought about it. ''You mean to place Mao, Chou, and General Chu on that plane?'' He was incredulous. ''How can that be done?''

"Listen to me,'' Yang said. ''Yenan has many underground tunnels. They are for safety in air raids and for quick access to different places. I know them all. Our Kempetai officers in Chungking duped the Kuomintang into believing the Red Army is preparing to move across the blockade and break out. The Kuomintang idiots are attacking at the blockade points. Then our officers convinced the Red Army that the Kuomintang means to break into their territory and force a disastrous battle with them.''

Oshima felt a surge of elation. ''Then they are at each other's throats!''

"At this moment the fighting is very heavy. It has been so all day long. They are moving troops around here like they are insane. The Americans will be forced to bring the courier plane in with information for their people here.'' Yang's crafty smile was enormous.

Oshima held out his empty cup. Yang filled it. ''The tunnels. What have they to do with the kidnapping of the Chinese leaders?''

"For years, my friend, we have been digging tunnels of our own. We have only to break through a place here, a place there, and we are at where they live. One tunnel goes directly to the wall behind where the Americans are quartered.'' His lips curled. ''Break through, and you are in their midst. No one will see you arrive there. You will go by tunnel.''

"And you?''

"I will be with other men, doing the same with Mao, Chou, and

General Chu. They will be moved, but I will know where. They will be greatly surprised!"

"But how do we get to the landing field? To the American plane? Won't that be dangerous?" Oshima bent forward in sheer confusion. The wine and the excitement of the conversation were too much for him. He knew he was trembling and couldn't stop it. "There are bound to be guards at their homes, with the battles going on and with everyone on full alert. We must be well armed. All I have is my Mauser. How do we get to the plane? And when we do, how do we force it to fly to Chungking? And if we get to Chungking, how do we explain yourself and me? What about the men who serve you?"

Yang sat relaxed, holding his wine cup. "We have all the weapons we need. You will have your pistol and a knife. We will use a gas weapon that renders them senseless. You will wear a mask that protects you. I will instruct you about the tunnels. We will all move in precision. Timing is vitally important. We have men who will drive a vehicle. They will meet us at an exact time in all locations. There will be bombs exploding all over Yenan. They have already been placed with timing devices. Another great diversion. We are to arrive at the landing strip at a time when the plane has landed and is being unloaded and refueled."

Yang pulled a sheet from his pocket. "Here, I have written it all down for you. Study it while I prepare our food. Then we will go over the entire project step by step until it is burned in your mind. We even have something planned for Miss Ho."

He smiled darkly. "Tomorrow will be a day that Kempetai men will honor in the years of history ahead!"

Oshima's hand trembled so much the wine spilled.

He realized Yang had not answered all of his questions.

CHAPTER TEN

Carr, tossing sleeplessly on the straw tick atop the kang in his cave room, heard the small creak of the tunnel door being opened.

He tensed and reached for the flashlight and the .45 automatic, swinging his bare legs out onto the floor. He flicked on the light. Loo was in its beam. She wore a soldier's uniform with leg wrappings. A rifle was slung across her back, almost as tall as she. Her hair was piled up under the shapeless cap with its red star.

She motioned for him to turn off the light. He did, and he heard her undressing. She came over, pushing him back in the dark onto the bed, a thick wide board propped up on cement blocks. He shoved the .45 into its holster hanging from a nail driven into the board.

"If they find out I have done this, they will banish me," she whispered. She cuddled next to him, and his hands ran down her smooth, silky body.

"My God," he whispered in turn, "how did you manage it?"

"Colonel Wu knows of my feeling for you. He brought me the uniform and rifle. That way I could move around without attracting attention."

"Wu?" He didn't like it. "Maybe he's trying to trap us."

She giggled. "No. He is a romantic. He has a lovely wife of his own. He has learned much from Colonel McHugh and Captain Beard. He now regards you as a much worthy person. He was impressed with what you said at breakfast."

"How will you get back to where you're staying?"

"There are soldiers moving about all over the place. No one will look at one more. My grandfather is in the hospital, and I am staying with a group of women in a large cave dormitory. They will not talk.'' She told him where it was, very close by.

Her arms were around him, and he stopped his mind to concentrate on her breathtaking closeness. They made love, easily and noiselessly, rocking the board perilously on its perches. When their breathing was regular again, he said, ''I want to see you.''

She pressed a hand over his eyes in the dark. ''Let's save that until we are alone again.''

''I'm sorry about your grandfather. Did you have a chance to speak to him about going back to Calcutta?''

''Yes. I saw him at the hospital. He believes the war will go on for years with the Kuomintang. He wants me to go back to the university and complete my studies, as my father wished.'' A note of sadness entered her voice. Her lips were near his ear, her words soft and mesmerizing. ''He made arrangements for me to leave this day on your courier plane. I believe he feels he will not live long. Colonel McHugh at his request, sent by Colonel Wu, will have the pilots drop me off at Chengtu, where I will talk to the British and return with them on one of their flights to Calcutta.''

He held her tightly, her hair flowing in his face, his hands alive with the sensation of her warm body. ''That is why you came!'' He kissed her long and hard, floating in the softness of her lips, thinking of ripe strawberries, wanting to savor the feeling for a very long time. ''When I was working in radio ops,'' he said, ''I talked to Lieutenant Dillon. He expects the mission to be canceled at any time. The battles at the blockade will delay it for a while, but the mission seems to be on its last legs.''

He stroked her hair, smelling the faint aroma of soap from it. ''I've done more than my time over here. Well over a thousand Hump hours. The lieutenant feels I might be rotated home.''

He felt her strong, lithe body stiffen in his arms. ''You would go to the United States?''

''No. I think I've got a lever to pull. That's my connection with Chairman Mao and your grandfather.'' He kissed her cheek, his voice low and reassuring. ''I've been thinking of you all night. It played hell with my sending and receiving, but I got the job done. They didn't relieve me until two o'clock. The people we report to are very concerned that we don't become involved in this stupid kidnap plot. There were a lot of messages.'' He let out a belly-deep breath. "What I hope to do is get assigned to some job at Hastings Mill."

"That is near Calcutta!" she whispered delightedly.

"I've been lying here trying to figure this thing out. Before I met you, Loo, all I thought about was flying. Now I've got to start thinking about my future and yours with me. Take the field promotion. They didn't give it to me because I'm a damned good radio/radar operator. They want to use me. It's my one good chance. If I play it right, I can make a deal with them. Even if this mission is kicked out, they'll need men like me, McHugh, Beard, Dillon, and the others to maintain some kind of contact with the Red Army." He nipped at her earlobe. "Now that I've found you, I've got to think about what happens during the rest of the war and afterward. I want to be something more than a flier."

She kissed him, a long sensuous embrace. "You've just got to be assigned to Hastings Mill. It would be wonderful. Both of us in Calcutta!"

"For the first time in my life, I'm beginning to see what responsibility really means. When we go home, if we go to the States, I want to set up a dealership. That means I would sell farm equipment. I've got an ag engineering degree. I know I can do well in that area, with my father's reputation behind me. Harry Carr is the best farmer in those parts. Or I could take over the farm and the one next to it. You'll love my mother. Her name's Ethel." He stopped, thinking. "If we stay in China, I can fly a plane, or I can be in communications."

He felt her full breasts, the nipples hard against his palm. "You keep one thing in mind," he said, "no matter what happens. I love you and I want you. Always remember that!"

She ran a hand over his stomach. "I didn't know you had such hard muscles. You have no fat at all." She giggled. "I tell myself I'm crazy. I'm in love with a white man. I can't believe it!" She pulled at the hair on his chest.

"I don't believe you," he said. "I don't believe anyone as little as you could be so perfect for me. You're a beautiful Chinese woman, and when you talk I feel as if I'm with an English princess."

Her voice was muffled in his arms, held tight around her. "I ask myself, why am I so attracted to a tall American with blond hair and blue eyes. Why am I not in love with someone of my own race? But in Calcutta I saw many Americans and many British, many other white men. I tell myself I have become cosmopolitan. I no longer am a little girl from Kunming.''

"How much of a problem will it be, adjusting to a capitalist?''

She sighed. "They have Communists in the United States?''

"They have. But it's like having capitalists in China. No one likes them very much if they're bang noisy about it.''

"Then they won't like me.''

"You're different. A Chinese Communist isn't like a Russian Communist. You're not trying to overthrow our government.''

"We can work it out,'' she said emphatically. "I'll make a Communist out of you.''

"Either that, or you'll make an American out of yourself.''

She sat up. "Turn on your light just to see your watch. What time is it?''

"A little past three-thirty.'' He clicked off the light, but not before he had seen the delightful brown of her taut nipples, the graceful swell of her breasts, the tantalizing curves of her body.

"I must leave!'' He heard her dressing in the dark, making sharp Chinese sounds as she got into the unfamiliar clothes and leg wrappings. He waited until he heard the sound of the rifle being picked up. He groped for her and his arms went around her. "I'll be at the field to wave goodbye to you,'' he said. "This kiss has got to last us a long time.'' He held her, feeling an immense loneliness. "Never forget, I love you, Loo.''

"And I love you! Will you find me? The university will have my address. I live with distant relatives. They will be shocked. But we can charm them into understanding us.''

"You know I'll find you, no matter where you are.''

They kissed again and she was gone. He heard the wooden door with its paper window creak again, and a cold draft made him get back quickly under the cover.

"Loo,'' he said to the silent walls in the darkness, "I love you!''

General Chu Teh, exhausted from the long hours in the command center, sat limply in a high-backed wood and bamboo chair in the emergency cave room, staring moodily at the flickering candle on the table before him.

His mind went over the battle orders, the long discussions with his aides, the flood of dispatches from the blockade area. He thought again of the kidnap story. He, Ambassador Chou, and Chairman Mao had been secretly moved from their regular homes to three adjoining cave rooms in a maze of such rooms dug well into the hillside. Only the most trusted people knew where they were. Outside, concealed guards protected the entrances.

He resisted the impulse to go again to the radio center, to learn how things were going. A night battle was being waged in three areas along the blockade. He had moved his men well—the 18th Group Army, the 8th Route Army, the people's militia—and he was satisfied that they would blunt the Kuomintang attacks. Still, there were nagging thoughts about the lack of air power for daylight retaliation, the lack of heavy guns to strike the enemy from a distance. The Americans, their Dixie Mission had reported, were attempting to pressure Chiang Kai-shek into stopping the assault and move his armies into areas where they could fight the Japanese. He knew their efforts would be fruitless.

He glanced at the bed, too tired to remove his uniform and get under the cover. His ears picked up a strange sound. It seemed to be coming from the far wall of the cave room. Perhaps his weariness was playing a trick on him.

Then a hole appeared in the wall. A hand reached through the hole, pushing the loess dirt away to enlarge it. He started to rise, seeing a large-barreled weapon being thrust through the hole. A massive pop and a hissing sound came. He was enveloped in a thin white gas.

He struggled to his feet. The last thing he saw was a face peering through the hole, an awesome sight of a black mask with lumimous eyes and a tube running where the nose should be.

Then he crumpled to the block-stone floor of the secret cave room.

Ambassador Chou En-lai awoke to the sound of digging as he lay on his bed.

He rose, lighted a lantern in the little cave room, and put on his wool-lined brown leather greatcoat. He slipped into his shoes and went to the far wall where the noise was coming from. He cocked his head, wondering who could be digging so late at night.

He was startled when a four-foot-square section of the wall burst outward before his eyes. A man stood behind the opening, a man wearing a gas mask with a long tube running to a canister at the waist.

Chou turned to escape to the tunnel. Something whizzed by him and exploded on the wall near the tunnel. He staggered, reaching for the wall to support himself. His fingers dug into the whitewashed loess and he slid toward the floor.

He felt hands reaching for him. He knew he was being lifted. He tried to cry out. Blackness came as his body reacted to the gas with frantic convulsions.

Chairman Mao Tse-tung watched somberly as the last of the political advisers left the overly large secret cave room.

He reached for a cigarette, then decided against it. He had smoked enough and the night was nearly gone. He thought of Chou in the room next to him, and of Chu Teh in the room next to Chou's. They were safe enough. So was his wife. She was away, fortunately, visiting a women's camp to the north. He would have a short sleep and return to the party headquarters for a breakfast meeting with his political and military staffs to make further decisions about the Kuomintang attacks.

He rose from his chair, looking at the sturdy kang which was to be his bed. He began unbuttoning his tunic, when a sound made him stop. It seemed to be a chipping sound. He looked around the large room, neatly whitewashed, the floor made carefully of fitted stone blocks. His greatcoat lay folded on the bed. The fairly long table had eight chairs, all of which had been filled during the night of interminable meetings. Where was the sound coming from?

A large knife came through the far wall, shocking him. It sliced up and down and across the wall, and loess dirt fell into the room, puffing immediately into a fine dust. He stared at the man stepping through the large hole, realizing the man held a strange weapon and wore a black gas mask.

He was going to be shot!

He moved quickly toward the man, trying to grapple with him, trying to get his hand on the weapon. It was raised, and he saw it flashing down at his head. He felt the terrible blow and his legs gave way. He tumbled backward, striking his shoulder with a jarring impact.

He saw another man, also wearing a gas mask, come through the opening. They moved toward him and he tried to rise, to fight. The nearest man raised the unusual weapon and fired it at the ceiling. A cloud of gas descended. Hands held him while he struggled. He breathed heavily, and a piercing sensation burst in his lungs.

He stared helplessly at the man kneeling over him until he entered a vast world of weird sounds of shrieking bugles and massively magnified cymbals.

Carr, finding sleep an impossibility after Loo had left, had gotten up and was now dressed in his still-clean winter uniform.

He had one thing in mind, to see her as soon as it was light. He had thought it all out—what he would say to Dean McHugh and Chance Beard at breakfast. He wanted to find out if Loo could be given U.S. transportation from Chengtu to Calcutta. Ho Ling-chi had been wise not to try to route her through Chungking, the Nationalist's headquarters, where someone might spot her and arrest her as his granddaughter. Especially not with the blockade battles going on.

He walked around the small table with its tiny bench, looking at his personal effects under the candlelight. His issue .45, the old A2 jacket, his knives, flashlight, the alpaca-lined suit that had kept Ho warm in the mountains, his wallet, and the carbine. The Japanese weapons had been turned in to McHugh and Beard. He wondered about Moffett's pistol with the silencer, which Beard had accepted. It was probably an OSS issue. He had regretted turning over the pistol; it was a beautiful firearm, perfectly balanced.

He leaned against the far wall as he surveyed the spartan room in the light of the candle placed in a metal reflector holder. A windowless room with a fifteen-foot-long tunnel leading to the outside. How had the Dixie Mission men been able to stand them? They were airless boxes dug into the hills. He knew there were many hundreds of such rooms in Yenan, some huge, some connected by a labyrinth of tunnels. One he'd been shown was large enough to hold several hundred men in a meeting. The wood furniture was simple, heavily varnished.

He felt a small trembling in his shoulder. His first thought was an earthquake. Then he put his ear to the whitewashed wall. Someone with a shovel was on the other side! He unsheathed his Gurkha knife and pulled the automatic from its holster. He stuck his wallet in a hip pocket and the flashlight in the other and blew out the candle. He felt along the wall, sensing the digging movement behind the loess dirt. The chipping pressure on it was getting stronger.

The wall gave way almost under his fingers. He heard chunks of it fall to the floor. He moved silently to one side, the knife and the automatic ready. A flashlight clicked on, and the far end of the room was lighted by its circle. The beam played back and forth on the apparently empty room.

Carr heard a mumble. He saw the hand holding the flashlight, another holding a Mauser. He waited until the man had pushed himself further through the hole. He raised the knife and brought it down, jerking it out quickly. It had hit bone. There was a sharp cry, and Carr realized that the intruder wore a dust mask. He brought the automatic down on the hand that held the Mauser. A scream of pain from the mask.

Then the head and bloody shoulder disappeared from the hole. Carr dropped the knife, grabbed the flashlight, and turned it into the hole. He saw a dust-shrouded interior of an inverted V-shaped tunnel, and through the dust he saw the blurred shape of a man crawling away.

He pumped the .45 and fired down the tunnel. The sound echoed with a great booming. He stared down the tunnel. The man was gone. He reached in and found the Mauser, covered with loose silt. The man's flashlight was nearly alongside it, still on. He turned it off and examined it in the light of his own torch. It bore Chinese markings.

He grabbed his flight jacket and ran through the tunnel to the outside. It was dark. He raised the .45 and shot three times into the air. He ran to the entrance of the cave room where Dean McHugh made his home. "Colonel! Colonel! It's Carr!" He slipped into the jacket to ward off the cold.

Pa lus, carrying rifles, ran toward him. He turned his flashlight on himself to let them see him. Lieutenant Dillon burst out of his tunnel, holding a .45. Then Dean McHugh appeared, struggling to pull up his trousers. He carried a .38 pistol. "What the hell!" he shouted. "What's going on?"

Carr told him, and they all ran back into the cave room Carr had just left. They examined the hole in the wall, the V-shaped tunnel, the Mauser, and the Chinese flashlight. "Holy Christ!" McHugh said. "How come there's a tunnel back there? Whoever he was, that guy could have gotten into any of our rooms! That tunnel runs along the back of them all!"

"It had to be someone who knew the tunnel was there," Carr said. "It wasn't dug tonight. There's an army shovel over there. He knew exactly where to dig. There are wood pegs in the wall of the tunnel to mark where each room is located."

McHugh spoke in fluent Chinese to the *pa lus* milling around the room. Two of them left on the run. "I've sent for Colonel Wu," McHugh said. He wiped the loess dust from his face and hands. The room and long tunnel were filled with its misting particles. "I've asked them to find out where it comes out." Three of the small soldiers entered the tunnel and crawled down it. "Let's get out of here. This dust is killing me."

Outside in the night air, they waited for Wu. They peered into the darkness. The running soldiers had alerted others, and soon there was a large group with lanterns and pitch torches moving in and out of Carr's cave room. A battered jeep, captured months before from the Kuomintang, roared up. It had no muffler. Colonel Wu hopped out, and McHugh filled him in. Wu examined the hole and peered down the long tunnel. He cursed in Chinese and ran to shout orders to his men outside. In minutes there were sounds of bells all over Yenan, an alert, a call to stations. He came back to Carr, McHugh, and Dillon, and Sergeant Broward, who had come running with a rifle. Other members of the mission, some in robes, joined them. All were armed.

"This is most serious," Wu said, breathing heavily. "I must go and see if Chairman Mao, Ambassador Chou, and General Chu are safe. They were placed in secret homes for this night." McHugh translated.

Carr shouted to the back of Wu as the officer ran to the jeep. "How could that tunnel be built without your knowing about it?"

Wu shouted back and McHugh interpreted. "They were dug by our Japanese prisoners as an escape if more mud slides or bombing should close off the front tunnels!"

The earth shook slightly as explosions burst across the city. They raised their weapons in reflex and stared at the eerie bomb lights in the sky, hearing the massive echoes around Yenan hills. "Good God!" Dillon said.

Carr held up a hand. "No sound of airplanes. There was no incoming sound from artillery. Those were planted bombs."

McHugh lowered his pistol. "Another diversion. That means the kidnappers must have worked this thing out pretty damned close. I'll bet they got into other tunnels wherever our hosts were hidden."

"What the hell did Wu mean about the prisoners?" Carr said.

McHugh waved a hand around. "There was a great loss of life some years ago here when a rainstorm hit. The loess gave way in a massive landslide. People were entombed in a lot of the caves. They felt that a bombing would do the same thing. I guess what he meant was that the tunnels were supposed to be a secret. Used only in a dire emergency. I imagine the Japs who dug them are all dead."

"If the chairman and the others were in rooms like this," Carr said, "maybe there was a tunnel behind their rooms."

"More than a possibility. They would want to have a secret escape route for them above all." McHugh made an abrupt motion. "It's cold out here and it'll be light soon. I don't want some crazy Chinese shooting at us because we're white men. Come on into my place." He led the way inside. They were all too electrified to sit. They moved about aimlessly, packing the small room. "Doug," McHugh said, "did you get a look at the guy?"

"Not much. He had on a blue padded jacket. He wore a blue cap with a peak and had a dust mask over his face." Carr demonstrated at the wall how he had stabbed the man and knocked the Mauser loose. They watched him, fascinated.

"So we got a guy with a knife wound in his left shoulder and probably a broken right hand," McHugh said. "Corporal, try to get that information to Colonel Wu. And find out, if you can, where that tunnel came out. Dilly, get on the radio and tell Chungking . . ." His voice faded. "Oh, boy, what will we tell them?" Corporal Broward left quickly.

"That an attempt was made on my life," Carr said stoutly. "We don't know about the chairman and the others. You don't want the Kuomintang to even guess at it." He looked steadily at McHugh. "This is the kidnap plot. You're thinking that somehow they intend to pirate the Yenan-run plane and get them out that way."

"That's exactly what I'm thinking."

"You've got enough to abort the flight," Carr said. "It can be turned around." He glanced at his hack watch. "From what you told me last night, they had a night takeoff and will be here by daybreak. They're a good hour to an hour and a half out, unless they're looping around to avoid a battle at the blockade."

McHugh made the decision. "Dilly, put it in today's code. Tell Chungking that an attempt was made on Carr's life by an unknown assailant. Say the flight is to come in on schedule."

Carr understood the reason. "If the plane doesn't land, Mao, Chou, and Chu might be killed?" Dillon edged his way out.

"If they've been taken, yes," McHugh said dully. "The plane gives us a place to concentrate our power." McHugh looked around at them. "Unless it's a feint. They might have another way to get them out if, indeed, they were surprised the way Carr was." He swallowed. "The thing against that is Wu will have every road and footpath out of Yenan and south of here covered with patrols in one damned hurry."

"So we wait until we find out if the Commies are safe?" one of the men said.

"We can't go running around outside. It's unhealthy out there." McHugh squinted at the map behind the tightly clustered bodies. "It's a hell of a long way to the blockade area. If they have ground transport, they'd have a tough time getting through, with those battles going on. Maybe they've got another plane coming in right behind the courier. They could shoot down ours and come in on its pattern."

The weather ops officer said, "It's a C-47, Dean. Coming in in the dark. How can it be shot down by a bomber on its tail? It would have to be a bomber to get the Commies and the snatchers out of here.''

McHugh brushed a hand over his face. ''Jesus! It's got to get here. You guys split up. Two or three to a room. Armed. Nobody by himself, not even to the latrine. Stay put until I get word to you.'' They moved out slowly. He turned to Carr. ''Doug, that guy wasn't trying to kidnap you. He was going to kill you.''

''I know. My gut feeling is that it was the same son of a bitch that got here on the motorcycle.''

McHugh blinked, his eyes still bothered by the loess dust. ''If he knew where the tunnel was and just got here yesterday, he's sure as hell in on the kidnap plot.''

Carr lowered his shaking body onto a bench. It wobbled under him. ''If the Commies are safe, that's one story. If they've been taken, that's another.'' He blinked his own tired eyes and rubbed them. ''Why would he want to kill me?''

The silence built between them as their minds worked at the problem. Outside they heard running feet, and two soldiers came into the room. One of them spoke to McHugh in rapid Chinese. He responded. The soldiers turned and left.

''That's it,'' McHugh said, slumping. ''Wu sent word. Mao, Chou, and Chu are gone!''

Carr sagged on the bench, leaning in shock on the table. ''Oh, Christ!''

''They got in the same way. A hidden tunnel behind their secret cave rooms. They were gassed.''

''Gassed!''

''The kind that knocks you out. Their places were filled with the fumes. The first soldiers that ran in are out cold.''

Carr looked at the sputtering candle. ''It only happened a short time ago. The bomb blasts were meant to stir things up while they made the snatch. That means they're still in Yenan. To me, the courier plane is the key. It'll be here in an hour or so. How the hell can we catch them?''

''Wu will have thought about the plane,'' McHugh said. ''If he didn't, I told those men to tell him our thoughts on it, that we've ordered the plane to come in if at all possible, that he should have every inch of the airstrip covered.''

"You told him about the guy with the shoulder wound?"

"I did. Corporal Broward would have gotten that word to him. You bet he knows about it."

"He might be part of the key," Carr said. "He's wounded and he's new around here. He might have a tough time making their rendezvous. You know damned well they had a split-second scheme. They knew about the tunnels. They had access to secret information. They had nerve gas of some kind. That's exotic stuff around here. That's the kind of thing intelligence people use."

Carr leaned across the table. "There was a stage over by the drill ground. What's it used for?"

McHugh's eyes narrowed. "Oh, the stage. For *kai hwei*, mass massings. They put on plays there. Lots of actors around here. The Chinese love plays. I've been to a lot of them."

Carr straightened. "There's one way we can stop them at the airstrip," he said. "Let's gamble that the Commies are alive. The nerve gas tells us that. Otherwise there would have been blood all over. The snatchers are betting Wu and his men won't open fire, that their audacity will work at the field. I think I know how we can call their bet."

McHugh leaned forward to hear.

Renya Oshima, staggering in pain, holding the dirty cloth mask against his shoulder, had made it with seconds to spare.

On a narrow dirt road, five hundred yards from where he had crawled from the tunnel's exit concealed in the thick underbrush of the hillside, he had been lifted into the long, ugly, hearselike vehicle used often by Chairman Mao. It was, in a city where there were few vehicles, a familiar sight around Yenan. Left unguarded, it had been stolen in the hour before midnight. It was now being driven in a circuitous route to the airstrip.

"The soldiers were right behind me," he said to Yang Ju-tung, who was bending over him. He had applied a medical powder to the raw wound after cutting away the dirty blue cloth. The wound was covered with gauze and a wide band of tape. The hearse-van was crowded with six other men, one of whom held a flashlight to help Yang. Three motionless bodies lay together at the end far away from the door. They were covered with army blankets.

"The American knifed me," Oshima said through clenched

teeth as the vehicle bumped and skidded. "I think he broke my hand. He shot at me as I crawled out of the tunnel."

"He shot well, my friend," Yang said. "There is a hole in your jacket."

Oshima eyed the three forms in the light of the torch just before it was clicked off. "It went well for you." He turned to feel the pressure of a pistol at his head. He sucked in his breath.

"My Kempetai friend"—Yang said the last word with disgust—"you failed us. You were to kill the Americans. The Communists would never have been able to explain their deaths. They gave the alarm and now all Yenan is on the alert, looking for us."

Oshima felt the pistol press harder against his skull. "But you have been victorious! You have them here!"

"You failed in your mission. You jeopardized your comrades. Two of our men are missing. They were not at their rendezvous. For you it is seppuku!"

Oshima tried to rise, and Yang pushed him down. "I know the code as well as you," he said bitterly. "If hara-kiri is demanded of me, I am man enough."

"You are an idiot! I did not trust you. I have an emergency plan. We have no seppuku knives here. You will still play a role in our great adventure here." Yang's white teeth gleamed in the darkness. "With the alarm, thanks to you and our two men who are missing, we must change our plan. We will go to the airstrip, where we will pretend to be guarding the chairman's vehicle."

Yang withdrew a sheaf of papers from his pocket and shoved them into Oshima's jacket pocket. "These papers," he said, "identify you as an agent of Tai Li. They are authentic in every way. I obtained them from our people in Chungking."

Oshima, his pain forgotten for the moment, the thought of hara-kiri in his mind, knew what Yang meant. "You do not feel now that you can capture the American plane. I am to kill them."

Their deaths would mean his death.

His body ripped by a hundred rifle bullets.

"How do you plan for me to do it?" he said in resignation.

The vehicle pulled into the airstrip area. "When the time comes, I will instruct you," Yang said. He opened the rear door and got out with the six men. In the faint light, Oshima saw that they were wearing Red Army uniforms and were armed with rifles. Before he closed the door, Yang hissed, ''Stay here! Keep an eye on them. If they move, stroke them lightly with this.'' He handed Oshima a pistol. The door slammed shut.

Outside, Oshima heard Yang shouting in Chinese to the soldier guards, ordering them to search the area and be quick about it. The pain returned to his body, and he stared moodily at the darkness around him. With his wound and broken hand he could never make it out of Yenan.

His seppuku was to be spectacular, at any rate.

Loo awoke to find two men standing over her, flashlights in their hands. One of them spoke harshly to her, demanding that she get dressed and go with them. They wore Red Army uniforms and carried rifles. She had never seen them before. The other women in the barracklike cave room peered from their covers. A small group of women in an adjoining room were working at sewing. As she dressed, she glimpsed the beautiful red silk they were using and the brilliant gold of the threads.

The men grabbed her arms when she was dressed and hurried her out the tunnel into the darkness of the night. She was bewildered and protested that she was the granddaughter of Ho Ling-chi. They paid no attention to her. They went a short way and peered back and forth as if expecting someone. They held her tightly. The smaller of the two spoke. She had difficulty understanding the words. Then she realized, with sudden shock, that the man spoke in Japanese!

She struggled to free herself. The larger one pulled a bayonet free from its sheath and fastened it on his rifle. His words were as guttural as the small man's. From their quick movements she understood someone was to have picked them up, someone who had missed the timing. Or the two men had missed it. Their distress was obvious, even in the darkness. She could smell their heavy sweat.

The big man pushed her roughly to the ground. He raised the rifle, bayonet pointed at her. She screamed.

There was the sound of heavy running feet. A body flew through the air and smashed against the two men. They went down in a heap. She rolled, feeling the sharp pain as someone's thrashing feet struck her in the hip. In the dimness she recognized the shape.

Carr!

Carr was on his feet. He held one of the rifles, swinging it in a huge arc. The stock crashed against the larger man's head as he was rising. His body whipped backward. Then Carr's big boot swung at the smaller man, missing the first time and connecting the second time. The little man, swearing in Japanese, struggled to reach his rifle. The boot stamped down on his hand. The rifle bayonet slashed into the hand, pinning it to the ground. The little man screamed and fainted.

Loo, stunned, tried to sit up. She felt Carr kneeling next to her, lifting her tenderly in his arms. He was breathing heavily.

"What the bloody hell!" she said loudly. "Those blokes were trying to kidnap me! They were going to kill me!"

When he could, Carr spoke. "Thank God you told me where you were staying! I'm sitting there with McHugh and all of a sudden I thought of you! I ran out of there so fast I knocked him over! All I could think of was getting to you!" He paused to take in deep breaths. "I was so damn dumb it didn't occur to me until minutes ago that they would try something with you!"

She hugged him tightly. "I said you had instincts! Oh, I'm so glad they work at night!"

"Come on," he said, "I'll get you back and have a guard posted over you. Then we'll find out who these bastards are."

He carried her back, refusing to put her down, feeling an enormous protectiveness scorched with burning love.

The uneasy dawn came with a brisk breeze that sent the thin broken clouds wisping through the blue sky.

Colonel Wu stood next to Carr and the full detachment of the Dixie Mission, wearing complete uniforms with theater ribbons and decorations, all with sidearms, arranged in parade order. A thousand *pa lu*s were standing in military formation along both sides of the crushed-rock runway. Other units stood at attention around the squat control tower and the few maintenance buildings near it.

With the sun's rays brighter, casting long shadows, there was a solitary bugle signal. A military band, small in number but loud, began to play a tune, strident in the morning cold. Overhead, the sound of a twin-engine aircraft grew in intensity. The C-47, old and oil-streaked, came into sight. It buzzed the field and then banked and began its descent. With its wheels and flaps down it seemed to float down onto the single runway.

Instead of turning at the far end and rolling up to the control tower and refueling station as it had always done before, it cut its engines at the far end of the runway. It was surrounded by one hundred armed *pa lu*s. Its nose was pointed away. Its crew, told to remain on board by radio, could see nothing back along the runway.

Another blast of the bugle. The ranks of the soldiers along the runway parted, and a long line of Japanese prisoners were marched by their armed escort onto the runway. There were about two hundred of them. When they were halted, they found themselves looking into the muzzles of a dozen field machine guns quickly placed and manned in a short crescent around them. There was no possibility of escape. They glanced at each other in deep apprehension. All had their hands tied behind their backs. The band stopped abruptly.

Colonel Wu strode over to Yang. His eyes glittered with hate. A motion of his hand and Yang and his men, standing around the hearse-van, were disarmed. Their hands were tied.

"What do you see?" Wu said, standing inches away from Yang.

"I see an impossible situation," Yang said softly. His eyes, shaded by the old felt hat, took in the long line of soldiers, the field machine guns, the stricken faces of the Japanese prisoners.

"Then free them at once!" Wu barked the command.

"It is out of my hands," Yang said. "If there is even so much as one shot, a man inside will kill your leaders."

Wu smiled, a malevolent twisting of his face. He raised his hand. From the far end of the runway, near the courier plane, three men stepped into sight.

"There is our chairman, ambassador, and general," Wu said.

Yang squinted in the sunlight. The distance was far, but the three men *did* resemble Chairman Mao, Ambassador Chou, and General Chu Teh. They were the right sizes. They wore the familiar clothes. An uncharacteristic alarm rose with him. "But these?" He motioned to the hearse-van.

"We have been prepared for years for an assassination or kidnap attempt," Wu said. "We had secret preparations that even you were not informed of, Captain Yang. We placed doubles in the secret cave rooms as decoys and let that be known to a few whom we suspected." He laughed. "If you had looked closely at them, you would have seen that your 'chairman' has no mole on his chin. The 'ambassador' does not have thick eyebrows. The 'general' is inches too tall." A lopsided grin. "But perhaps through your gas masks you did not notice these important details."

The door of the hearse-van burst open and Lieutenant Oshima leaped to the ground. He held the pistol in his left hand, aiming it at Yang. The nearby *pa lu*s raised their rifles, and the deadly sound of bolts being thrown back filled the air.

"You fool!" Yang shouted at him in Chinese. "It is over!"

"*You* are the failure!" Oshima screamed in Chinese. "They outwitted you! The great Honda!" His eyes flicked to the end of the runway, to the American plane and the three men standing alone by it. "They did not bring the plane here as you said! We could not commandeer it! And the leaders are there, not inside!" The pistol was pointed at Yang's felt hat. "Still you wanted these three men dead inside there!" His voice was out of control. "You would sacrifice all our men here to kill three Communist decoys!"

Yang, frozen in place, stared at the pistol. He said in Chinese, "Yes, I failed. I did not know about the doubles. Put the pistol down. It is over."

The pistol in Oshima's left hand shook. He tried to steady it with his crippled right hand as he pointed it at Wu. He crouched, his eyes wild as he shouted in Chinese, "This one will die! He made fools of us! He will die!"

Something whacked against the wavering pistol. It flew from Oshima's hand and skidded along the dusty ground. He bent and reached for it. Something whipped cruelly against his left hand and he yelped in pain. He looked around savagely. There had been no rifle fire. No pistol fire.

Then he saw Carr.

Carr stood, Moffett's pistol with the silencer raised and pointing at Oshima's head. With a scream, Oshima charged at Carr. Yang stuck out a foot, and Oshima went sprawling.

Wu motioned, and the soldiers fell on Oshima, holding him to the gritty ground, until his frantic thrashing subsided. One tied a short rope as a tourniquet to his arm to stop the flow of blood.

"Take the doubles to the hospital," Wu ordered. Two intelligence officers leaped into the hearse-van, and it moved away quickly. Wu turned to see Carr standing face to face with Yang.

"It was a stupid thing to do," Carr said. "How could you outwit the Red Army? They have the best intelligence in the world. Your men who tried to kidnap Miss Ho are wounded and telling all they know about your Kempetai cell."

Yang shrugged, looking down the field. The three men had disappeared. "Now we will never know if we had the right ones or not." He spoke in passable English.

"No, you won't," Carr said. "As far as they're concerned, the doubles were the ones you took."

"Word will get out," Yang said defiantly. "My people will learn of it." His teeth were bright in the sunlight. "The name of Honda will be honored!"

"Yes, word will get out," Carr taunted. "They will put it out that a blundering, inept Honda posing as a Yang made a terrible mess of an attempted kidnapping by taking the wrong people. How will that sound to the Kempetai leaders in Tokyo?"

Carr looked down at Oshima. "You are the one who followed me. An idiot's journey. Think of what this has done to the honor of your name. They will laugh when they speak of you in Japan."

Wu barked an order. The Japanese prisoners were removed. Oshima, bloody hands tied, white-faced with pain, was led before the machine guns, Yang and his men a few feet behind.

Carr joined the Dixie Mission men. They marched in formation away from the airstrip. At a distance, Carr turned to look over his shoulder. The *pa lu*s had moved in a mass behind the machine guns. Then the Dixie Mission went down a hill.

Behind them they heard the sharp chatter of the machine guns.

They crowded into Colonel McHugh's room. He faced them sternly. "This never happened," he said softly. "You are sworn to secrecy. That is a direct order. If any one of you talks, I will see that you are court-martialed for disobeying a direct order of your commanding officer." He turned to Carr. "Give me that."

Carr handed him Moffett's pistol. McHugh held it up. "A brave man who carried this died in an effort to get here," he said. "Lieutenant Carr worked with Colonel Wu to set the stage for the show at the airstrip." His voice strengthened. "The Chinese have a great sense of drama. No one will ever know which were the doubles, in the van or at the end of the strip."

He looked into their eyes, swinging around to face each man. "We're not going to screw it up by talking to anyone about it. Do you read me?" He waited for them to nod, each in turn. "I have no idea how much longer this mission will remain here. But while we do, and for as long as we wear a uniform, what we saw this morning remains nothing. Nothing! It did not happen!"

He sighed and relaxed. "That's it, men. I know I can depend on you. You've done a splendid job here. You saw China at work. I don't know if we're going to end up on the side of the generalissimo or the Red Army. I only know I'm proud to have served with you in Yenan. There aren't many people back home who even know we're here, or what we've been trying to do. But goddamn it, we're part of a slice of history!" He went around, shaking all their hands. "Now get back to your quarters and stay there until mess time. Give them a few hours to calm down. Then go about your duties as if you'd just gotten out of the sack."

They filed out, all except Carr. "Well, it worked," Carr said. He sat down wearily in a chair, the only one in the room. "Damn it, it worked!"

McHugh sat down on a bench and leaned against the table on his sturdy arms. "When you came up with that idea I thought you were nuts. The prisoners, and the actors as doubles."

"But you took me to Colonel Wu with it," Carr said quietly. "He bought it. What I said about Yang put him on to the guy."

"I've been up here for months. I've lived in China for years. I speak the language. You just got here. How did you get to know so much about Chinese mentality?"

Carr shook with silent laughter. "I'm in love with a Chinese girl!"

The door at the end of the tunnel opened and Colonel Wu entered. He motioned for them to remain seated and placed his haunches on the kang, swinging his legs over the side. "Your men?" he said in Kuo-yu.

"They all slept in this morning, Colonel," McHugh said easily in Chinese. "I'm damned mad about it. They should have been working. They've seen and done nothing all morning long."

"You run a very poor military establishment," Wu said with a conspirator's smile. He looked at Carr. "You are from—?" Mc-Hugh translated.

"The state called Illinois. A city called Bloomington. A farm near there." Carr decided he liked Wu. The officer was a different man from the one he'd met on the road into Yenan.

"The hunting is good?" McHugh translated it into English.

"Every kid learns to shoot at an early age. Shotguns, rifles, pistols if they have them."

"You had a pistol?"

"My father did. He taught me how to shoot."

"He taught you very well," Wu said. He was silent for a moment. "Colonel McHugh, how difficult would it be for you to cut orders for Lieutenant Carr to return at once to his command at Myitkyina?" The Chinese words were laced with seriousness.

"As quick as I can cut them."

Wu slid down from the kang. "The courier plane is being unloaded and refueled. Your supplies will be delivered soon. With the battles under way at the blockade area, it is a good idea to have it return as soon as possible. I believe it would be most important to have Lieutenant Carr on that plane when it leaves."

McHugh understood. Carr would be a man marked for revenge by Japanese agents not uncovered by the disastrous kidnap plot. Or by Kuomintang agents who would see the value in Carr's death, with the blame being placed on the Red Army. "My thought exactly, Colonel," he said. "He'll be on it."

Wu nodded solemnly. He shook McHugh's hand. Then Carr's. He held it for a second longer. "Ho Ling-chi feels he does not have long to live and wishes his granddaughter also to be on that flight," he said, with McHugh translating. "Until we work things out at the blockade area, Yenan will be in great danger from bombers. It is safer for her to go to Chengtu and then to Calcutta." His face beamed. "Perhaps you would be so kind as to see that your American people take her with you to Myitkyina and from there to Calcutta? I will act as her family representative if Ho Ling-chi dies. I will care for her interests here."

Carr felt a grin spreading on his own face as he listened to Mc-Hugh finish the translation. "I believe it is possible. The colonel can work that into my orders."

Wu stepped back. "Then it is all arranged," he said to Mc-

Hugh. "I will say goodbye now to Lieutenant Carr. I must attend to many things. I will not be there to see him off." He looked into Carr's eyes.

"Tell Colonel Wu," Carr said to McHugh, "that I would like him to give my deepest respects to the chairman, the ambassador, and the general. I was most honored to meet them. I have been honored to meet Colonel Wu."

McHugh interpreted and Wu nodded. "Remember us and what we seek to do." He moved down the tunnel. "Perhaps one day we will meet again. Good luck, Lieutenant." The door closed behind him.

McHugh blew out air after he told Carr what the officer had said. "That's a side of him I never saw before." He flicked a finger at Carr. "Get packed, Doug. I'll get your orders cut. I'll radio Combat Cargo that you're coming in. I'll set it up at Chengtu."

Carr pointed to Moffett's pistol on the table. "Why do you suppose he brought that with him?"

"Who knows, Doug? Maybe he had a premonition it would come in handy around here."

Carr saw that McHugh was studying him closely. "It's been a real experience for you, hasn't it?" McHugh said. "What has it meant to you?"

Carr felt shaken. He took time to form his words. "In the year I've been in the CBI I thought China was a garbage dump. I felt superior to the Chinese. I called them slopeheads, coolies, pigtails, all that. I thought they were little stupid bastards who let the Japs run all over them." He sifted through his emotions. "I see them differently now. They have their own culture, going back thousands of years. They have their own problems and they mess up like any other nation. But they're human just like us and they deserve our respect and consideration. I don't feel so damned superior anymore."

"I've changed the same way," McHugh said. "even though I've been in China a long time."

"The Dixie Mission," Carr said. "It's a damned shame it didn't work out."

McHugh shrugged in disgust. "Major General Patrick J. Hurley came over here thinking he could arm wrestle the Reds and the Nats into an agreement to work together. All the old China hands told him to go easy, to remember what had gone on before. He misplayed it. He got mad when they wouldn't kowtow to him.''

"So you've missed the chance to unify China and get it all on our side?''

"We sure as hell have, Doug. Like I said, we're winding down here. Mao doesn't trust Americans. How could he when Hurley killed his proposal to go to Washington and meet with President Roosevelt? When he hasn't gotten a damned thing from us but a lot of conversation that went nowhere?'' The words were seasoned with a strong dose of bitterness. "China will go one way and we'll go another. We'll pay for it.''

Carr shook his head. "Why did they send your mission up here if they didn't intend to back it up?''

"Oh, Christ! Indecision. Politics. Bullheadedness. Our brass have been like gamblers at the racetrack. They keep betting on the same horse and losing, but it's a habit and they can't break it. Everyone over here knows Chiang can't make it, but Washington keeps putting its bets down on him out of habit. They tied our hands here because they didn't want another horse to win.''

McHugh rose and straightened his uniform. "Come on, I've got to get you on your way.'' His face softened into a smile. "You've got a good thing going with Miss Ho. I hate to think of what would have happened if you hadn't run the hell out of here last night. You're really tuned into that little gal.''

Carr stood, feeling a little giddy. "I know China, this part of it, has changed me. I don't know how much. It's as if I can see the whole world and not just a small part of it.''

McHugh stuck out a hand. Carr shook it. "That's the first step. The next is to see ways you can help this poor, miserable world settle some of its problems. Now, start getting ready.''

Carr followed him out and went to his own room. He packed the old barracks bag and waited. Lieutenant Dillon came for him. The Dixie Mission men, in small groups, shook hands with him as they went into the different rooms to say goodbye. Corporal Broward handed him a scrap of paper. "If you get to San Francisco, go to Chinatown. There's where my folks and kid sister live. They'll see you get the best American-Chinese food in the States.''

Carr and Dillon walked the long way to the airstrip. It was empty except for the Chinese mechanics working on the C-47, moved now to the refueling station. The pilots stood by the ladder reaching up to the cabin.

"Well, Doug," Dillon said, "sorry your stay here couldn't have been more exciting." He looked around the empty airstrip. "It's sort of boring in Yenan. Nothing much happens."

"I know," Carr said. "Maybe things will pick up."

"Sure," Dillon said. They shook hands. "Say, here are some letters the guys would like you to put into the mill when you get to Myitkyina." Carr stuffed them into his jacket pocket and climbed up the ladder. At the top he said, "Hey, where's home?"

"Indianapolis."

"Christ! Then we'll get to see each other."

"Count on it."

The crew chief and radio operator came up the ladder, followed by the pilots. The chief pulled up the ladder, stowed it, and closed the door.

Carr saw Loo. She sat in a jump seat near the cabin bulkhead. He heard the pilots calling off the checklist. He sat down next to her, putting the barracks bag to one side and snapping on the safety belt. The port engine fired, then the starboard. The cabin shook rudely under the efforts of the warmup. The plane moved to position on the runway, then began to roll along it. Its nose leveled and its tail came up. It was airborne, with Yenan rushing by under its wings.

Loo lifted a package wrapped in rice paper and handed it to Carr.

"What's this?"

"Colonel Wu told me what happened," she said. "I still don't believe you? What you do shocks me! The plan you worked out! How do you think of such tricks?"

"It seemed the thing to do." He hefted the package. "What's in it?"

She giggled. "Open it and see."

He unwrapped the cotton strings and pulled the paper away. It was a magnificent red silk robe. He held it up. Dragons in gold leaped from the beautifully embroidered cloth. The symbols of Chinese royalty.

"Oh, my God!" he said.

"The women helped me. They worked day and night on it. I

got your final measurements when I visited you. Isn't it beautiful?''

"The Robe of the Emperor of China," he said. "No, the Dragon Robe of the Emperor of China!"

Her eyes glistened. She wet her lips, making them lush and irresistible. He kissed her, holding her as tightly to him as he could while they sat side by side in the wall jump seats. He held the robe so that it didn't touch the floor.

When he released her she said, "Will you wear it at our wedding?"

He held it up high to marvel at it again. "You know I will. We'll do it in Calcutta and we'll have another one back home."

Her eyes were wide. "You decided that?"

"Not totally. We'll go there. You have to meet my folks. We'll see about that dealership or about the farm. Then we'll think about coming back to China." He looked at her, knowing that the future was not predictable. "The thing is, we'll be together. That's what counts."

She laid her head on his shoulder. Her long black hair was loose and fell across him in a glistening cascade. "Do you think we're going to make it, Doug?"

He started. It was the first time she had called him by his first name. He glanced out the small window behind him, seeing the last of the brown hills around Yenan, seeing the snowcapped mountains in the distance, seeing the roads below filled in the bright sunshine with marching troops moving south and long lines of peasants moving north.

"Look, honey," he said, "there were times I didn't think we were going to make it to Yenan." He put his fingers under her chin and lifted her face toward his. "Now I know that Wu will work for us here and Ho Ling-chi won't come between us. My people won't, either. We're going to make it all the way, to Calcutta, to the States, to Bloomington." He kissed her, feeling a great weight fading away from him, feeling a new sense of destiny, a surging ecstasy of eagerness for life.

The radio operator came through the doorway and halted abruptly as he saw them embracing. He looked at the message from Colonel McHugh confirming the orders. And the line that read "Chance Beard has affirmative your assignment OSS training unit at Hastings Mill, Calcutta. Congratulations.'' He grinned and went back to his seat.

The message could wait.

The big blond second lieutenant and the gorgeous little Chinese doll didn't look to him as if they could.

THE ADVENTURES OF
SKIPPER GOULD

BLOODRUN Robert Kalish   88021-0/$2.75 US $2.75 Canada
Skipper Gould said his goodbyes to Asia after Vietnam. There he had become a man, but like the lover who never forgets his first woman, when Asia called to him again, he came, came back to find out who killed his brother Ricky. Skipper's only link to the killers was a sensual Oriental beauty—a link strong enough to lock Skipper into a spiraling game of oil politics, KGB intrigue and corruption.

BLOODTIDE Robert Kalish   89521-8/$2.95 US $3.75 Canada
The second novel featuring tough, ex-navy fighting man Skipper Gould is an explosive, high-voltage thriller of murder, intrigue and atomic espionage off the coast of Maine.

Skipper was the editor of a small town newspaper now. But the woman came to him because of what he had been. And finding a dead man's body floating in the bay was enough to sweep him toward a giant maelstrom of evil and violence.

BUDDHA'S RETREAT, the third Skipper Gould novel, will be published in August 1985.

AVON Paperbacks